The Lone
and
Level Sands

Being the First Movement of the Song of the Crickets

Emmett Burgess

Table of Contents

For Poppyseed.
—EB

For Uncle Silas.
—EG

For the only two people from my old life
whose names I still remember.
—JT

The dream was marvelous
but the terror was great;
we must treasure the dream
whatever the terror.

—*The Epic of Gilgamesh*

The Lone and Level Sands:

Being the **First Movement**
of the
Song of the Crickets

as told by
John Talbot

to
Emerson Grey

—here transcribed by
Emmett Burgess

Prelude

At the peak of a lone mountain lives a song. No one knows how it came to be there, or how long ago it was written. No one has heard it in its entirety. It is difficult to find, and were you to find it you would be lucky to hear a single verse.

Those who have heard it say it is as subtle and soft as thoughtful humming, accompanied by the soft ringing of small bells. There are movements to the song, and the melody ranges from slow and meandering to a thundering staccato. Some hear the strings of a lyre being plucked while others hear the whimpers of a wounded bull. You may even hear lyrics, though few have.

The song itself is a mystery. Those who hear only the music cannot agree on which instruments are being played, and those who hear its lyrics cannot understand what is being sung. No one knows why the song is there, what purpose it serves, or whether one should hear it at all.

But the song is there. You can find it yourself if you listen for it.

Often it can be found at night, when the moon is cloaked and the stars are bright.

From atop a mountain, miles from the nearest city and surrounded by a vast desert, you may hear the call of an eagle searching for its mate, or watch as it brings meat back to its nest.

Then, al azif. This is what the people who live near the mountain call the chirring of insects. If the night is warm, which is often the case near the mountain, al azif will be steady. When you have listened to al azif long enough that you lose focus on all that surrounds you, then the song will begin. Or rather, you will hear it then—the song has no beginning.

The melody will rise and encircle you. Perhaps you will hear brass horns and the crash of cymbals, or the long sigh of a violin like wind through dried reeds. Or perhaps you will feel the thumping bass of drums, of giant footsteps running toward you from within a shadowed cave. And yes, you may even hear lyrics. Don't worry if you don't. Those who do are often disappointed when they realize they cannot understand the words.

Regardless, you will feel love—love for your children begotten in sacrifice, and the lengths to which you would go to protect them.

Shame, also, of disappointing your father, although you have the strength of a god.

Pain from losing your brother to an ancient evil, forever wondering if it could have been helped. If you could have done more.

Strain of guiding a boat over poisonous rapids rushing over grey pebbles covered in algae.

The color orange.

The smell of burnt almonds.

You will forget what brought you there, the choices that shaped and formed your sorrows and joys, that determine where you will journey next. And later, you will forget the music. You will forget the lyrics, if they did in fact come to you. The experience will fall through your memories like sand through bony fingers. You will only remember that the song exists, and that you were lucky to have heard a single measure.

I am not lucky.

I have heard the entire song.

This is a small piece.

1

The Mountain at the End of the World

Shifting sands slid through the rib cage of the skeletal cow. It reminded Tarlos of his brother. He was seated, resting his tired legs on the small hillock when the loose earth fell away to reveal the dead animal. Small bits of fur clung to its bones on strips of dried leather. Its jaw gaped, neck bent backward. The legs stretched out in a sort of running position, like a dog bounding through a field as it dreams. Its death must have been slow and painful. Likely of thirst.

Thirst.

I'm thirsty.

He tipped his water bag to his mouth, let the water briefly pass his lips before pulling back. He was not sure how much longer it would take him to reach the mountain, and the hide bag was almost empty.

Tarlos knelt beside the cow skull and stared into its empty eye sockets. He narrowed his eyes, allowing anger to well up inside him.

Hello, Krastos.

He traced the cow's jaw with a dry finger. He imagined sticky saliva on its once-full lips. He could see it standing. Walking. Breathing. It bellowed in the desert, letting its presence be known. Its heart beat, its tail swished the flies away, and sweat ran over its back and down its shoulders. One day it was alive. Next day it was dead.

How seamlessly life leads to death.

The ground beneath it was dry and hard, the perfect cow hide impression in the packed earth. Tarlos could see individual hairs. He had no way of knowing how long ago this cow had died, but the image in the ground erased all sense of time between him and the living animal.

He shook his head. So much evidence of life, or the absence of it, right before his eyes. Would anyone or anything remember this cow? Tarlos doubted it. But he would.

The cow's jaw was long and white, lined with thick square teeth that clung to the bone. Some of the teeth had loosened over time, yellowed, or disappeared entirely. Tarlos poked at them, feeling how loose or intact they were, and one fell easily from the jawbone. It was a larger tooth and oddly shaped. Instead of flat and smooth for grinding plants, this tooth was sharp with a deep chip in its side. Tarlos picked it up, ran his thumb over it before dropping it in his pocket.

He stood and clapped the dirt from his hands. The bleached-white skeleton would be a part of him so long as he kept the tooth.

"My condolences," said Tarlos.

The desert stretched out behind and ahead of him, and in every direction; it met the horizon, merging in the distance with the grey-blue sky. Tarlos grew up here, but his home had food and water—the desert outside of Kesh was cursed and barren. It had not rained since the start of his journey. He'd lost track of how many days ago that was. Possibly thirty.

He carried with him two skins of water, one empty now for two decans. Each time he thought about taking a drink from the second bag, he forced himself to think about other things. The water must be saved for when he could not continue without it.

Tonight, when I bed down, I'll have another drink.

Shar-shu-ma, Shar's Mountain, rose in the distance. The air shimmered, the heat playing tricks on the mind. When Tarlos first saw the mountain, he thought it must have been a mirage. But there could be no doubt about it: the mountain had grown larger, its image clearer. He was getting closer.

Tarlos's feet and legs ached, and sometimes he could barely

walk at all. He was not used to having to walk such a distance. Being a Holder, he'd never had to before. He fingered the tooth in his pocket, pulled it out and held it flat in his hand. He was tired, and his mind needed focusing, but with a little effort he managed to lift the tooth. It hovered a few inches above his palm, wriggling a bit before dropping again. It seemed so long ago that he'd been able to do that with his own body; there were entire days that his feet never touched the ground. When was the last time he had flown? He could not remember. Before Krastos died, surely. Perhaps in the fight against Bawa.

Tarlos closed his eyes, shutting out a flash of violent memory.

I miss it. The wind in my eyes, screaming past my ears. Seeing the world so tiny below me.

He returned the tooth to his pocket and looked ahead. The mountain resembled the tooth. What might have been a triangular peak was now cracked down the middle, creating a V-shape. Every morning for the last several days, Tarlos had watched the sun rise, stretching forth from that V in the peak. It was Shar's doorway from the dead country to the living world.

Tarlos envied those who lived beneath the mountain, in that country from which no man returns. At least they were at rest. They did not get thirsty or hungry. Here in the living world, there were only sore feet, sand, and skeletons.

A small dusty whirlwind passed in front of him, and he paused to watch. It was beautiful in an odd way, twisting and silent. He saw them sometimes, on days that were especially hot and dry.

The sun beat down on him as he made one step after another. All the while the mountain in the distance loomed over the desert. He would get to that mountain if it was the last thing he ever did.

His feet screamed and his thighs cramped. Tarlos thought about what awaited him if he could only make it through the Tunnel of the Sun and to the dead country beyond.

As the day went on, Tarlos forgot about his promise to save his water only for emergencies. He let water touch his lips twice and made a silent prayer that there would be more on the mountain.

Why would there be? The mountain belongs to the gods, and the gods don't drink water.

He hoped for it nevertheless. Hope was all he had, other than his ragged clothes and meager provisions.

And a tooth.

He must not forget his tooth.

He rested during the hottest part of the day, when Shar was at its highest, and he pushed as far as he could until the sun set behind him and the desert turned a dark shade of purple. Above, the stars blinked, silently watching him.

Night set in, but Tarlos did not bother to build a fire. There was nothing to burn anyway. He slept in the open, chilly desert air with his bent arm as a pillow and the sky as his blanket.

The last three miles were the most difficult, and he felt every step of that last stretch toward the mountain. He'd drank the last of his water the day before. His mouth was full of cotton. He tried to swallow but had no saliva and gagged on his fat tongue. The beginnings of sores dotted the inside of his mouth, behind his lips and in his cheeks.

It had been three days since the cow. Or so he thought. He gripped the tooth in his pocket and pressed on.

The mountain was now taller than he had imagined it being. It loomed menacingly over him. *How dare you come to me*, it seemed to say. Tarlos craned his neck toward the peak: two points that cut the sky above. The sun rose from between them, from the dead country. The sight made him dizzy, and he stumbled backward. For a moment the loss of balance returned to him a memory. He slapped the sides of his face until Krastos's frown left his mind.

You're here, came the voice of his twin brother. *Now what?*

"Be quiet, you're dead," Tarlos said. His dry and cracked voice didn't sound like his own.

Brittle grass grew on the gentle sloping foothills. The area around the mountain was a strange island in this ocean of sand, the off-yellow of the prickly grass stark against the monotone tan of the desert that surrounded it. The mountain lightened as grass gave way to rocks white as bone. It all seemed so alien to Tarlos. He did not linger. That the grass here was brittle and yellow meant only one thing.

He heard a trickle then and smelled the water before he saw it. The sound and scent woke his exhausted, dehydrated mind, and he jumped to search for it.

A crack in the dry earth ran down the foothills, thicker bunches of the brittle grass growing along its sides. Tarlos crouched low and placed his hands in the dirt.

It was dry and cool, indicating water just beneath the surface. He could hear the trickle but could not see it. He stood, not bothering to clap the dirt from his hands. His tongue clicked dryly in his mouth. He followed the trickle up the hill. That sweet sound—it was like bells.

It led him farther up into the hills, to where the grass grew a mote greener. He kept the trickling to his left, following the sound of it ever onward. He jogged, then walked, then slowed to a shamble. At last, he fell to the ground crawling, and he followed still on his hands and knees until the sound was right below him.

He could hear it. He could smell it. He could almost taste it. The air closest to the ground was just the tiniest bit cooler. Tarlos pulled at the grass and dug at the dirt with his chewed fingernails.

The water was there, its sound sweet. His tongue flopped in his mouth as he took out scoop after scoop of dirt, digging closer to the water.

Perhaps eight inches into the ground, Tarlos stopped digging. He could hear the water clearer—it was not much farther. He started digging in another place, just right of the first hole. He yanked at the grass and clawed at the dirt. He dug ten inches only to find the ground was dry.

He dug a third time. Dry. A fourth and a fifth.

All the while the sound and smell of water surrounded him. Tarlos's temples pounded, his mouth was numb, his head spinning.

Now what? came the voice of Krastos.

"Be quiet, you're dead," Tarlos tried to say, but the words came out garbled and incomprehensible.

There was no water here. Tarlos rolled onto his back and stared up at the split peak above. The white rock face was tinted pink in the late afternoon light. He grimaced then looked west to the sun. Dusk was a few hours away yet—it was the hottest part of the day.

"Damn you, Shar," he meant to say. His slurred speech offended the very thought of language.

"And why do you say that?" asked a voice.

Tarlos's heart was already exhausted, and the voice made it leap in his chest. He closed his eyes and gasped at the sudden rush of adrenaline. He was dehydrated, probably dying, and the gods had made him hear the voice of a young boy before he died. He could not guess why.

"Are you asleep?" asked the voice. Tarlos opened his eyes and forced them to roll to the left. The hazy shape of a small person appeared beside him. Tarlos blinked a few times. It was indeed a boy, a very young one. Perhaps ten years old. "Can you hear me?"

"Who are you?" Tarlos rasped.

"Father never gave us names," said the boy. "At least none we wanted to keep." He was naked but for a white tunic around his waist. "Everyone just calls us 'the twins.' Are you thirsty?"

Tarlos nodded. The boy reached into a small pocket in his tunic and took from it a silver cup the size of a cedar nut. He dipped it in the empty hole Tarlos had dug, and Tarlos groaned.

"Wuh . . ."

"Here you go." The boy gave the small cup to Tarlos, taking care not to spill it.

Tarlos narrowed his eyes at the cup and then at the boy.

"Do you want it or not? You think getting water is easy? Here." The boy pressed the cup to Tarlos's lips. Tarlos's eyes widened as he tasted cool, clear water.

He took the cup from the boy and tipped it back. Water,

fresh and clean, gushed into his mouth and down his throat. His shriveled tongue soaked it in, the sores on his cheeks and gums screaming at its touch. Tarlos ignored the pain.

After several long seconds, Tarlos brought the little silver cup away from his mouth and breathed. He looked into it and saw that it was only half-empty. "Is this magic?" he asked the boy. His voice was a broken whisper.

"It's water," the boy answered. "What did you say before?"

Tarlos took another long drink, relishing in the ecstasy of quenched thirst. "When?"

"Before. You cursed the sun. Why?"

Tarlos shrugged. "He never did anything good for me, I guess." He handed the cup back to the boy, and it disappeared into his little pocket.

"Have you met him?" the boy asked.

"Shar? No. I don't plan to, either."

"He never wanted to meet us," said the boy, "even though we guard his precious gate." He smiled at Tarlos, a strange and somehow half-given gesture.

"Who else is here?" Tarlos asked. "Your parents? Where do you live?"

"It's just my sister and me. Father left us."

Tarlos scanned the area. There were no signs of a camp or provisions for living. "Has he been gone long?"

"I think it might be coming up on ten thousand years, now. But I really don't keep count; I just take life as it comes."

Tarlos straightened up. His head cleared as the water worked its way through his body. He took a better look at the boy sitting in front of him. He was average in almost every way—no older than twelve, wearing a common loose tunic. His hair was black, curly, and cropped short. There was no dirt on his face or hands, although he was barefoot and sat on the ground.

Then he noticed them—the boy's eyes were entirely black. Dark like obsidian, empty like the night sky. If there was any light within them, it was sad.

"You're a jinn," said Tarlos. "A child of Ablis."

"Yes, my sister and I." The boy smiled again. Darkness hung in his eyes. "She's up at the gate. I should be there, too. Would you like to meet her?"

"The gate," Tarlos said. "You mean Shar-shu-ka? The way to . . . the other side?"

"The Scorpion Gate." The boy nodded. "Come, I'll show you. Can't go through it, of course. Only Shar and Moresh do that. But you can look just the same."

The boy rose and gestured for Tarlos to follow. As Tarlos stood, his knees and spine crackled. The boy led him the rest of the way up the foothills until they came to a sheer rock face—the start of Shar's Mountain.

"This way." The boy walked around a large outcropping of rock. Behind it was a narrow path that wound upward until it disappeared behind the other side of the mountain.

Tarlos followed. The boy was small and thin, and he jogged without effort through the narrow rock canyon. Tarlos struggled in the tighter places. He sucked in his breath and squeezed between the walls.

The path ended at the top of the mountain, almost at the split peak. It opened up into a small green clearing, bordered on one side by a large flat wall of tan rock. The hike had taken more than four hours, and Tarlos sat down to rest.

"Are you thirsty?" the boy asked. "I only ask because we hardly ever do. Get thirsty, I mean."

Tarlos nodded. In truth, he was fine without another drink, but he had no idea when he would again be able to fill his water bags, and he doubted the boy would give him the magic silver cedar nut to keep.

The boy knelt in the grass, which Tarlos ventured to call a proper green, and dug a small hole in the dirt with his hand. He dipped the tiny cup into the hole and handed it to Tarlos. Again, Tarlos stared at the cup in disbelief at the water it held within only a few visible drops. He was grateful for it and took another long drink.

He gave the cup back. "Was that a gift from your father?"

The boy almost laughed. His mouth opened into a splitting grin as he hid the silver cup away in his white tunic. His teeth were small and sharp, and there were dozens of them. "Father never did anything except give us to Shar to guard the gate. No, we have our own power. What little we were born with, anyway."

Four short trees covered in broad green leaves grew in the small clearing. Tarlos guessed that there must be water beneath the ground for the trees and grass to grow so green. He wanted that tiny silver cup.

The boy shouted into the trees, "We have a visitor!"

The leaves on the branches rustled, and a small pale girl the same size and apparent age as the boy dropped down to a low branch. She hung there, upside down, her legs grappling the tree. Her arms fell down over her head, and her black hair fell longer still. She regarded Tarlos with curiosity and dropped to the ground with a flip. She landed soft on her small feet and stood beside her brother.

"Who is this?" she asked, staring at Tarlos. Her voice was hardly a whisper.

"He came from the desert," her brother said, lowering his voice. "I haven't asked what his name is."

"What is your name?" the girl asked. Her eyes were as black and solemn as her brother's.

Tarlos hesitated. "My name is Tarlos."

"Why are you here?" asked the girl. "Why have you travelled so far over miles of desert? Tell me."

Tarlos's neck stiffened. "None of your business, jinn."

The boy scratched his chin and mumbled to himself. "Tarlos." He turned to his sister. "Does that name sound familiar to you?"

The girl nodded. "Tarlos, son of Ninsun?"

Tarlos drew back at the sound of his mother's name. "How did you—"

"Oh, we know all about your family back in Kesh," said the boy. Both he and his sister smiled. "Your mother, Ninsun . . . sorry about that, by the way. She was a wonderful queen and a lovely woman. So we've heard on the wind."

"And your brother," said the girl. She stepped closer. Tarlos wrinkled his nose and leaned away. "Krastos, was it? Oh yes, we know all about him, too." She giggled. Tarlos felt the bile in his stomach rise.

"Sorry about him, too," the boy said. "I wish I could say I know how you feel, to lose a sibling. But we're immortal, and we don't know any of our father's other children."

Tarlos did not respond. He had no desire to speak of his mother or his brother to anyone, much less these jinn. He pointed to the split peak. "How do I get up there?" he asked.

The jinn followed his finger. "Why would you want to go up there?" asked the boy.

"I need to get through. To the other side."

"Why? Are you dead?"

"No."

"Are you a god?"

"No."

"Then you can't." The boy shrugged. "Rules are rules."

"Are you trying to rescue your mother and brother?" the girl asked. "That's very chivalrous of you, but I'm afraid it doesn't work like that."

Tarlos shook his head. "I'm going for myself, and not for the dead country but for what lies beyond."

"The Ageless," whispered the boy. He held his sister's hand and sneered. "You're looking for the Ageless. I can save you the trip—you can't achieve eternal life." The boy laughed, and the girl joined him. Their little bodies shook, and Tarlos had to look away. The sound of their laughter was painful to his ears. They were not human children, he reminded himself. They were demons. Children of Ablis, the Discarded One. Half-siblings to the monster that killed his mother and brother.

Tarlos said, "My business is not your concern, jinn. I'm going through that mountain, with or without your permission."

"Oh no," said the boy. He wiped a tear from his obsidian eye. "It's not a question of whether you have our permission or not.

You simply can't go through the mountain."

"I don't care about the rules."

"I didn't say may not. I said cannot. Do you see that peak?" The boy pointed. Tarlos nodded. "What comes out of it every morning?"

Tarlos lifted his hands in a half-shrug. "The sun, of course. Shar, father of gods."

"And how long does it take for him to climb through the earth every night?"

"It depends on the season, but this time of year, I'd say about eight hours."

The boy nodded. His sister held her brother's arm and giggled. The sound sent a clammy shiver up Tarlos's back and neck.

"If it takes the father of gods eight hours to make the journey, how long do you think it would take you, son of man, before he finds you in his passage and burns you to something less than ash?" The boy lifted one eyebrow and smirked. "You'd have to be able to fly to have a chance of making it."

Tarlos smiled back at him. "But I can fly."

The smirk left the boy's face, and the girl stopped giggling. "I suppose that would make sense," he mumbled. "You are the son of Lakaeus, after all." He shook his head. "I still don't understand what you could possibly have to gain by crossing the dead country. There's nothing useful for you there. Why don't you just go home? Back to Kesh, your kingdom, your people. I'm sure they miss you. Don't you have any children? A wife?"

Tarlos swallowed, and he felt heat rise through his throat. "Are you going to show me the way through the mountain or not? I've wasted enough time as it is. Maybe I should be going."

"No!" the girl screamed, still clinging to her brother's arm. She looked at her brother. "This man is driven by despair. He's exhausted and burnt by the desert. Look at him. He can barely stand. He's been so brave to have come this far. We have to help him."

The boy nodded in agreement. "I've never seen such a desperate man. You're dedicated to your goal then, Tarlos? To cross the dead country and find the Ageless?"

Tarlos gave a single nod.

"And you know that they probably can't help you with your problem?"

"That's for me to find out," said Tarlos. "Show me the way."

The boy sighed and turned around. The girl lowered her head at Tarlos, staring at him through her long black hair. She turned with her brother, and they faced the sheer tan rock wall that bordered one side of the small clearing. The jinn raised their hands to the wall, and the sunlight shimmered over it.

Tarlos blinked, sure that as the wall began to ripple it was the hot sun playing tricks on his mind. The desert wall warped and moved in tiny waves, the rock becoming bone white to match the rest of the mountain. Small spindles of black lines crawled around the wall as if drawn by some invisible hand. They began at the ground and curved upward, rising several feet above the jinns' heads. When the drawing was finished, two scorpions faced each other on the wall, their pincers locked together.

The rock began to dissolve along the black lines, matter becoming steam. It boiled until the wall had been carved and cut away in chunks and fissures, leaving three-dimensional likenesses of the two scorpions. Between the creatures' pincers, between their legs and stinging tails, the mountain appeared hollow and dark.

Tarlos stared in amazement at the gate that had materialized before him. The two jinn faced him. They both wore malicious grins, exposing their sharp teeth. Their faces were drained and exhausted.

"Rabu-zorak," Tarlos whispered. The Scorpion Gate. He had grown up hearing tales of the magic gate that led to the dead country.

The boy and girl spoke together in one voice, and Tarlos squirmed at the sound.

"The tunnel leads downward into darkness," they said. "All will be black behind and before you and to both sides. You have eight hours to reach your destination. If you do not emerge from the tunnel before Shar enters it in the morning, his fire will engulf you. There is no refuge. May the tunnel of the sun lead you safely to the end of the living world."

The jinn ceased their speech and stepped aside. Between them, the stone scorpions vibrated. With a loud *CRACK* they separated from each other at the pincers. They folded outward, and Tarlos stepped back to give them room to open.

Behind him to the west, the sun's last rays cast out across the desert in orange and pink fingers. Tarlos could almost feel the eyes of Shar on him, daring him to venture into his mountain and see what awaited him.

Tarlos stared into the abyss and saw no light at the end of the tunnel.

"I wouldn't waste any time if I were you," the boy said.

"It was nice to have known you," the girl said.

Tarlos ran.

2

The Holder and the Demigod

Hestos lived to be ancient; no one knew exactly how old, but Lakaeus was aged himself by the time his father finally died. Lakaeus met Ninsun when they were both young, but they were permitted by law to marry only after Hestos was gone. And by then, Ninsun and Lakaeus were afraid they could not produce an heir.

They tried for many years, but the gods would not grant them a child. News spread that the king and queen of Kesh were having trouble. The kingdom feared for them. Much of the world feared as well.

Each Holder passes the Power to their eldest child. If this fails to happen, it is said that the universe itself will come apart and all life will cease to exist. Everyone in Edorath knew this. They grew nervous as the years passed with no heir to the Power of Space.

Lakaeus and Ninsun tried for twenty years for a child. Other women were brought to Lakaeus—concubines, and princesses from far-off kingdoms—but he refused to give a child to anyone but Ninsun, his beloved wife.

They prayed and sacrificed to the gods until, eventually, unto them a miracle was given.

Moleg, the god of strength, came to Ninsun in a dream as she slept beside Lakaeus.

"Ninsun," said Moleg, "I have heard your prayers and have received your sacrifices. You and your husband have served the gods well. You are both old, but the king must have an heir."

Ninsun cried out, "Yes, lord, give us a child, I beg you!"

"I will give you a child," said Moleg, "but you must give me something in return."

"Anything, great god."

"Come to me on your child's twelfth birthday, the day his Power reveals itself. I will await you in the Cedar Forest. Then I will ask a favor of you."

Ninsun awoke in tears. She shook Lakaeus awake to tell him about her dream. He was happy, and they embraced in love.

Nine months later, Tarlos was born. He was small, pink, and perfect, and he cried and wriggled like a baby should. Lakaeus held Tarlos and grinned. His firstborn son! He would inherit the Power of Space and the throne of Kesh.

And then, something unexpected happened—another son appeared! Krastos held onto Tarlos's foot, entering the world mere moments after his brother. Krastos was a large baby and already covered in hair. He never cried as a baby. Ninsun often referred to him as a peaceful old soul.

A few years later, just after the twins began to walk and speak, the king and queen noticed that Tarlos and Krastos were quite different from one another. Tarlos was a normal, average child. He was the expected size and weight for his age, and he looked like his father with his narrow feet, slender hands, and lean face.

Krastos, however, looked like neither parent. He grew faster than a wolf cub. By the time he could stand, his arms could lift a cedar chest. While other children tripped over their own feet, Krastos sprinted faster than a bull. Most full-grown men struggled beneath a plow, but Krastos dug tributaries with his bare hands.

The king and queen knew that Tarlos was their son, the next Holder of Space and future King of Kesh. But what had become apparent was that Krastos was the son of Moleg.

Ninsun loved both boys fiercely and would have done anything for them. She denied the traditional service of a wet nurse to help change their soiled clothes or tuck them into bed. She was present for every moment of her sons' lives until her death.

The night before the twins' twelfth birthday, Ninsun gathered her servants and soldiers. They made ready to set out toward the Cedar Forest, two days' journey west of Kesh.

Only one soldier survived to tell what happened next.

Before Moleg came to Ninsun to ask his favor, the monster Bawa attacked her and all who'd accompanied her—Bawa, the monster spawn of Ablis, who was discarded from the sight of Shar and Moresh.

Bawa killed Ninsun before Moleg arrived.

Lakaeus wept.

Four days after the twins' birthday, Lakaeus came to their bedroom and sat on a chair across from their beds. "Sit and be quiet," the king said. He ran a hand through his greying beard and did not look either boy in the eye. "I will tell you why your mother is dead."

Tarlos and Krastos sat in silence as they listened to their father's story. They did not interrupt, only nodding whenever the king looked up—which was seldom—to communicate their understanding. When the king finished recounting the events that led to his wife's death, the two boys stared at him with blank faces. Lakaeus said no more about their mother, whispering, "Sleep well, boys," as he left.

Tarlos did not cry that night. He wanted to, but the tears would not come. He thought of his mother, and of Bawa. A seed of anger was planted deep within him then, one that would not surface for many years.

Krastos did cry, but Tarlos heard his brother try to stifle his sobs with his pillow. Tarlos never told anyone that Krastos had cried that night. Indeed, he was envious that his brother was able to cry at all. He often wanted to weep for his mother but was never able to.

Ninsun's body was never recovered, but a golden sarcophagus was buried all the same. It was filled with treasures, its outside inlaid with lapis lazuli that the goldsmith had shaped into a likeness of the queen. Tarlos did not think it looked like his mother.

The sermon at her funeral was from an ancient text. It was the same funeral reading that was received by all the dead—royal or not. After the sermon, the sarcophagus was sealed away in a stone tomb in a secret place in the desert. No one stayed long afterwards. Even Lakaeus departed the scene before the stones were set in place.

Tarlos stayed, as did Krastos. Krastos cried again as the stones and mortar were placed around the gold coffin. Snot and tears ran down his face, and he wiped himself with his huge hands and linen tunic. Tarlos did not cry. He knew that what they were burying was not his mother. She was gone forever, and all who had attended the funeral knew that. The goldsmith could not remember her face. Whatever memories anyone had had of Ninsun were buried in that tomb.

The morning of their twentieth birthday, Tarlos was sound asleep in his bed when Krastos pounced on him like a jaguar. Krastos was a huge man, heavy like a boulder, and he managed to knock the air right out of Tarlos, who woke with a breathy shriek, kicking and punching. Krastos put a hold on him from behind, and Tarlos saw then that the room was full of laughing guards and servants. Krastos had brought them all to watch Tarlos be humiliated.

"Krastos!" huffed Tarlos, still catching the breath that had been knocked out of him. "Let me go!" He tried to move, though his arms were pinned behind his head, his legs squeezed together between Krastos's feet.

"Happy birthday, brother," said Krastos. He put a finger in his mouth, sucked on it, then stuck it in Tarlos's ear. Tarlos growled, and the bed levitated into the air. "Hey! None of that! I want to wrestle you fair today. My birthday gift to you."

The curtains and the bed sheets floated like smoke, the adrenaline having triggered Tarlos's Power. The bed tilted on an invisible axis and they toppled over the side. Krastos crashed to his shoulder. He rolled away, stood, and cradled his arm.

"How am I supposed to complete my trial with a dislocated shoulder?" he asked. His smile never faltered beneath his beard.

Tarlos had not landed at all. He floated down, touching his toes to the wood floor before settling his full weight on his feet. He grimaced and rubbed his wet ear.

"I hate when you do that," he said. "There's nothing you can do when the inside of your ear gets wet. You just have to wait for it to dry, and that takes forever and a day." He gave up and nodded to his brother. "But you're right. We have a hard day ahead of us, so let's not wrestle this morning."

Krastos laughed, and the servants and guards stepped back. "No using your Power, and I won't use my strength."

Tarlos looked at his hairy hulk of a brother and laughed. "You can't choose to abandon your strength, son of Moleg, any more than Katla can abandon her beautiful legs." He winked at his servant. Katla was from the north, and her skin was pale as milk. She blushed, and her freckled nose and cheeks turned hot pink.

"Well, I'll restrain myself as best I can," said Krastos. "As long as you don't lift me so I can't touch the floor, or suck the air from my lungs like you did last decan."

"It was entertaining, watching you squirm like a fish."

One of the guards laughed at that. Krastos shot him a glance and the guard choked.

"You're on *his* side, Lugal?"

Lugal shifted his weight and gripped his spear. "Forgive me, Prince."

Krastos pointed at Tarlos. "You turned my friend against me!"

"They have their own free will, same as you and I." The brothers were now circling each other in the center of the room. Tarlos's ear was still wet, but he ignored the discomfort. "Surely, they have only chosen the cleverest, strongest, and most handsome prince to support. It's natural they would want to see the slower, uglier, hairier brother lose."

"Who are you calling slow?"

Lugal pumped his fist into the air and laughed again.

Tarlos emptied the space between them of air, bringing them

together in a temporary vacuum. Tarlos drove a punch into his brother's gut, catching him unaware.

Krastos laughed. His muscle was like iron, and he could hardly feel his brother's blow. He reached over Tarlos, his shorter and smaller twin, and grabbed him by the waist. He lifted Tarlos upside down and above his head as a child would lift a housecat.

Tarlos in turn lifted Krastos with his mind, and the two of them hung suspended in the air. Having been in this situation many times before, Krastos let go of Tarlos and simply stood upside-down on the ceiling.

"Behold, the strength of a demigod!" he shouted, and pushed off from the ceiling. Krastos almost reached the floor but Tarlos's Power slowed him to a stop. Tarlos felt the full weight of Krastos, and his mind gave way. Krastos crumpled to the ground. He lifted himself and rolled his shoulders.

Tarlos remained on the ceiling, a safe ten feet above Krastos. "Give in, brother?"

Krastos sneered and jumped. The wooden planks in the floor groaned as he propelled himself upward. He grabbed Tarlos around the shoulders and pushed off the ceiling with his feet. The two of them fell in a heap with Krastos on top.

"Just let me know if this gets too uncomfortable," said Krastos. He held Tarlos's arms behind his back and pulled.

Tarlos let out a roar, and the hot water his servants had been preparing for him jumped from the stove and flew at Krastos's face. He let go of Tarlos and rolled away. The water splashed on the wood floor near the bed and steamed in the cool morning air.

"Hey!" Krastos yelled. "That would've actually hurt me!" He leaped at Tarlos, and the two of them locked hands. Their feet drove into the floor, and they growled against each other's strength.

"You're too kind-hearted," Tarlos said. Sweat beaded his temples. "That's why you never win. You're afraid of hurting me."

They snorted like bulls locked in combat. The walls shook with Tarlos's Power while the floor vibrated under Krastos's weight and strength.

Tarlos bent his knee with one foot planted and threw Krastos to the floor. He sunk his feet onto Krastos's hairy chest. "Do you submit?"

Krastos's chest heaved, and for a moment he looked at his brother in anger. But only for a moment, then a smile spread over his bearded face. He laughed and held out his hand, and Tarlos helped him to his feet.

"There's none in the world like you, brother," Krastos said. "Not even a demigod can best a Holder." He took Tarlos in for a hug, Tarlos's head coming up to his chin.

"Even still," said Tarlos, "only a Holder can best the son of Moleg, the man who could carry the Sun himself on his shoulders."

The servants and guards applauded them, and they each gave a short bow.

The bedroom door flew open and slammed into the wall behind it. The High Priestess, who spoke on behalf of the gods, charged into the bedchamber. Tarlos's room servants, Katla and Mez, backed away with their heads down. The four guards who had come to watch them wrestle stood erect and clutched their spears.

"As Shar himself sees you behaving thus, I wonder why he does not burn you all where you stand!" She pointed with an elegant finger through the window to the rising sun. Her painted eyes burned with fury, her skirt dusting the floor as she approached Tarlos and Krastos. "I thought the end-times were upon us, the way the palace was shaking and creaking and thundering. You've woken everyone here, royal and servant both! And did you think of your father? Sick in his bed, needing all the rest he can get? He thought Ilshu had come for him at last, the way the walls were swaying around him. And on the anniversary of your mother's death, no less! You should know better."

The twins averted their gaze; their bowed heads hid their smirks. They risked a humorous glance at each other.

"And you!" She turned to Katla and Mez. "Why is the stove lit? Why are the tea leaves out? Today is the day of the princes' trials—today they are not to eat or drink until they are men."

Katla and Mez kept their eyes on the floor. "Forgive us,

High Priestess," said Mez. "We lost track of the day."

"You will both be punished accordingly," said the High Priestess.

"No," Tarlos said. "I asked for it, Priestess. Don't blame them."

"Why would you ask for tea, Tarlos? You know the commandment."

He nodded. "Forgive me."

Krastos said, "We're sorry things got out of control. We're both anxious for our trials today, and we wanted to let out some energy."

"You'll need all the energy you can muster," said the High Priestess. She stood defiant, legs far apart and hands on her hips. Her eyes were lined with blue and red paint, drawn down her cheeks in three lines. The ends of her black hair were dyed green. On every finger was a ring, and bands of bronze and lapis lazuli adorned her thin arms. Standing before them in her splendor and authority, the brothers felt, in the presence of the High Priestess, more like rebuked children than princes.

"Come," she said with a wave of her arm. "It's time to prepare."

As she led them from the room, Tarlos gave a friendly smile to Katla, and the Northerling girl simply shook her head and smiled in return.

Krastos punched Lugal's shoulder on the way out, and the guard grunted in pain. Krastos snickered and patted Lugal's arm. The guard smiled and nodded at the prince, and the twins followed the High Priestess through the palace.

The bathhouse was all cedar wood, as was the palace and most of the city-state. The bath itself was a small swimming pool set above a natural hot spring.

Krastos and Tarlos undressed and eased into the steaming water. Body servants scrubbed them down with soap, lathered their hair with oil, and smoothed out their tangles with cedar wood combs.

Tarlos asked his body servant, "What do you think they have in store for us, Basmem?"

"I couldn't say, Prince," the servant replied as he washed Tarlos's hair. Basmem was probably about fifteen years old, but even he did not know his exact age. When he was much younger, he was caught stealing an apple from a merchant. He had lived as a servant and without thumbs ever since.

Basmem poured a red liquid soap into Tarlos's hair. As he had difficulty holding objects, the small vase slipped from his hand and the soap dripped into Tarlos's eyes.

"Gah!" Tarlos rubbed his stinging eyes with wet hands.

"Prince—!"

"No, no, it's all right. But if I fail my trial because I can't see, I'll cut off the rest of your fingers."

Basmem chuckled.

Tarlos said, "I imagine a giant boar for me, or maybe an aurochs. Have you seen the mammoths that the traders from the north ride? I'd bet I could take one of those. Krastos, though, they probably have a dairy cow for him, eh, Basmem?"

Krastos sent a splash toward Tarlos, and Basmem laughed. He wiped water from his forehead with a thumbless hand. Tarlos moved a small wave back at Krastos without lifting a finger. It drenched Krastos and his body servant.

Krastos sighed. "Patnu spent *hours*, probably, getting his hair perfect this morning, and now it's ruined. I hope you're happy, brother." He made one more tiny splash at his twin, for the sake of having the last move.

"Will you forgive me, Patnu?" Tarlos asked, still rubbing soap from his eyes.

"Nothing to forgive, Prince." Patnu ran his hands over his face and curly black hair. He was the only servant in Kesh from the south, across the deserts and jungles. Neither Krastos nor Tarlos had ever known how Patnu had managed to find himself in Kesh, thousands of miles to the north in the middle of a vast desert.

"Unless," Patnu added, "you'd like to apologize for not thinking of inviting me to this morning's wrestle. I always enjoy seeing Krastos put in his place."

Tarlos exploded with laughter. Krastos reached a giant hairy hand behind him and pulled Patnu over his head and into the water. Patnu surfaced, sputtering and laughing. Krastos laughed as well in spite of himself.

The last thing to do was to rub a special oil on the princes' faces to help their beards to grow. A good beard was a symbol of power and authority. Tarlos had never been able to grow much more than stubble, and Basmem gave his face an extra rub. Krastos, who'd had a beard since he was thirteen, as well as being covered in hair everywhere else, received a trim before his own oil rub.

The twins lifted themselves out of the bath, and Patnu and Basmem wrapped them in hot towels and brushed their hair. They wrapped cotton tunics around their waists.

The High Priestess was waiting for them outside.

"It's time for your blessing," she told them. "Follow." She spun around, and her braided black hair flew in an arc, colored beads snapping against one another.

"High Priestess," Krastos said. "Couldn't we have just some bread and water, at least? Slaying a beast will be tiresome, and I'm already starving."

"You will eat and drink nothing until you have completed your trial. That goes for you as well, future king."

At the same time, both twins realized where she was taking them. "Why are we going to see Father?" Tarlos asked.

"Isn't he too sick to have visitors?" Krastos asked. "And on the anniversary of our mother's death, no less!"

The High Priestess caught Krastos's satirical tone. "How dare you?" she said, turning on him. "May Moresh, goddess of motherhood, with whom your mother now lives, forgive you for taking Ninsun's death so lightly." Her voice was not loud, nor was it angry. There was disappointment in her words.

Krastos frowned and nodded, lowering his eyes.

"I expect more of you, Prince," she added, then turned back around and continued to lead them to Lakaeus's chamber.

The guards at the massive cedar doors stepped aside and opened them. Light hurt the King's eyes, so his chambers were kept as dark as possible—heavy black curtains covered the windows, and no flame was allowed in the room. For more than three years, Lakaeus had been weak and sensitive, symptoms of his blood disease. He would cry out in pain, gripping the sides of his head if the light of a single star squeezed into the room.

The king himself lay on his bed with the curtains pulled back. Servants and a healer tended to him.

The doctor saw the princes and the High Priestess approach, and bent close to the king. "Your majesty," he whispered, though in the silence of the room his whispers still bounced off the walls. "The High Priestess has come with the princes."

The king emitted a low grumble, and the healer nodded to the servants. They left his bedside, bowing to the Priestess and to the princes as they departed.

Leeches covered the king's arms, legs, torso, and neck. Tiny trickles of blood snaked between him and the leeches, staining the white sheets below. Old, brown stains from previous leeching sessions dotted the sheets.

"Your majesty," said the High Priestess. "The princes have come for your blessing. Today they take the trials of manhood."

The king's white, naked eyes rolled in his head. He looked at Tarlos and Krastos. He held out a bony hand, and Tarlos took it. His skin was like moth wings, Tarlos thought.

"My son," Lakaeus said. His voice was dried leaves in the wind. He swallowed, licked his lips, and looked to Krastos. "Brother of my son, son of my wife." A small smile played at the corners of his mouth. "You have come to visit me?"

"Yes, Father," said Tarlos. He had not been permitted to visit his father for several decans. Now that he saw him, he was filled with dread.

Soon I will lose my father as I lost my mother.

Lakaeus's cheeks were sunken, his lips thin and pulled back, revealing yellow teeth and grey gums. His eyes were round, and they swiveled in their sockets like birds' eyes. His face was almost skeletal—fleshless and white. The rest of his body was not so different: skin dried like papyrus covering bones as soft as mud.

"I do not look well," the king mused. "Your eyes tell me."

Tarlos shook his head. "You look wonderful, great king. Healthy as Moleg, who gives you strength."

Lakaeus smiled. "I am happy to see you. Why have you come now, after all this time? How long has it been since I've seen your faces?"

"We didn't want to disturb you. You need your rest."

"I need death, that's what I need." The king laughed, and it was a sound like a headless swan attempting to breathe underwater. "I am too old to have lived this long. The only mercy I pray for is Ilshu to ferry me across the river."

Tarlos patted his father's hand, frail as a child's, and looked into his pasty eyes. Regret surged within him. He didn't really know his father. After Ninsun died, Lakaeus retreated within himself, hardly speaking to anyone, least of all his sons. Her sons. They reminded him too much of her. Tarlos blamed no one for his father's distance, not even him, but he did regret it. King Lakaeus's time was not long for this world, and for a moment Tarlos felt it as heavily as the king.

Krastos remained silent at his brother's side. Although Lakaeus had raised him as his own, Krastos was not blood and therefore was not permitted to speak unless spoken to. Only the High Priestess and Tarlos were allowed that privilege.

"Our trials are today," Tarlos said. "We are to become men. We ask for your blessing before we begin."

"Ah-h-h . . ." Lakaeus lifted a thin, clawed hand to Tarlos's head, resting it in his hair. "And so you have it. May the gods bless you as I do. May you be a greater king than I, and a greater father."

Tarlos took his father's hand from his head and held it in his own. "No one could be a better king or father than Lakaeus the Great."

The king did not respond. He took back his hand and gestured to Krastos. "Come."

Krastos lowered his head to the king and allowed the feather-light hand to rest in his hair.

"I am not your father," said the king, "but I have raised you and loved you as my son. And as surely as your father, the great god Moleg, blesses you, so too I bless you as your foster father. May your life be fruitful. May men and women sing of your deeds forever."

Tarlos saw the beginnings of tears in Krastos's eyes, which Krastos quickly wiped away. He was thankful for the blessing and had not hoped for a better one, nor had he expected it—not from a man who had never wanted him but had nonetheless raised him as his own.

Krastos took Lakaeus's hand and kissed it. "Thank you, my king. May you live forever."

The king laughed once more, an awful, wheezing sound. Krastos drew back in confusion.

"No, dear boy," he said. "To live forever in my state would be a curse. I have lived a full life and am at peace with my death, which is soon to come. Only gods and Ageless live forever." The king pointed to a small dresser at the other end of the room. "Tarlos. The first drawer. Bring me the little box."

Tarlos did as his father instructed, finding a small black wooden box in the drawer. He set it down on the bed next to the king. Lakaeus opened it and pulled out two small talismans on silver chains. They were identical, made of bronze and stamped with the seals of Moresh and Shar, half blue and half red. Lakaeus gestured for the twins to put them on.

"A gift from a dying father to his boys," said the king.

They put the necklaces over their heads. Tarlos let his drop to his chest, keeping his eyes on his sick and dying father. Krastos inspected his for several moments, running his fingers over the stamp and feeling the weight of the bronze. He wore the talisman on the outside of his tunic while Tarlos placed his underneath and against his skin.

Lakaeus took a hand from each brother and smiled. "Good luck with your trials. Gods, has it been twenty years already? I will forever think it the greatest shame that life lingers so slowly when we suffer, while the time we spend with those we love is more fleeting than sunshine in a storm."

Before anything else could be said, the High Priestess swept in and placed her hands on the twins' shoulders. "Your majesty, the princes must prepare for their trials."

Lakaeus gave the smallest of nods and waved the princes

away. "Don't worry about me. I've still got a few decans left, I'm sure of it." He gave them one last smile, then fell asleep.

The High Priestess led them through the king's chamber and outside the palace, through the courtyard and gardens there. The courtyard, shaded from the hot summer sun, was filled with palms and Yeshu trees, conifers, lilies, and roses. The gardens buzzed with hummingbirds and honeybees.

She led the princes to the temple on the other side of the gardens. Unlike most structures in Kesh, the temple was built from stone, each block weighing over a ton and dragged from a quarry fifteen miles away, on the border of the Fertile Valley. It was in the temple that the gods spoke to the priestesses and gave them commandments that they in turn conveyed to the people of Kesh.

When they were young, Tarlos and Krastos thought the temple reached to the heavens, to the throne of Shar. They'd had to crane their necks back to see the top-most block scrape the sky. Now that they were older and bigger, the temple did not seem so large. In fact, their own palace was taller.

A few servants worked in the gardens in the courtyard and in the smaller gardens surrounding the stone temple, and some worked on the structure itself, sealing cracks in the old rock with mortar. They all paused their work and touched their foreheads to the ground as the princes walked by with the High Priestess.

Krastos spoke to one of the servants. "Good morning, Namgan. How is your family?"

The servant did not lift his bald head from the ground but answered just the same. "Healthy, with full bellies. Thank you for asking, Prince."

"For as long as I shall live," said the High Priestess, "I will never understand your friendliness toward servants."

"It's not their fault they were born servants," said Krastos. "They're only people. Like us."

Tarlos elbowed his brother. "Says the man whose father is a god."

Krastos continued, "If I were king, I'd give them wages. The royal family has enough possessions. We can afford to pay them."

They climbed the stone stairway to the matching door above.

"You will not be king," said the High Priestess. "Your brother will." Tarlos thought he heard resentfulness in that last bit.

Tarlos said, "Maybe we will rule together. A Holder and a demigod. Co-rulers of Kesh."

The High Priestess chuckled in her throat, clearly disgusted at the notion. "Such has never been heard of."

The door was open and dark before them. The High Priestess extended her slender arm, motioning for the princes to enter.

The inner room was lit with candles, and statues of the gods lined the walls. There were more than a dozen in all, though Tarlos cared for only a few. The dancing light from the candles gave the gods menacing stares and grimaces—it seemed as if they were judging the twins with their stone eyes.

Priestesses—young girls who had devoted their lives to the gods and had vowed never to marry or bear children—came to help the princes into their ceremonial clothing: a sleeveless leather shirt, belt, sandals, and a copper headband.

At the end of the room were the statues of Moresh and her husband, Shar—the moon and the sun. The High Priestess motioned for the brothers to kneel before their gods, which they did.

Shar wore the sun as his crown, and he held the sun in his right hand, and he himself was the sun.

The moon was in Moresh's right eye, and she cradled the moon against her bosom, and she herself was the moon.

In the beginning there was nothing.

And then there was chaos, and from that chaos came Moresh and Shar, the moon and sun, and together they formed the stars and the Earth. They separated the stars from the Earth, and had children, who were the lesser gods, and the gods came together to create mankind from clay and fire.

A brazier stood before Shar, and another before Moresh. The High Priestess brought a torch and first lit Moresh's, and then Shar's. The flames on Moresh's brazier turned blue, and her husband's flames were red.

The High Priestess lifted her hands to the goddess of the

moon. "Moresh, two children come to you this day to receive your blessing that they may become adults. As they use their skill and cunning during their trials, look upon them in favor."

A young priestess, perhaps seventeen years old, held a bowl to the High Priestess. She dipped her fingers into it and smeared blue paint on the princes' cheeks.

The High Priestess lifted her hands to the god of the sun. "Shar, two boys come to you this day to receive your blessing that they may become men. As they use their strength and force of will during their trials, look upon them in favor."

Another young priestess stepped forward with her bowl, and the High Priestess smeared red paint on the princes' foreheads and chins. Tarlos saw the young priestess give a tiny smile to Krastos, and Krastos winked at her in turn. Tarlos glanced at the High Priestess, hoping she did not see the exchange, but it appeared that she had.

She shook her head. "Gods save us from the future king and his brother," she muttered under her breath.

She motioned for the twins to stand. They did so, bowing to the gods—first to Moresh, then to Shar, then to each god and goddess that lined the walls from right to left.

At Moleg, Krastos stayed a bit longer. The statue depicted Moleg as grinning, with pointed teeth and huge round eyes. Tarlos watched as his brother looked upon his father with wonder and respect, and knew that Krastos was giving one final prayer especially for Moleg. Tarlos had overheard him many nights leading up to this day praying to his Moleg idol in the privacy of his bedroom: "Give me strength. Show the king that I am Ninsun's son, and let him be proud." Krastos always kept his pain hidden away, behind a smile. Only Tarlos knew how much Krastos wanted Lakaeus's love.

The day was dry, and the hot sun beat down on the princes as they walked through the streets of Kesh. All through the city, people lined the roads and cheered for them. They shouted the princes' names, tossed lilies and palm leaves at their feet, threw red and blue chalk powder on them to bring favor from the gods.

Tarlos smiled, even as his heart beat madly in his chest. He had waited many years for this day, and now that it was here it felt surreal. He thought he would have been more excited than nervous, but he was wrong. The closer he and Krastos came to the arena, the more Tarlos's heart thumped, the more sweat dripped from his forehead and armpits, making tiny trails in the chalk powder.

Krastos ignored the cheering crowds, and the blue and red chalk dust that clouded the streets and covered him from head to toe. He was never one to be distracted by applause. He had always been focused when he needed to be, and he was focused now. His brow pointed low over his dark eyes and his jaw was set beneath his bushy beard. His strength had never failed him, and he knew it would not fail him now, in the arena. He was the son of Moleg. No beast could best him.

The arena lay on the outskirts of Kesh, without the wall that encircled the city-state. It was a great bowl in the red and yellow rock of the desert, partly carved from the living stone, partly built from quarried granite and cedar wood. It was more oval than circle, six hundred feet by five hundred in the arena itself, its walls reaching upwards more than two hundred feet. Its thousands of seats were already filled with the citizens of Kesh.

The guards who'd escorted the princes through the city led them now through a small private gate in the city wall, then down a path kept off-limits to civilians.

Tarlos punched Krastos's shoulder. "What do you think?"

"I think I'm ready." Krastos did not look at his brother; he was focused.

"I mean, what do you think it'll be?"

Krastos shrugged. "Doesn't much matter, does it? You'll fly above it, whatever it is, and throw it around with your Power. Maybe toss a boulder at it. I'll grab mine and wrestle it to the ground, choke it until it passes out."

"And then you'll kill it."

"Not if I can help it. Whatever it is, it's just an animal. I'll tell them to release it after."

Tarlos shook his head and grinned. His fingers and hands

vibrated with adrenaline.

A trial of manhood for a Holder happened once a generation. The firstborn of a Holder was also a Holder, and therefore heir to the throne. If a king and queen had multiple children, they were also expected to complete a trial. Holders faced a monster, such as a dragon or a gryphon. A Powerless prince or princess would only have to fight an animal—a gorilla or an adolescent elephant—and would be given weapons. Holders were not given anything.

Today there would be two trials, and both initiates were more than human. Tarlos was a Holder, able to move things at will with his mind; Krastos was the son of Moleg and had inherited his godlike strength. Today's trials would be of a kind not seen before in Kesh, or perhaps the world.

The path led them behind the arena, into a small room in which initiates would prepare themselves and pray. Above them, Krastos and Tarlos heard the thundering of the crowd, their cheering and shouting, the stomping of their feet. Small puffs of dust drifted down from the stone and wood ceiling above.

The guards stood at attention as Tarlos and Krastos each made one last silent prayer to Moresh and Shar. Tarlos was sure that Krastos included Moleg in his prayer. They finished their supplications and looked to the guards.

"Are you ready, princes?" asked the captain, standing in front of the rest and holding a spear taller than himself. Both princes nodded. "I will let them know. Prince Tarlos will be first. Best of luck to both of you." Before turning away, the captain paused for a moment to take one last look at Krastos. His eyes lingered, and then he and the other guards bowed, and he led them from the small room. The brothers were alone.

"Did he seem worried?" Krastos asked.

"I don't see why he should be." Tarlos crossed the small room and leaned against the door there, knowing that it would open at any moment—to the arena, and to the cheering crowd and the monsters that would try to kill them. "We're the ones facing possible death."

Krastos took the talisman from beneath his shirt and looked

at the image of the sun and the moon. He ran his fingers over the outside edge.

"I forgot we had those," said Tarlos, and he grabbed his own talisman. He took it from around his neck and stuffed it in a pocket.

"Don't you like it?"

Tarlos shrugged. "It's just a necklace. Nothing special."

Krastos frowned and squeezed the talisman in his fist. "Don't laugh, but . . . since Mother died, this is the first time I've really felt like family. Lakaeus almost treated me like I was his son." He hid the talisman back under his shirt and inhaled shakily. "So, you're first?"

"I'm older."

Krastos nodded. "Good luck."

Tarlos returned the nod, hoping this would not be the last time he saw his twin. "See you on the other side."

Outside, great drums *boom-boom-boom*'d, and the sound carried through the arena, causing the crowd to cheer ever louder. Their stomping dropped more dirt on the princes. The sound of chains rattling made Tarlos's heart race as the door was pulled open.

The roc was already there when Tarlos stepped through the door into the hot and sun-bright arena. Spectators filling every seat called his name and applauded. The door shut behind him. There was no handle on this side.

A giant bird stood over an aurochs, tearing into it, its beak sharp as obsidian. It ripped the beast's flesh with its enormous talons, blood pouring from the dead aurochs, puddling around both the bull and the bird in a thick red pool.

Tarlos swallowed and scanned the area. The roc had not yet seen him—they were on opposite ends of the arena. Tarlos had a few seconds before the roc smelled fresher prey. An aurochs was but a morsel to a roc, whose wingspan spread over two hundred feet, and was no doubt only meant to keep the roc occupied until Tarlos had formulated a method of attack.

Tarlos was not allowed a weapon. In the trial of manhood, a

Holder was allowed only his or her hands and wits. He stepped lightly around the edge of the arena, spotting many boulders littering the space. He made note of them but decided against that plan. Using his Power cost energy—he knew he could not throw boulders for long. Krastos might have better use for them.

The only other object in the arena was a wooden scaffolding holding a narrow ladder that connected the arena floor to the stands above. The ladder was used by guards in case someone was seriously injured and needed a quick escape. If, however, Tarlos were injured, he would not need the ladder; he could fly.

But I won't be able to fly if I'm unconscious or exhausted. And what if Krastos needs a quick escape?

Stop worrying about your brother and worry about the roc instead.

The last of the aurochs went down the roc's long neck, and the giant bird stretched its wings and screeched. Everyone in the stands covered their ears and grimaced at the sound. Tarlos closed his eyes and put his arms over the sides of his head. The sound was like a copper knife being dragged over rough granite, and it made his teeth rattle.

The roc flapped its wings, and a thunderclap shook the stadium, blowing dirt and small rocks outward in a circle. The shockwave knocked Tarlos off his feet and sent him flying into the stone wall behind him.

He grunted as he hit the wall, then once more when he fell to the ground. He stood and stretched his neck. It popped, and he sighed in relief—he was still intact.

The roc folded its wings and craned its head upward. It cawed at the people above, and with another thundering flap of its wings attempted to fly up to them. The people screamed as the sharp, gaping beak of the roc soared too close. But a short chain attached to its feet jerked it back down just shy of its prey. The spectators continued to scream, many fleeing to different sections of the arena.

Tarlos dropped to his belly to avoid the last bout of thunder as the roc returned to the arena floor. He felt wind and tiny rocks graze his back, but he was not thrown.

The roc hovered down, disappointed. It preened its black and brown feathers.

Tarlos regarded the beast's talons. It was difficult to tell from a distance, but he judged them to be at least a few feet long each. They were silver, and they glinted in the sunlight. He had seen how the talons had torn into the aurochs as if it were made of soggy papyrus, and he knew he must avoid them. But Tarlos would get nowhere near the bird if he did not take care of those wings first.

The roc hobbled around, pacing the circumference of the arena and testing its confines. It considered the audience with passive interest, more concerned with the chain holding it to the ground. It pecked at the stone wall of the arena, and great chunks of red rock came loose and fell to the ground in puffs of red dirt. As it paced the field, Tarlos moved with it, keeping himself to the opposite end of the arena at all times. He stayed low and quiet.

Maybe he could rip its wings off. That would stop the thunderclaps. But no, that would be too messy. Although it was a monster, Tarlos would prefer to leave his opponent some dignity.

With another tooth-rattling screech, the roc lifted its head and stretched its neck. It stared directly at Tarlos. Its obsidian beak opened, the pink tongue within clicking against the roof of its mouth. It unveiled its enormous wings, and Tarlos once more fell to his belly.

The thunderclap hit him like a galloping horse, and he felt the weight of the air as it launched him to the wall at his back. Even lying flat, he stood no chance.

Tarlos stood, groaning, and shook the stars from his head. The roc trotted over to him from across the arena, its huge clawed feet sending out ripples of sand with each step.

Tarlos jumped in the air and flew above the roc's head. The bird looked up at him with confusion, and then leapt to meet him in the air. The chain pulled it back down, and the roc landed hard. It cried and screeched, watching Tarlos in the air with a swiveling head and eyes like black marbles.

Reaching out with his mind, Tarlos selected a medium-sized chunk of rock that the giant bird had pecked loose from the wall. He brought it up to his height—he had been lifting rocks this size since he was young. The audience followed the boulder with their collective gaze, as did the roc. Beside him now, the boulder was about half his height, and many times heavier than himself.

Tarlos steadied the boulder over the roc and let it fall. It struck the bird in the back but did not injure it at all, which was exactly what Tarlos wanted.

The roc screamed in pain and in annoyance, and flapped its huge wings. The arena rocked and the people cried out and ducked between their seats to shield themselves. The roc carried itself as high as its chain would allow and screamed at Tarlos.

With a flick of his hand, Tarlos removed the creature's restraints, and the bird soared at him as fast as wind itself. The people screamed, and Tarlos grinned.

Up, up, up—Tarlos led the roc high into the sky, speeding toward the noon sun as fast as his mind would allow. Just below him, the roc flapped its mighty wings. It bared its talons and opened its razor-sharp beak. Its large pink tongue wriggled in its mouth like a serpent, eager for the meal to come.

Tarlos stopped, hovering a few thousand feet above the ground. The arena was a tiny oval, no bigger than his little fingernail. A few inches to the east lay Kesh, surrounded by a great wall as thick as a hair. It was cold this high up, and the air was thin. Tarlos's next move had to be quick—before he fainted and fell from the sky.

He allowed the roc to reach within a few feet of him before he pinned its wings to its sides with his Power. The roc squawked once more, struggling to spread its wings. It lingered in the air for a moment, and then it fell.

Tarlos stayed beside the roc as it plummeted, watching it roll around in midair and thrash at nothing. The tiny oval of the arena below grew larger and more defined as they approached. The bird swiveled its head to watch the ground rise to meet it.

Tarlos halted at the top-most level of the arena and rested

there while the roc crashed into the red dirt of the arena. A spray of rock and sand and feathers bellowed up from the point of impact. When the dust settled enough to see again, the audience and Tarlos beheld a crumpled mass of feathers and twisted broken limbs. Tarlos floated down and landed on the great roc's head. He waved to the crowd as the people of Kesh cheered and shouted his name.

These were his people smiling at him. "Tarlos! Tarlos!" they chanted. He drank it in; he felt their praise in his bones and in his blood, and knew then that there was no greater life to be lived than his own.

Tarlos flew to the top of the stands, to the highest of the seats. The arena was small below him. He rested on the roof and dangled his feet off the edge as he waited for the soldiers to clear away the mess of the roc in preparation for Krastos's own trial.

Tarlos's heart was sprinting, the adrenaline in his body making him nauseated. He had never felt a rush like he did at that moment. Any moment now, that heavy stone door would open and it would be his twin's turn to face whatever monster awaited him in the arena.

Tarlos sent up a small prayer to Moleg on behalf of Krastos. *God of strength, lend your strength to my brother.*

Krastos must have been afraid and anxious. He never enjoyed fighting unless a friendly wrestle. But Tarlos knew that whatever creature he was about to face, Krastos would wrestle it into submission. He had seen Krastos do it before with cave lions and wild bulls.

Only a Holder can best the son of Moleg. Tarlos had said that earlier this morning, and he only half meant it. He knew that Krastos let him win those wrestling matches, but he never said anything about it and neither did Krastos.

He heard the sound of metal against metal, chains rattling, and the stone door pulled open. Krastos stepped into the bright sun and shielded his eyes with his huge arm. The crowds erupted in applause.

"Krastos! Give it hell!" Tarlos shouted. He did not know if Krastos could hear him or not.

Then, on the opposite side of the arena, more chains rattled. The *click-click-click-click* of gears brought Krastos's attention to a large metal gate in the section of the arena that housed the large animals.

Krastos planted his feet firmly in the ground and crouched low.

The metal gate opened to darkness. Several silent seconds passed, and the crowd grew anxious. Tarlos found himself chewing on a fingernail.

From above the gate, two guards threw a dead sheep into the arena. It landed in front of the dark hole like a limp doll. A huff and a sniff came from the darkness, and then a monster walked out on all fours to inspect the dead sheep.

Tarlos's heart stopped. It was a manticore—a huge, demonic animal with the body of a lion, the tail of a scorpion, and the face of a man. Its body, from mane to tail, was covered in sharp poisonous quills. Krastos would not be able to wrestle it. He would not even be able to touch it. Even a Holder would have trouble fighting a manticore.

Krastos crouched low, hiding behind a boulder as he gathered his thoughts. The manticore nibbled at the sheep. Although it had the body and teeth of a lion, it did not have a lion's snout, and it slowly and methodically tried to fit its man-like mouth around the carcass.

Lakaeus used to tell the brothers stories about the monsters and demons that roamed the desert. The manticore was said to have huge bat wings and three rows of sharp teeth on each jaw, and it could shoot poisonous quills from its tail like arrows from a bow. But this manticore did not have wings, and although Tarlos could not see well from his vantage point, he did not think it had three rows of teeth on each jaw. So, could it shoot quills from its tail, or was that too an embellishment?

Krastos could not risk it. Tarlos knew he would attack the tail first. Krastos looked around from his hiding place. All there was around him were boulders and dirt and the stone door behind him that would not open from this side. Then his head stopped as he caught sight of the narrow scaffold and ladder against the arena wall.

Tarlos swallowed—if Krastos was about to do what Tarlos thought, he would only have one shot.

Krastos wrapped his massive arms around the boulder he was hiding behind. With a slight grunt, he hefted it from the ground and up over his head, then tossed it. As the boulder soared through the air, he sprinted for the ladder.

The boulder collided with the manticore's face as Krastos grabbed the first rung of the ladder. The monster's mannish nose broke beneath the rock. Blood sprayed in all directions. The manticore roared, displaying its sharp teeth, as blood ran from its nose and into its mouth.

It saw Krastos climbing the ladder and galloped toward him. It leapt through the air, claws extended from its furry toes. Krastos neared the top of the ladder and was almost able to see over the wall and into the stands when the monster jumped. Krastos turned.

The manticore's mouth opened so wide that it seemed almost flat, and even from a distance Tarlos could see that it did indeed have three rows of teeth on both the top and bottom.

As the manticore flew through the air, Krastos reached the top of the wall and planted his feet on the last rung of the ladder while steadying himself with one hand. He bent his knees and jumped, using all his strength to push from the ladder, and soared over the manticore. Too late the beast caught sight of its foe—Krastos drifted over its spiny back as the monster pummeled the red stone wall.

A large crack stretched from ground to spectator seat, letting out a *pop* and a *crack* so loud that Tarlos saw the audience recoil in a wave, spreading from the bottom row to the top. He felt a small rumble under himself as the shockwave reached the topmost level.

Krastos slipped beneath the manticore, grabbing hold of the end of its scorpion tail. He was dangerously close to the stinger, but it was the only place not covered in quills. Using his momentum, Krastos pulled the scorpion tail to the ground. The manticore, still stunned from its collision, lay motionless for a few short moments.

Krastos landed, pulling on the tail. With a tug, a jerk, and a twist, the stinger ripped off. The entire tail wriggled like a beheaded snake, and shudders rippled up the manticore's back. Green ooze bled from the wound. Krastos jumped away—he could not remember whether manticore blood was poisonous or corrosive and would always rather be safe than stupid.

The monster raised itself from the cracked wall, its tail still flicking around like a lizard's tongue. The manticore shook its head, its spiny mane ruffling. It brought its tail around to its face, gave it a lick with a long black tongue, and whimpered.

Oh no, thought Tarlos. *It feels pain*. Now he knew Krastos would not kill it, though he prayed that he was wrong.

The manticore shifted its attention back to Krastos. Its lips peeled back from its three sets of triangular teeth. It growled. Leapt. Krastos somersaulted out of the way, landing hard on a rock. He stood back up, clutching a bleeding shoulder.

The manticore roared and swiped at Krastos with one of its giant paws. Krastos jumped over it and landed beside the manticore, then jumped away again as the tail swooped in. He landed beside the discarded stinger. The base of it was round, the stinger itself more than several feet long and curled at the end to a gruesome point still dripping with yellow venom.

The manticore puffed its bristly mane, which inflated to three times the size of its head. Then, just as quickly, it seemed to pop, shooting dozens of yard-long quills in all directions.

Krastos held the stinger in front of him like a shield. The quills hit the arena walls with a few dozen hard thumps. Several quills hit Krastos's makeshift shield, and the force pushed him back. His feet carved tiny channels of dirt as he slid.

If Krastos had known it felt pain, Tarlos was sure he would have killed it quickly—if he was going to kill it at all. Now that the monster was agitated, Tarlos had no idea what his brother was going to do.

The beast fired more quills, accompanied by a roar, and then leapt at its prey. Krastos blocked the quills and rolled out of the way just in time to avoid a paw full of claws to the torso.

He stood again, and more quills came at him. Around and around they danced.

"What is he doing?" Tarlos wondered aloud. "Throw the quills like spears!" He wanted to yell it, but aiding Krastos would forfeit his trial.

Krastos was doing nothing to fight the manticore, and the manticore was doing everything it could to kill Krastos.

Tarlos hovered around, leaving his stoop and circling the top of the arena. He scratched his chin and chewed his thumbnail again as he watched Krastos narrowly escape death dozens of times.

And then, Krastos made a mistake.

The manticore shot its quills, and Krastos lifted his stinger-shield to block them. Predicting the manticore's next move, Krastos rolled out of the way to avoid the inevitable pounce—only the manticore did not pounce and instead shot more quills, one of which caught the edge of Krastos's shield as he rolled.

The shield flew from his grip and skidded to a halt several yards away. The manticore grinned, lips pulled back in a sneer and hind legs bent.

Tarlos put his hands on his head and shouted the first thing that came to his mind: "Behold the strength of a demigod!" Krastos looked up at him with absolute fear in his eyes, but with this fear came understanding.

The manticore pounced.

Please see your chance, Krastos.

Tarlos reached down with his mind, and with all his strength he stopped the manticore mid-leap. He groaned under the mental strain, willing Krastos to act.

Krastos saw his opportunity in the two seconds in which it occurred. He sprinted, spraying a wave of dirt behind him, and grabbed the broken stinger before leaping straight into the path of the manticore's mouth.

Its maw was open in a halted roar. Krastos dropped the stinger into its gaping jaws and then vaulted off the monster's broken nose.

Tarlos released the manticore to great relief. He was a hundred feet closer to the ground and had to will himself to not fall the rest of the way.

The manticore landed on one side of the arena and Krastos the opposite. The manticore closed its mouth. It paused. Turned.

Krastos met the monster's human eyes. They were blue. Not clear like the sky but opaque like sapphires.

The manticore fell over on its side. Its hind leg twitched, and then it was dead.

To the audience, the pause in the manticore's leap was almost non-existent. It all happened so fast, from start to finish, and then the monster was dead and Krastos stood victorious with nothing more than a scraped shoulder.

The crowd erupted with applause and cheers. Krastos's chest heaved as he struggled to steady his breath, and he wiped his sweaty hands in the dirt. He looked at the dead animal and shook his head. He did not smile.

Tarlos came down and landed in a small crater, beaming. Krastos smiled at his brother, and they embraced tightly. The civilians cheered them on as they grasped each other's hands and thrust them into the air.

They were men.

3

Dead Country

When Tarlos set out on his journey, he'd had an idea of how long it might take to get through Shar's Mountain. This is why he did not fly at all as he crossed the desert. Flying cost him almost the same amount of energy as running, though it was his mind that became tired instead of his body. He guessed that the tunnel through the mountain would be a fair distance, but he was wrong.

He thought about Shar's path through the sky and about the dead country. Surely the dead had sunlight for the same amount of time as the living—night there is roughly the same length as day in the living world. So then, how far could the tunnel possibly be if the lands of both the living and dead have days of the same length?

But then, what if he was wrong? What if a day in the dead country was in fact shorter than one in the living world? What if time was irrelevant on the other side?

Tarlos cast the thought aside—it did not matter. He was ready for the task ahead, and he knew he would make it to the other side before it was too late.

He ran into the tunnel and the Scorpion Gate closed behind him with a heavy thud. The light in the tunnel faded as the holes in the rock between the two scorpions melted back into solid rock. Tarlos was not prepared for the darkness.

This is what it's like to be blind.

He inched forward with his hands outstretched. The darkness

was thick as tar. This worried him. If the tunnel was short, he should be able to see light on the other end, the light coming from the dead country. But there was none, and Tarlos could see absolutely nothing.

He kept his hands in front of him as he walked. Twice, he walked into the wall on the right side and had to adjust his course. A few times he waved his hands above his head to guard against low ceilings, but there were none. This made sense; the sun was enormous, and the tunnel must be large enough for it to fit.

He was comforted by this realization, for if the tunnel was large enough for the sun, he could fly if he was careful. Slowly, he lifted himself into the air. The feeling of weightlessness was great—he had not experienced it since before Krastos died. He could not see the walls or floor of the tunnel, so he could not be sure how high he was. It was disorienting.

It was always a secret pride he'd kept within himself, knowing how birds and dragons felt to soar hundreds of feet from the ground, seeing huge cities as tiny dots and great forests as green splotches in the red desert sands. In this tunnel, though, there was nothing. As far as he could tell, he was floating in empty space that extended forever.

He propelled himself forward, keeping his hands in front of him all the while. He tried to keep his flight speed slow yet faster than he could run without slamming into the walls. There was no way to tell how fast he was flying, though, as there were no landmarks. The air moving past his ears and through his hair was enough to tell him he was advancing quickly, but how quickly was hard to tell.

There was no way to measure time inside the tunnel. After what felt like several hours, he began to worry. What if he had seriously miscalculated? There was still no light to be seen, so he could not be close. And yet he knew he had been flying for a while. He pressed on, harder, faster, feeling the air whip past.

Hours later, or at least what felt like hours, Tarlos had grown weary. His feet grazed the smooth rock of the tunnel floor. He flinched at it, realizing he had been drifting off to sleep.

Tarlos slapped himself across the face. The sound echoed loudly through the tunnel, bouncing back and forth a thousand times before dissipating.

"Get up," he told himself, and his voice joined the echoes.

Tarlos lifted a few inches from the ground and then felt that part of his mind give out like a pulled muscle. He cried out in pain and crumpled to the ground. His temples throbbed. He pressed the heels of his hands to them, rocking back and forth on bent legs.

He tried again, hovering for a moment. He'd barely cleared the ground before the searing pain of a hot knife pierced his head and he screamed in agony. He fell once more.

No more flying.

He stood, still pressing his hands to his temples, and swallowed. His mouth was dry. He went to grab for his water bags only to find that they were not there. After a moment's panic, he remembered he had left them in the clearing with the jinn. They were empty anyway; they would have only slowed him down. He pressed his fist to his forehead and squeezed his eyes shut.

Tarlos took a few steps forward. His legs were sore, even though he had not used them for several hours. He jogged on. No more flying.

He had no idea how much time he had left, and so he ran. He kept one arm outstretched ahead of him, the other pumping at his side to help push his legs faster.

He guessed he had run for about half an hour before his heart made a funny rushing feeling, and he paused to catch his breath. Sweat poured down his forehead and into his eyes, dripping from beneath his arms and down his back and torso. He bent down, placed his hands on his knees, and vomited. Perhaps running so fast for so long without water was not such a good idea after all.

The sun would rise any moment, now. He had to move no matter how much it hurt.

He tried to run, but he felt stitches on both sides of his belly.

His throat was raw, and his dry nose stung when he breathed. He walked, keeping a brisk pace, always one hand out in front of him.

Tarlos felt wind on his face again. He rubbed his sweaty brow, feeling the breeze cool him, and thought how amazing it felt to fly. He stopped, remembering that he had been walking for a long time now. He should not be feeling the wind at all.

But it was there. Faint, but he could feel it.

Tarlos raised his hands in front of his eyes. It was too dark to see. He brought them closer until they were no more than half an inch away. He could almost see the faint, blurry shapes of his hands. Light. However small an amount, light was coming from somewhere up ahead. He was almost there.

He ran, ignoring his screaming sides, his burning throat and lungs. Yes, there was a breeze, and it was picking up.

Farther and farther. *Follow the breeze.*

He ran for another mile before noticing that he no longer needed to stretch his arm ahead of him. He could now see the ground.

A flicker of light twinkled up ahead. His breath caught. He paused and stared down the tunnel, moving his head from side to side. The tiny speck of light seemed to blink on and off.

He forced himself forward. The end was in sight. A stiff breeze blew across his face. He closed his eyes and smiled at it, loving how it felt. The light grew brighter, and before he reached the end of the tunnel, he had to shield his eyes from its intensity.

The tiny prick of light grew into an opening as large as the sun, and Tarlos found the energy within himself to sprint. The cavern opened up into a mountain face. It was almost a mirror image of Shar's Mountain on the other side. Just below the tunnel opening, foothills covered in lush green grass rolled away from its wide foundation. Tarlos reached the opening of the tunnel and collapsed. He rolled down the grassy hill there and only stopped when he had reached the bottom, well away from the yawning mouth of darkness from which he'd emerged.

Tarlos panted and swallowed as he lay in the green grass and stared up at the evening sky.

I'm here. The dead country.

He reminded himself that no living person had ever reached this place, not since the creation of mankind. He took pride in that fact.

Trees of green and yellow leaves surrounded him, lining the foothills that led to the mountain. They shimmered and shook in the breeze. Tarlos rubbed his face as the wind cooled his burning skin. Above him, the sun was setting.

Shar, the sun god in his fiery chariot, soared over Tarlos and dipped down toward the mountain. The fire of the sun was bright and burning, and Tarlos turned away to save his eyes. He opened them again after the light had faded and looked to the mountain above. The tunnel glowed brightly and then faded to black. Shar had moved on—soon the living world would once more see the sun.

Tarlos did not know what the dead country would look like, but he had imagined something grimmer than what stretched out before him. He had pictured grey skies, cold wind, and sprinkling rain that both never let up and never quite became a full shower. He thought the landscape would be painted in tones of brown and grey, and that the sun and stars would always be hidden behind an overcast sky. There, souls would wander without having anywhere to go, but desperate to get there all the same.

None of this turned out to be true. There was more life in the dead country than in the desert Tarlos had crossed to get there. A lush green forest that began at the mountain sloped into a great valley, green from horizon to horizon. Although he could see no birds, he could hear them chirping in the distance. There were no animals that he could see, but if there were birds then certainly there must be other creatures in the forest.

From his vantage point halfway up the mountain, Tarlos saw over the tops of trees and all the way to the edge of the valley. There the mountains fell into flatlands and disappeared into the distance. With the sun gone through the mountain to the living world, the sky was falling into darkness. Tarlos squinted down into the valley, his eyes adjusting to the fading light. Moresh rose far to the east. She was almost at full face, for which Tarlos was grateful.

Down in the valley, perhaps two miles from the mountain and nested in the foothills, a light flickered through the trees. Tarlos peered through the forest, widening his eyes as much as he could against the dark. There was a white light from which a faint line of smoke floated up and disappeared into the sky.

Tarlos made his way down the mountain. The slick rock underfoot transitioned to gravel and grass, and then dirt as the trees grew thicker around him.

The birds had stopped singing. Tarlos assumed it was because they were sleeping.

Do the dead sleep? He tossed the question around in his mind for a few moments and then cast it aside.

Ahead, the sound of rushing water could be heard. Tarlos's pace quickened. He batted away low-hanging branches and kicked at the waist-high ferns and conifers. The moon was bright, and Tarlos found that it was easier to see at night in the dead country than it was in the living world.

Tarlos stopped and listened. Water streamed a few feet away.

A river.

He came to it and saw rapids through a small stretch of it. The water bubbled up over the rocks, creating small eddies and white foam. The river was about twenty feet across, and to the left and right appeared much deeper.

At the sight of the water, which seemed fresh and clean, and at the cool mist on his face, Tarlos felt his thirst grow more pronounced than ever. He wanted nothing more than to plunge his sunburned head into the river and drink long and deep.

But it would kill me. This is the Styx. This is the river Ilshu uses to ferry the dead to his country.

The water tempted him. Tarlos licked his dry and cracked lips as he stared into it. But he held himself back. He had not come all this way to kill himself in the Styx.

The white light he saw while still on the mountain appeared on the opposite shore, just beyond the tree line. The clear outline of a building broke through the forest, the shadow of smoke rising from its chimney. He looked up and down the river, searching for a bridge. If there was one, it was not close by.

He walked upstream, keeping the river on his right. He would not get lost as long as he stayed within sight of the Styx.

To his left, in the forest, a cricket chirped. Tarlos paused and turned to the sound. The cricket chirped again, and Tarlos raised a corner of his mouth in a half-hearted smile. He had heard nothing but birds since arriving in the dead country, and he did not know how long before then it had been since he had heard anything but the calls of vultures. He entered the forest, keeping his eye on the river. The cricket chirped again.

A tree with round green leaves stretched high into the night sky, the stars shining through its branches. At the base of the tree was a boulder, flat on the sides and top. Tarlos crouched beside it. A small green cricket sat there, still. Its tiny antennae wiggled at his presence, and the cricket chirped again.

"Are you alone?" Tarlos whispered.

The cricket sprang away, disappearing into the undergrowth. Tarlos frowned. Now he knew for certain—there really was life here. That was something he would never have imagined.

He moved to stand and caught sight of something on the boulder. Marks had been carved into it, strange letters that Tarlos did not recognize. But while he did not recognize the foreign writing, he could still read it.

John Talbot was here

Tarlos ran a hand over the carved sentence. A cricket chirped behind him. He turned. The river rushed before him, moonlight glinting atop the water. A small footbridge, only a few feet wide, stretched from the near shore to the far bank. Tarlos was sure it had not been there a moment ago. The cricket was nowhere to be seen.

He walked across the bridge, listening to the Styx rushing beneath him. At the other shore, Tarlos stepped off the bridge and looked around. On a small sign to his right, sunk into the ground on a long post, were two words:

Windmill District

4

Who but the son of Moleg?

Some hours after their trials, Tarlos's belly was full of spiced beer and his head was full of ideas. He looked at the tilting and rippling room ahead of him, seeing the people talking and walking every which way, drinking and dancing and singing. Music drifted through the room, high-pitched strings and deep drums. It all gave him a headache.

A huge bonfire roared in the center of the great hall, and eight boars roasted on four spits above the flames. Servants turned the spits, and the grease and fat dripped sizzling into the fire. The boars' bellies were filled with apples and cinnamon, and the room was full of the aroma of baking pork. Tarlos's stomach lurched at the smell.

Someone hit him on the back and almost broke him in two. A huge hairy arm draped over his shoulder, hot breath whispering into his ear.

"Brother, that was some kind of thing you did, the way you killed that roc." Krastos's words were slurred, and the goblet in his hand spilled as he swayed. Tarlos looked up at his giant demigod twin brother and smiled with hooded eyes.

"Of course," Krastos continued, "I didn't see it. Stuck behind a door, yeah? But I heard it all. And Lugal saw it—he told me all about it, how you put that giant chicken in its place, yeah? Flying all over the place, throwing stuff. Did you throw stuff? I threw stuff. Did you see me? Yeah, of course you did. I almost died."

Krastos swirled his beer around in his cup, and more spilled over the rim. Tarlos said nothing. He hardly ever spoke when drunk—Krastos spoke enough for the both of them.

The smell of cooking meat was too much for Tarlos. He bent over and vomited. It was brown and all liquid.

"Oh wow," said Krastos. "You need something to eat. Be back, yeah?" He left Tarlos staggering, heading to the table that ran the length of the great hall. It was covered in cheese, fruit, and bread.

Tarlos wiped his mouth and swallowed the sour spit. He was thirsty and drained the rest of his beer, then tipped the cup upside down over his face. A drop fell out and stung his eye. He quickly rubbed it.

"More mead, Prince?" said a sweet voice.

Tarlos looked to his left and focused his double vision. Katla stood there with a pitcher. Tarlos realized for the first time how small she was, with her narrow hips and tiny feet. Her straight blonde hair was always pulled back revealing her stark blue eyes. No one else in Kesh had blonde hair. No one had blue eyes, either. And now that Tarlos was really seeing her, her skin seemed almost milk-white. Meanwhile all those native to Kesh were chestnut-skinned with dark curly hair.

"Where are you from?" he asked.

"A small village called Hirnhyo," she said. "I'm sure I've told you before. Can I refill your cup?"

"Did you see me today?" Tarlos held out his cup and Katla filled it with mead.

She shook her head. "Mez wanted me to. I refused." Her neck and face turned a light shade of red. She regarded Tarlos with sad eyes. "I couldn't. What if you had . . ." She cleared her throat.

Tarlos placed a hand on her bare shoulder. "I'm sorry if I worried you. But I'm okay." He took a sip of mead. "Have you ever seen a mammoth?"

Katla shook her head. "If I ever did, I was too young to remember."

"Traders say they're dying out."

"That's a shame." Her eyelashes were long and dark, and they fluttered with shyness. "Can I get you anything else?"

Tarlos shook his head. "I think I'm going to bed soon. I'm really tired."

"You had a long day. Congratulations, Prince." She started to walk away but turned back. "Tarlos, I . . . there's something . . ."

He burped in his mouth and smacked his lips, grimacing at the taste of vomit. "Yes?"

She stared at the floor. "Perhaps now isn't the best time. Goodnight, Tarlos." Katla left to attend to the other banquet guests.

Krastos returned a moment later with a wooden platter stacked with cheese and red grapes. "Eat," he said, dangling a hunk of white goat cheese in front of Tarlos's face. It stank. Tarlos waved it away. "You have to eat, brother. You can't drink the night away. There's dancing to be done and girls to bed and songs to sing and stories to tell! You can't do any of that if you're sick or asleep." He shoved the cheese into Tarlos's mouth.

Tarlos glared at his brother as he realized he was actually a little hungry. He had not eaten since the previous night. He ate the cheese and some grapes as well.

"There you go," said Krastos. He slapped Tarlos on the back. Tarlos choked on a piece of cheese for a second, then swallowed it and chased it with some beer.

Tarlos sighed. "Why aren't you doing all that stuff?"

"What?"

Tarlos pointed to the party all around them. "Singing and dancing and all that."

"Brother! We have to stay together tonight! It's our night. Not yours and mine separately. After all, if it wasn't for you, I'd be dead, yeah?"

Tarlos raised a finger to his brother's lips. "I would advise you . . ." He belched. It tasted like beer and cheese and grapes and vomit all at once. He scowled. "I would advise you not to talk about that. I broke the rules. As did you, taking the chance I gave you."

"Aww . . ." Krastos brought his brother in for a rib-cracking hug. Tarlos held his cup to the side so as to not spill any beer. "I'm too drunk to remember that!"

"Not as drunk as this one." Tarlos nodded to a woman sauntering over to them.

"Oh, Tarlos, save me," whispered Krastos.

The woman was in her forties, and in her younger years was Lakaeus's favorite concubine. Now, she covered herself in bracelets and jewelry in her ears and nose. Her face was painted at least half a dozen colors, thick like a mask. The skin under her arms was loose and flabby but reminiscent of younger, more youthful days. She wore a purple robe, loose in all the wrong places, and held the largest goblet in Kesh.

The twins grimaced as she approached. She placed a red-tipped hand on Krastos's shoulder and moaned.

"Oh, boys, boys," she said. Her breath reeked of beer. "That was some display of strength today." She squeezed Krastos's shoulder. He drew back and she stepped closer.

"Thank you for the compliment, Kamhat," said Tarlos.

"It's only the truth. Everyone knows it." She shot a smile at Tarlos. A few of her teeth were missing and the rest had yellowed. She gazed at Krastos and bit her bottom lip.

Krastos cleared his throat. "We haven't seen you in a while, Kamhat. How are you?"

"Oh, fine, fine." She took a long drink from her goblet, draining half of it in one gulp. "The king treats me so well, being his favorite, you know. Gods bless him, he's too tired for me to visit him anymore. Moleg give him strength."

Tarlos and Krastos both rolled their eyes. They knew for certain that Lakaeus had not made physical contact with any concubine for more than five years. And he most definitely was not avoiding Kamhat for his health.

"And speaking of Moleg," Kamhat said. She ran a finger down the length of Krastos's arm. "What are you thinking about, demigod prince?"

Krastos pulled away and stepped to one side. "Thinking

about those hogs on the spit! They're almost ready by the smell of them. I think I'll go and have a word with the servants tending to them—I like my pork bloodier than most." He nodded to Kamhat and frowned at Tarlos, then made for the bonfire.

"That Krastos," mused Kamhat, following him with her eyes, "is surely his father's son."

"Have you seen my father recently?" Tarlos asked, bringing her attention away from his brother.

"Oh, dear prince, no. Hardly anyone has but for his healer, a few servants, and the High Priestess." She smiled at him. "You miss your father."

Tarlos shrugged. "As any son would. I worry about him. I wish he could have been there to see me—us—today. But I understand. This day is difficult for him."

Kamhat nodded and grabbed his bicep. "Your mother, of course. Such a great queen, Ninsun was. And so beautiful. A great loss." She made a *tut-tut* noise with her tongue. "It was thought among some of us privy to her lineage that she would live for a thousand years."

"Mm." Tarlos took a drink, swallowed, coughed. "Why's that?"

"Her ancestors, of course. She was descended from the Ageless."

Tarlos raised an eyebrow. The small motion seemed slow and difficult given his drunkenness. "From . . .?"

"But evidently it was not true." Kamhat shrugged, staring into her goblet. "That small thing you were talking to, is she yours?"

"Katla? Yes. She and Mez are my room servants."

"I shouldn't have to guess then." She gave him a sideways glance and a smirk.

Tarlos narrowed his eyes at her. "No, you shouldn't."

Kamhat gave him an apologetic look. "Forgive me, Prince. I forget my place when I've had too much to drink." She bowed her head. "Congratulations on your becoming a man. You will make a great king someday."

Tarlos nodded and took a drink, and Kamhat made her exit.

Krastos came back some time later with a bronze plate

loaded with a pile of red pork. He was chewing on a slice, blood dripping down his chin. He wiped it away with a hairy hand and swallowed his bite, then licked his lips and tried to reach his bloody chin with his tongue.

"Mental, that one," he said.

Tarlos nodded. "I'm not feeling so well."

"You need to eat." Krastos held out a slice of bloody meat.

Tarlos gagged at the smell. "I drank too much," he said. "I think this is my eighth cup." He drained the rest of it.

"Did you talk to Katla?" Krastos asked.

"Yes."

"What did she want?"

"Nothing, why?"

Krastos pointed toward the middle of the hall, where people danced with goblets in hand, holding on to one another as they swayed to the rhythm of the music.

"I saw Lugal a minute ago, or maybe an hour ago. I can't really tell. I'm less drunk than I was. I think it's because I've eaten something. You really should eat something. It'll make you feel better. What was I—oh, yeah. Anyways, Lugal told me that Katla had something to tell you, but I told him that's none of my business."

"Nor his."

"Told him that, too. Did she tell you something?"

"I don't remember. My head is swimming. So's the room. I think I'm going to sleep. Hopefully the room doesn't sway too much while I'm lying down."

"I've got some herbs that Shala gave me a few decans ago—"

"That priestess girl? Are you still seeing each other?"

"—she gave them to me for bad dreams. It helps you sleep really, really deeply."

"You're having bad dreams?"

Krastos shook his head and shoved another piece of pork into his mouth. He chewed quietly and did not speak again until he'd swallowed. "Not anymore."

"Goodnight, Krastos."

"Goodnight, brother. I'll see you tomorrow. If your head isn't hurting too much, yeah?"

Tarlos nodded and put his empty cup on the table next to the food, and made his way out through the crowd of people who had gathered to celebrate his coming of age. He climbed the steps to his chamber, fell into his white cotton sheets, and was asleep as soon as he'd closed his eyes.

Lightning cracked and forked over a mountain, and the sky was for an instant illuminated in white and purple. The mountain laughed at the lightning, and Tarlos covered his ears.

"Why do you cover your ears?" the mountain asked. "Do you fear the sound of laughter?"

"Why do you laugh at the lightning?" Tarlos asked the mountain.

The mountain bent down to speak with him. Tarlos saw the mountain with two sights—in one, the mountain was a mountain, unmoving, while with the other he saw a man of black rock and red clay.

Rain began to fall then and the rock-and-clay man glistened in the night. He smiled a smile filled with rocks and mud and twigs. "Because the lightning lives only for a moment, while I will live forever. Will you live forever?"

Tarlos lay in his bed, covered in leeches while blood trickled from beneath and stained his sheets. His once-long, black beard was now sparse and white.

"Only the gods and Ageless live forever," Tarlos told the mountain. But the mountain was no longer a mountain. It was Krastos who now stood beside him, at his deathbed, holding his frail hand.

"Do you fear the lighting?" Krastos asked.

"Because it lives only for a moment?" Tarlos—or was he Lakaeus?—asked.

"Because I can bring down the mountain," answered Krastos. Now, Krastos had become a rock-and-clay man. He stood tall and broad, transformed into a mountain, looming and great, silhouetted against the stormy sky.

Another crack—lightning struck the mountain, and the mountain crumbled from the shock. Rocks avalanched from the peak until there was no more peak, and the rest of the mountain followed suit, huge boulders cascading down in a thunderous gale of dust and debris.

"Tarlos."

"Father?"

No. He lay in his bed, helpless and sick and dying, watching the mountain crumble. The boulders and smaller rocks that once made up the mountain now rolled on top of him, crushing the air from his lungs, cracking his ribs and skull.

Tarlos felt his tongue pop out of his head, his heart and lungs and intestines explode from his torso and squish under the weight of an entire mountain.

He could not move. He was dead. He knew he was dead and could not leave this stone prison. He was trapped and would remain beneath this mountain until chaos returns to the cosmos and the Earth dissolves alongside the Powers that be.

Tarlos woke with a scream and clutched his beating heart. His cotton sheets were drenched with cold sweat, sticking to his naked body.

When did I get undressed?

He tried to swallow, but his throat was dry and his tongue stuck to the roof of his mouth. The room was dark, the moon outside a thin sliver.

"Mez?" he called out. "Katla?"

A stirring in a dark corner by the door. "Prince?" It was Mez. "Are you alright?"

"Did I scream?"

"Yes. Bad dream?"

Tarlos rubbed his eyes with the heels of his palms. "Yes. Could you get me some water?"

"Of course." Mez's dark shape stood from his bedroll and crossed the room. Tarlos heard the trickle of water from pitcher to brass cup. Mez gave the cup to Tarlos.

"Where's Katla?" Tarlos drank the water and returned the cup to Mez. His head pounded with the pain that came after a night of drinking.

Mez lit a candle, and the room flooded with soft orange light. "She wasn't feeling well."

"Probably drank too much."

"I don't think so, Prince. Can I get you something else? Some tea might help."

Tarlos nodded. "Thank you, Mez. Tea sounds good."

Mez built a fire in the small stove, and the room was cast in dancing shadows. Orange and yellow light lit Mez's face as he set the pot on the stove and mixed in the tea leaves.

"What time is it?" Tarlos asked. He sat up and hung his legs over the side of the bed.

"A few hours before dawn."

"When did you come to bed?"

Mez stirred the tea as it heated. "I didn't attend the dinner. My regrets, of course."

"You didn't miss much. I was just wondering if you had seen Krastos. He gets to drinking too much and becomes a different person."

"I've noticed he talks a lot." Mez added more kindling to the fire. The kettle began to steam.

"Krastos's greatest strength is his kindness. Sometimes that goes away when he drinks. I was just wondering if that happened last night. He was doing fine when I left."

"I couldn't say, Prince." Mez poured the tea and gave it to Tarlos.

The prince took a cautious sip. The tea filled his body with warmth, and the clouds in his head dissipated a bit. "Get yourself a cup."

"Thank you, Prince." Mez poured himself some tea and sat on the floor across from Tarlos. He let his tea cool and watched the steam rise.

"How old are you, again?"

"Fifteen."

"And Katla?"

"Sixteen."

"She looks younger."

"Hers are fair-looking people."

Tarlos blew on his cup and took a sip. Mez did the same.

"She was worried about you, you know," said Mez.

Tarlos watched as his tea steamed. "Do you talk to each other about your lives before? Has she told you about the north?"

"No. We do our duty, and our lives are here, in Kesh, with you. Anything that happened before is irrelevant."

Tarlos shrugged. "If that's how you want to go about it . . ." His tea was cool enough to drink now. He quickly downed the last of it and gave Mez his empty cup. "Make sure no one wakes me tomorrow. I have a feeling I'm going to be sick in the morning."

"Of course, Prince."

"And don't you dare let Krastos in here. If he tries to pounce on me tomorrow, tell him I said I would have your teeth pulled out if he so much as crosses my doorway."

"Would you?"

"What?"

"Have my teeth pulled out?"

Tarlos heard the smile in Mez's words. "Go back to sleep, Mez."

"Sleep well, Prince."

Tarlos was awakened by a guard shaking him. He rubbed his eyes and sat up. "What is it?" His head was full of cotton, as was his mouth. He licked his chapped lips. The sun shining through the open window sent spears of light into his eyes and brain.

"Prince Krastos has been arrested," said the guard. "The king has summoned you to his room."

Tarlos scratched his hair and looked up at the guard. "What about Krastos?"

"Please, Prince. The king is not in a waiting mood."

Tarlos nodded and wrapped himself in a clean tunic, then splashed some water on his face. Mez was sitting up on his bedroll, hair sticking up in the back. His eyes were puffy with sleep.

"What time is it?" Tarlos asked the guard.

"Two hours after sunrise."

"What did you say about Krastos?"

"King Lakaeus wishes to speak to you about it."

Tarlos said no more as the guard led him across the palace to his father's chambers. His arms and legs were heavy, like deadweight pendulums. His head was foggy and his eyes stung. He needed a drink, and to relieve himself in the worst way.

The guards in front of Lakaeus's chambers opened the cedar door for Tarlos, who entered alone. In the dark room, Tarlos heard the clash of something light and metal on the floor. There was another clash, and a copper plate skidded across the wood floor and came to a rest near his feet.

"Father? Are you in here?"

"Tarlos, why in gods' graces did you take so long in getting here?" the king shouted. He did not sound as sick as he had the day before. His voice was impatient, furious, and energetic.

Tarlos proceeded into the room, frustrated to have to adjust to the darkness as he'd only just gotten used to the sunlight. When finally his eyes did adjust, he saw, through what little light seeped through the curtained windows, his father leaning on his bedpost, chest heaving, hair in a chaotic halo.

"Are you alright, Father?" Tarlos approached slowly.

"Curse that boy's father, that's all I can say. And to think I raised him as my own. Brother to my son, son of my *dead* wife, and I raised him as my own. *My own!*" A gold candle holder atop a nearby chest floated up and flew into the wall behind Tarlos. He was startled—he was still a child the last time he'd witnessed his father use his Power.

"Where is Krastos?" Tarlos asked.

"In the dungeons, where he'll rot for the rest of his life unless I come to my senses and have him executed!"

Tarlos smiled. "What's really going on?"

The king hobbled over to Tarlos, keeping a hand on his bed to balance himself. He grabbed Tarlos's shoulder and leaned close. Dried spit and mucus had yellowed in the corners of his mouth. Tarlos smelled his putrid breath—malnutrition.

"He *raped* Kamhat," the king hissed. "He took her unaware

when she was drunk and defenseless! She's lucky she survived."

Tarlos lay one hand on his father's, the other on his shoulder. "Father, surely you don't believe that. Kamhat . . . she's a harlot."

"She was my best concubine when we were younger. Your brother knew the penalty for taking her! And to say nothing of our laws against rape—"

"So maybe she was raped," Tarlos interrupted. His head was beginning to clear, and fear and doubt began to creep into his heart. "But you can't believe it was Krastos. He wouldn't hurt anything. *Couldn't* hurt anything. Father, he didn't even want to kill the manticore. He told me before our trials, if he could find a way . . ." He shook his head. "Krastos would never. He wouldn't take her if she begged him. What makes you think it was Krastos?"

"Her pelvis is shattered." The king stepped back, his mouth knit into an angry line. The tips of his ears were burning red, and he ran a hand through his thin beard. "Both wrists broken. Her back and neck and chest—all bruised. Now you tell me, Tarlos, who in Kesh—who on Earth other than Krastos could have done such a thing?"

Tarlos simply shook his head. "I don't believe it. There's no way."

"The penalty for rape alone is death. To lay with one of the king's concubines is also death. If he were any other man, he would have been beheaded twice! He should be dead now, Tarlos, and he would be had I not raised him as my own." This time it was a bowl full of grapes that flew across the room and clattered to the floor, spilling fruit in every direction.

"Where is he?" Tarlos asked.

"The dungeons, like I said. Chained to the wall with our strongest irons until I can figure out what to do with him. But even our strongest irons may not be enough to hold the son of . . ." He coughed. ". . . Moleg." He looked at Tarlos with disappointed eyes. "He was like a son to me. I was like a father to him. Moleg didn't raise him, didn't show him how to hunt, how to fight. He was *my son*." This last part he whispered, and Tarlos thought for a moment that the king might cry.

"I didn't want to do it," the king continued, his voice softer now. "But the law is the law. If only he would confess, then perhaps I could call upon the High Priestess to ask the gods' forgiveness. Then Krastos may only serve a life sentence in chains. Then he wouldn't have to die." He nodded, then turned away from his son. "I would like to know your opinion."

There was a beat, and then Tarlos almost laughed, a short chuckle escaping his nose. "You already know my opinion. Krastos is innocent!"

"The time for judgement has passed!" Lakaeus shouted, crossing his arm as if to dismiss the matter. "The only hope Krastos has now is to confess to his crime."

Tarlos braced himself for another dish in the air, but this time his father only put both hands over his face and shook his head. He sighed deeply.

"Talk to him, Tarlos. You're his brother. His best friend. If he would confess to anyone, it would be you."

"He didn't *do* it."

"Damn your stubbornness!" the king screamed. "Do as I command! Go!"

Tarlos stared at his father almost a full minute before he reached beneath his shirt and plucked the talisman from around his neck. He threw it across the room. Lakaeus watched with sad eyes as it clattered. Tarlos turned and jogged from the chamber.

The door to the dungeons opened into darkness. A shaft of orange light was briefly projected on the floor, thinning as the door closed. A guard took a torch from a sconce on the wall and lit it with a piece of flint, then handed it to Tarlos.

"I'll wait back here," he said. There was worry in his voice. All guards, soldiers, and servants in the palace loved Krastos. "He's in the cell down at the very end." He pointed.

Tarlos started down the hall, splashing through small puddles that dotted the ground. The cell at the end of the hall came into view, and Tarlos caught Krastos's grey shape behind the bars. He was chained at the wrists, arms raised above his head, which hung low and miserable.

Krastos looked up and stared at Tarlos through his long, matted hair. "Hello, brother. It's good to see you before I die."

Tarlos stared at his twin, chained to the wall, feet barely touching the cold stone floor. Krastos's eyes were sad and empty—they were the eyes of one who had given up. All at once, Tarlos hated his father.

"Get those chains off," Tarlos said. His voice was even—he kept himself from shouting. "Why are you still in them? Break free."

Krastos shook his heavy head. "I deserve them. Don't you know that? Don't you know what I did?"

Tarlos reached into the shackles with his mind and felt around for the tumblers. With two clicks, the restraints unlocked themselves and Krastos crumpled to the stone floor.

He sighed. "I told you, I want to be in chains. I deserve to be in chains. Don't you know what I did?"

"I refuse to believe it," Tarlos said. He bent down to help Krastos stand, but Krastos pushed his hands away and slumped against the wall.

"Who else could have done such a thing?" Krastos looked away, passively inspecting his tiny cell. "Only the son of the god of strength."

"You're an idiot if you believe anything they tell you," Tarlos said.

"The king believes it."

"He's an idiot, too."

Krastos frowned at his brother. "How could you say that?" Krastos brought a hand to his chest and touched the talisman that hung around his neck.

"Because he's stupid enough to believe this. Stupid enough to have you put in chains when you could tear them off like cotton."

"What was I supposed to do? Fight the guards? Run away? That would only cement my guilt."

"Did you even try to defend yourself?" Krastos shook his head. "Why not?"

"I don't know that I didn't do it."

Tarlos sighed and sat next to his twin. He set the torch to the side, and the shadows of the cell danced in its flickering light. "I know you didn't do it. The Krastos I know never could."

"I was drunk. I have no memory of last night. How do you know I didn't do it?"

"The same way I know the sun will rise tomorrow. Because it always has. Krastos, the idea of you doing a thing like this is like . . . it's like suggesting that a swan ate a lion."

"You're comparing me to a swan and Kamhat to a lion." It was not a question. One corner of Krastos's mouth twitched upward.

"I'm not so good at analogies." Tarlos tried to smile but found that he could not.

What might have been a hint of hope on Krastos's face faded. "But the swan had just finished defeating a monster, and he was mad with drink and the thrill of accomplishment. And the lion was old and drunk, and was not afraid of the swan. I think, in that case, the swan might have killed the lion."

"She's not dead. Just . . ." *Broken.*

Krastos sighed shakily. He covered his face with a hand and inhaled deeply. "He must hate me," he whispered.

"Who?"

"The king."

Tarlos stood up and kicked a small chain on the floor. "Ablis take my father. He's an old fool. You shouldn't seek his approval."

Krastos looked up over his hand. "A stranger wouldn't know you loved him only yesterday."

"Yesterday my brother wasn't in chains!" Tarlos screamed. His voice reverberated through the stone halls. "He's old and sick, that's all. If he were young and healthy, he'd see that you could never do this and would investigate further. But the man I call Father would never accuse my brother of rape."

"And the man I call Father has never shown me his face," said Krastos, his voice rising. "He's never spoken to me. He didn't help raise me or teach me. As far as I know, he never loved me. But Lakaeus did. He was more of a father to me than anyone else I've known, and it upsets me when you take him for granted."

Tarlos crossed his arms and chewed his bottom lip in contemplation. "I don't understand why you seek his favor so much. You already have it. He told me himself, he considers you his own son."

"I seek his favor because I know that I am *not* his son, and he is not my father, but he took me in just the same, even after Mother died—his only wife, and, I'm certain, the only woman he ever loved. So why don't you help me put these shackles back on and leave me alone? I deserve my fate."

"He's going to have you put to death." Tarlos stared at Krastos, legs and feet stretched out in front of him, hands in his lap, staring straight ahead.

"There's nothing I can do about that," Krastos whispered.

Tarlos paced around the cell, kicking aside the skeleton of a large rat. It skittered into the dark. "I have an idea," he said at length.

"To end my existence sooner?"

"Listen." Tarlos crouched beside Krastos, resting his elbows on his knees. "You want the king's favor, right?"

"Yes."

"And neither of us want you to die."

"Get to the point."

"Gain his favor—and regain your honor—by avenging Mother's death." Tarlos stood.

Krastos stared at him, mouth agape. "What?"

"Go into the Cedar Forest," Tarlos said, his mouth stretching to a smile. "Bring back the head of Bawa."

There was a silent beat, and then Krastos closed his eyes and laughed. His chest shook with quick, deep breaths. He ran his hands through his messy hair.

"What's so funny?" Tarlos demanded. His hands balled into fists at his sides. "Why is that funny?"

Krastos wiped his eyes. "You want me to just wander into the Cedar Forest with the intent to kill Bawa. You know what Bawa is, don't you?"

"He's a monster. So what? We each killed our own monster

just yesterday, and it wasn't such a huge task."

"Don't you pay attention to the High Priestess's sermons?"

Tarlos raised an eyebrow. "Really?"

Krastos sighed. "Bawa is the son of Ablis and the Mountain. Since cast out from the presence of the gods, Ablis doesn't have the power of godly creation. So, he mates with the creations of the other gods and produces bastard offspring—nature mixed with evil, manifested in physical form. Ablis's children are all evil, but Bawa is the most neglected and despised. They say his voice is the flood, his words are fire, his breath is death."

It was Tarlos's turn to laugh. "They're just stories, Krastos. Sure, there's a monster in the Cedar Forest and its name is Bawa. He's been there for a thousand years, and he killed our mother. He killed the king's *wife*. Isn't that the perfect way to regain his favor?"

Krastos stood and regarded Tarlos, standing before him with arms crossed and a stern look on his face. "You're serious, aren't you?"

"I wouldn't joke about your life," Tarlos said, and he meant it.

Krastos shook his head. "No. Absolutely not," he said, waving away the suggestion. "I'm not going against a demon. Not by myself."

"Who said you'd be doing it by yourself?" Tarlos laid a hand on his brother's shoulder. "No way I'd let you have that thing alone. And stop calling it a demon."

"But it is—"

"—just a story."

Krastos shook his head again and turned away. "I can't. Bawa has killed more men than any other dem—monster. He's bigger than anything we've ever faced, Tarlos. We don't even know what to prepare for."

"Of all who've tried to kill him, not one was a Holder or a demigod. He won't be able to take us both. Just like the manticore, yeah?"

Krastos spun around and pointed a finger at Tarlos. "And about that! You shouldn't have helped me. The manticore was my right to kill, my trial—"

"Gods, Krastos, are you with me or not?" Tarlos yelled. Krastos stepped back. "You're being a coward. Your spineless words are really discouraging, you know that? The gods have our days numbered, brother. We aren't meant to die in the Cedar Forest by the hands of Bawa. He's just a monster. And you! No one has ever bested you in a fight."

Krastos sneered. "You never lost to me."

"The gods have given me a Power to wield, so that no one can ever defeat me." *And you let me win anyway.* "But you are the son of a god, Krastos. Or have you forgotten that?"

Krastos said nothing. He stared at the wall, avoiding Tarlos's eyes. Tarlos crouched beside his brother and grabbed his arm.

"Mother died for us. If you die now, she will have died for nothing. Please, Krastos. For her sake."

Krastos groaned and scratched his head. He sighed deeply and stared at the wet stone floor. The torchlight was fading. Krastos nodded, looked up at his brother, and extended an arm.

Tarlos grinned, reciprocating. The torch went out and the dungeon went black.

Tarlos said, "There will never come a day when the names Tarlos and Krastos are forgotten from the minds of mankind."

5

Where the Dead eat Burgers

The building sat at the edge of the trees several yards from the riverbank. It was wooden, two stories with a few windows in front and a porch and steps leading up to the door. Orange fire light glowed through the windows on the first floor, and shadows crossed on the inside. Above the door hung a sign written with more strange letters that Tarlos did not know yet could understand.

Tavern

Tarlos looked around and saw no one. He was standing on a dirt path wide enough for a cart, which led up and down the river. Upstream, Tarlos could just make out the shadowed shapes of more buildings partially hidden within the cover of the trees. They were smaller than the tavern, and smoke rose from a few of their chimneys. The smokeless buildings were devoid of any light.

He climbed the steps and approached the tavern door. The handle was strange to him. It was not brass like the door handles in Kesh. This one was round and brown, shiny with use and sticking directly out from the wood as a growth. He touched it. It was cool and hard. Metal. He grasped it, feeling the cool metal in his palm, and tried to move it down as he would have in Kesh. But this one did not slide down. He bit his lip and twisted it instead. There was a click, and the door swung inward with a low and slow creak.

Smoke billowed from the hearth in the wall. Above the fire, a rack with garments dripped dry. There was, too, a sour smell of alcohol, though it was like no alcohol he had smelled before. The bitter sensation was stronger than the mead and beer he was used to in Kesh. But the aroma of drink reminded him of his dry throat, and his thirst returned stronger than ever.

And then there was the aroma of cooking food. A counter near the back of the tavern was covered in dirty plates with leftover bits of food on them. A door behind the counter swung freely on a hinge, and more whiffs drifted out from whatever room was behind it. Meat, vegetables, bread, and fruit—Tarlos recognized them all and then some, though he had words to identify the rest.

The tavern was one large room with more than a dozen tables littered around. Tarlos guessed that on a busy night, this tavern could hold more than a hundred people. Tonight, however, there were only a few. One man sat in a far corner, farthest from the counter, with a wide-brimmed hat that shadowed his face. He was drinking an amber-colored liquid from a large clear cup. Another man and a woman seated at a table in the center of the room were enjoying a plate of meat with what appeared to be small carrots and a brown sauce. Tarlos's mouth watered at the sight and smell of it.

A woman stood behind the counter, rubbing a transparent cup with a small towel. She was the only one who looked up when Tarlos entered the tavern.

"Welcome," she said, waving the hand that held the towel. She jerked her head to the side. "Have a seat."

Tarlos stepped toward the counter, weaving between the tables. None of the other patrons looked at him as he passed.

He sat on a cushioned stool and placed his arms on the counter. He looked at the woman and wondered what part of Edorath she came from. Her hair was brown and thick, and fell in waves over her shoulders. Her nose was small and freckled, and her brown eyes were lined with dark eyelashes. Her lips were full, her face round and childlike. She was not as tall as Tarlos, but she carried with her an air of authority regardless of her physicality.

"Hungry?" she asked. She set the cup and towel to the side and smiled at Tarlos.

He nodded. "More thirsty than hungry. What is that?" He pointed at the strange cup.

She glanced at it. "What?"

"That . . . cup."

"What do you mean, what is it?"

"What's it made out of?"

She raised an eyebrow as she smiled and flicked the cup with her finger. It gave a small, delicate ring. Tarlos leaned back in surprise.

"They don't have glass where you come from, huh?" she said. "You want some water? You look like you need it."

Tarlos nodded, and the woman held the glass cup under a small metal pipe. She twisted a knob on top, and water gushed into the cup. She handed it to him, and he drank slowly. It was delicious.

When the cup was half-empty, he paused and stared at it. "Where does this water come from?"

"The spring, a few miles away. Why?"

He shrugged. "Just making sure." But he knew that if the water had come from the Styx, he would be dead already. He gave her back the empty glass cup and asked for another, and the woman complied.

"Hungry?" she asked again.

"Yes, I'd like some meat. Do you have boar?"

She laughed, sweet and friendly. It made Tarlos smile, although he was also confused.

"How about a burger?" she asked, then disappeared behind the swinging door.

Tarlos did not know what a burger was, but he waited patiently for it as he sipped at his second cup of water. He chanced a glance behind him at the others. The man continued to drink alone in the corner, and the couple still ate their meal.

The woman came back a few minutes later with a white plate. She set it on the counter in front of Tarlos. He stared at the thing she had brought him.

"What is this?" he asked. He poked the top. It felt like bread, but it was wrinkled and covered in small seed-things. There was some kind of meat between the bread, but the rest he was not sure about.

"They don't have burgers there either?" she replied, shaking her head. "Man, where *did* you come from? Or I guess the better question would be, *when?*"

Tarlos raised an eyebrow. "I don't understand." He picked up the bread on top of the pile and smelled it. There was yellow and red slime on the other side, and he grimaced at it.

"It's just ketchup and mustard. I hope that's okay." The woman turned and grabbed another dirty cup and began cleaning it. "Who doesn't like ketchup and mustard on their burger? I guess someone who's never had one. Don't eat it like that! Here." She set her cup and towel down and slid the plate over to her side of the counter. "You don't mind cooties, do you?"

Tarlos did not know what a koo-dee was, so he shook his head. The woman grabbed the burger in her hands, keeping the slices of bread on each side of its innards. She brought it to her mouth.

"Like this." She mimed biting and chewing, then gave the burger back to Tarlos.

He grabbed it as she had and brought it to his mouth. It seemed too thick to fit, but he opened his jaws wide and did his best. He bit down, feeling the soft crunch of the green vegetable and the hot juice of the meat, which he guessed was beef. There were other tastes he could not identify, but they blended well. He chewed and swallowed, and his stomach roared in response.

"Good, huh?" the woman asked. "Better than McDonald's, anyway." She went back to cleaning her cups.

Tarlos nodded, not sure what she was talking about. He ate his burger in silence. He had no idea how hungry he was until he tasted this food. It was then that he realized he had not eaten anything for several days. Perhaps more than a decan.

The woman set the glass cup on a shelf beside her, which held dozens of others just like it. She smiled at Tarlos, inspecting him. "Are you okay?" she asked.

Tarlos almost laughed. Instead, he returned her smile and

shook his head. "No, I'm not okay. Not yet."

She nodded. "You look . . . well, you don't look good. Usually when people come here, they look refreshed and sort of . . . refurbished. Know what I mean?"

"Yes." He did not know what refurbished meant, but he understood her. His cheeks were hollow. His face was frost-chilled from the cold nights and sunburned from the hot days, and his arms were thin and tired. And of course, there was the depression. He'd carried it with him since Krastos had died. It sat heavily on his shoulders, causing him to slouch. He knew he must have been a sight.

He finished his burger, and the woman took the plate away to the back room. When she returned, she reached beneath the counter and brought up a green glass bottle. She used a special metal tool to pop the lid off, and she gave the bottle to Tarlos.

"I think you need a beer," she said.

Beer was something Tarlos knew. He drank with eagerness. After a few gulps, he took the bottle from his mouth and looked at it. He smacked his lips.

"This isn't like any beer I've had before."

"Is there a lot of beer where you come from?"

"We invented it." He drained the rest of the bottle, and the woman gave him another. Tarlos raised a hand before she could take the lid off this one. "Please, I'm already very tired."

She smirked and put a hand on her waist. "It's not like you can get drunk or anything. Go on, it's free. In life I'd never turn down a free drink."

Tarlos nodded and took a sip from the second beer. He cracked his neck, which was painfully sore, and rolled his shoulders to try and relax his muscles. All at once his body reminded him how exhausted it was, and Tarlos let out a heavy sigh.

He took the tooth from his pocket and held it in his open palm. It hovered a few inches above his hand, spinning slowly in the air before dropping again.

The woman stared. "That's some trick."

"It's not a trick. I'm a Holder."

The woman seemed nonplussed. She regarded the tooth with fascination. "Where did you get that?" she asked. She ran a finger through her thick brown hair, pushing a loose strand behind her ear.

"I found it in the desert."

"When?"

"A few days ago, I guess. Maybe a decan. Why?"

She shrugged, still staring at the tooth. "It looks familiar."

"Teeth do look similar."

"I guess. What's a decan?"

"Ten days," he said. "What's your name?"

She looked from the tooth to Tarlos's eyes. "You're new here," she said. "You have a lot to learn. Wait a minute—" Tarlos put the tooth back in his pocket as the woman put a hand on the side of her face. Her eyes grew wide. "How do you have that with you? You don't get to bring anything with you. That's impossible."

Tarlos licked his lips and took another sip of beer. "Listen," he said. "This is going to be strange to you, but you should know."

The woman nodded. "I know." She gave Tarlos a friendly smile and patted his hand. "It's not easy for anyone. You come down here, you have no idea where you are or who you are, no idea how you got here. It gets easier with time. Eventually your memories come back. You get to remember your life—but not your name. That's lost forever. Maybe it makes it easier knowing we all had to go through it at some point."

Tarlos looked down at the woman's hand. It reminded him of another he liked to hold back in Kesh, in the privacy of his own room. He pulled away. "I see what you are getting at. But there's something else."

The woman nodded. "What's that?"

"Well, I'm not dead."

The woman stepped back, making a short noise through her nose that sounded like a laugh. "That doesn't . . ." She shook her head. "I mean, it usually takes a few days to know that you *are* dead, and it's common not to believe you're dead at first, but . . .

how did you know what I was talking about anyway?"

Tarlos squeezed the glass bottle in his hands, perspiration travelling down its neck. It was cold in his dry cracked palms. "Because I know where I am. I know what this is. I know you're dead, and they're dead." He threw a finger behind him, indicating those still eating and drinking at their respective tables. "But I'm not dead. And if I can help it, I never will be."

The lock of hair behind the woman's ear came loose once more and she pushed it back again. "I got some bad news for you. You are dead. No one thinks so at first. That's normal, so don't feel bad. You get used to it. Really, being dead isn't all that different from being alive. We still eat the same food, and the company isn't bad. Don't believe me? What's your name? Can't remember, can you? None of us can. That's part of being dead."

"My name is Tarlos." The color fell from the woman's face. She stepped back. Tarlos continued: "My father was Lakaeus and my mother was Ninsun, king and queen of Kesh. My twin brother was Krastos. They're all dead. I'm not."

The woman said nothing for several seconds. Her eyes were wide and white, her lips pressed together in a thin line. She kept her distance from Tarlos. "If that's true, how did you get here?"

"I went through Shar's Mountain."

"Where is that?"

"At the edge of the desert, where the sun rises. It opens up not far from here. Haven't you seen it?"

She shook her head. "I grew up in Oregon. Newport. There was definitely no desert there. Not on that side of the state, anyway."

It was Tarlos's turn to look confused. He leaned back on his stool. "Where is Org-en?"

She returned to the counter and placed a hand on his, gave it two soft pats. "I know this is a lot to take in. It's better to just accept it. I don't know how you remember your name and the names of your family members, but . . ." She looked around the tavern, at the people eating, drinking, speaking in low tones. "Trust me, it'll all make sense eventually."

"I'm not dead," Tarlos said. "I'll never die."

"Oh? How's that?"

"On the far side of this country, at the end of the Styx, is the Ageless country. I will find the Ageless and discover their secret to immortality."

She nodded. "Well, I've never heard of anyone who lived forever. Except gods. I guess if that's what you feel would be best . . ." She shook her head and sighed. "I can't imagine that, though. Living forever. I had a good, full life. I honestly feel satisfied and rested now."

Tarlos took another drink. "If you had been through what I've been through, you would say different."

The woman threw her head back and laughed. "I could tell you stories from my life," she said. "Not to discredit what horrible things you've no doubt been through—I'm not saying your life hasn't sucked—but I had myself a doozy. More pain and heartbreak than anyone should ever have to go through."

Tarlos nodded in understanding.

"But," she continued, holding up a finger, "I would never want to live forever. Even if it meant I could right all the wrongs that happened in my life."

Tarlos said, "I don't think you understand, then. Have you ever actually known someone who died? Have you seen their dead husk and tried to shake them awake, knowing they will never breathe again or speak your name?"

The woman stared at him, unblinking, unsmiling. Her eyes glazed over as if her memories were flashing over her, a river of images. She nodded.

Tarlos sighed. "And yet you say you would not want to right those wrongs or live forever."

"Tarlos . . ." She turned away, picked up another glass cup and began cleaning it. "People are born. They live, they die. That's just the way of things. Until your end comes, you should just enjoy your life. Sure, mourn those you lose, but don't lose your own life over them. Eat good food, take hot bubble baths, dance and sing and love . . ." She inspected the cup in her hands and nodded. "That's what you should be doing."

She set the cup down. "I wish I had done more of that, honestly. It's funny, when it's all over, what you really regret is not doing more of the little things."

"What are you trying to say?" Tarlos's voice came out louder than intended. The woman drew back in surprise. "My heart is *sick* for those I've loved! What you say, it means nothing. I'm going to the Ageless country, and there I *will* find the way to immortality. I will never die as my mother and father and brother did."

The other tavern patrons turned their heads as Tarlos spoke. He could feel their eyes on him, and he lowered his head. They quietly returned to their conversations, drinks, and meals.

The woman raised an eyebrow at Tarlos. "Do what you need to do. A person's goals are important, no matter how misconstrued they are."

Tarlos turned his head and scanned the three people in the tavern, then looked back to the woman. "Is there anyone here who can take me down the river? I've travelled a long way, and I'm exhausted. I'd rather take the trip by boat than hike the rest of the way down the riverside. I have no idea how much farther I have to go."

"You're going to the very end of the river?" the woman asked.

"Yes. The Ageless country is on the other side of the land of the dead, at the end of the Styx."

She looked at him sidelong. "You sure you're not from Greece?"

"I don't know what that is."

She nodded and took up her cleaning again. She tipped her head to the side, toward the corner where the lone man sat drinking out of a mug. "That guy has a boat. He trades up and down the river with the other communities. He knows he doesn't have to—we have everything we need—but I guess it gives him something to do. Maybe he can take you where you need to go."

"What's his name?"

She let out a chuckle. "Very funny."

Tarlos moved to stand. The woman grabbed him by the wrist.

"Woah, woah," she said. "You trynna leave tonight?"

"As soon as possible." He tugged his arm free from her grip.

She smiled sympathetically. "I promise you, he won't want to leave now. People around here tend to sleep at night. You told me yourself that you're exhausted. There's a spare bedroom upstairs with a shower. Get a good night's sleep and talk to him in the morning."

Tarlos considered this a moment. "He'll be here?"

"Oh yeah," she said with a nod. "He's here every day, for all three meals and sometimes more, unless he's out on the river. Here." She reached below the counter and retrieved a key, which she handed to Tarlos. It was the smallest key he had ever seen, half the length of his finger, and it was thin, light, and made of silver. "Take a shower and get some sleep. I know you need it."

Tarlos took the key and nodded. "Fine. This is your tavern, I'll respect your wish."

She patted his hand once more. Her eyes were deep with memory and experience, and when she blushed the freckles on her nose stood out. "I just work here," she said. "Goodnight, Tarlos."

Tarlos climbed the steps to the second floor and found the empty bedroom at the end of the hallway. Inside was a large bed with thick blankets, a dresser, a table with a single chair, and a door at the back of the room. Tarlos opened it and looked inside. He recognized the huge white oval bowl to be a tub, although it was much smaller than he was used to. Over it hung a pipe, much like the one the woman used to give him a cup of water, and the knobs on it looked similar. He guessed they worked the same way.

He twisted the knobs as he had seen the woman do, and water gushed from the pipe. Tarlos put his hands beneath it then withdrew them in surprise. The water was hot. He moved a small lever on top of the pipe back and the water stopped coming from the pipe and instead came from above, becoming a thousand drops of rain through a piece of metal with several holes.

"Must be the 'shower,'" Tarlos said to himself. Feeling the warmth of the water, he stripped off his clothes and climbed into the tub. He combed his hands through his matted hair. Not seeing any soap, he scrubbed himself with his hands as best he could. The water became thick and muddy, and it spiraled down the drain. His neck and nose pained at the water's touch, having been sunburned worse than the rest of his body.

He twisted the knobs the other way, and the water stopped. He squeezed the water from his hair as best he could, grabbed a blue towel from the rack on the wall and patted himself dry. The towel was warm and soft, softer than any towel he had ever used.

A sort of fold-up knife sat on a basin beside the bath. He picked it up and tested the edge with his thumb—it was razor-sharp. He ran a hand across his cheeks and chin, feeling stubble that had grown too long. He used the knife to shave.

The bed beckoned to him, and he climbed beneath the clean, fluffy sheets. The mattress was more comfortable than any bed he had slept on, and the pillow was like a cloud beneath his head. He was asleep in less than a minute.

6

Bawa

As they ran from the dungeons, Tarlos fought the urge to laugh. His smile was big enough, but he had to suppress his joy and excitement that was rising from his belly and through his chest and up to his throat.

Tarlos had never told anyone, but he had kept a secret desire in his heart to hunt down and kill Bawa since he was a child. The exact reason for it, he could not pin down. He told himself it was for his mother. He would kill Bawa to avenge the death of Ninsun, the death of his father's true love, the death of Kesh's queen.

But running through the palace, ignoring the shouts of his and Krastos's names, and ignoring the guards that jogged after them for a few yards and then gave up, Tarlos realized something that he had never admitted to himself. He wanted to kill Bawa for the sport of it. For the glory of it. So that for all eternity people would remember that King Tarlos son of Lakaeus, then prince of Kesh, had slain the dread beast Bawa, offspring of Ablis the Discarded One.

The armory was a small building beyond the courtyard, across from the palace. It was attached to the blacksmith's house, and he worked solely for the royal family and their guards.

Nekhte, the blacksmith, was awake and already working, scraping a wooden tool at an antelope hide stretched across a wooden frame. He turned at the sound of footsteps and greeted the twins.

"Majesties," he grunted. Nekhte was a huge man, with a

bushy black beard that he kept tucked into his belt. His shoulders were massive, making his large head seem small in proportion. His right arm was a degree more muscular than his left, as was the norm with all hammer-wielding blacksmiths. "What brings you to my humble establishment?"

"We need armor and weapons," Tarlos said. "And we'd appreciate it if you were quick about it."

Nekhte nodded and waved an arm, inviting them into the small building. "May I ask what it is you'll be fighting? Or would you settle for some cheap practice armor? I know how you two can get—you wake me up almost every morning with your wrestling." His tone was gruff but lighthearted. Neither Tarlos nor Krastos had ever known Nekhte to harm a person, verbally or otherwise. When they were out of the palace, they sometimes caught Nekhte slipping sweet rolls to children, whether royal or servant.

Nekhte rummaged around the place, opening and sifting through wooden chests.

"We're just going on a quick hunting trip," Krastos said. "For a day or two."

Tarlos punched his twin on the shoulder and Krastos drew back. "Don't lie to the man," he said, then turned to Nekhte. "We're going to kill Bawa."

Nekhte stopped what he was doing and looked at them both in turn. He was silent and expressionless for a while. The princes glanced at each other, uneasy.

And then, like a sudden clap of thunder, Nekhte exploded with heavy, booming laughter. Tarlos and Krastos waited patiently for the blacksmith to catch his breath and wipe the tears from his eyes.

"Are you done?" Tarlos asked.

Nekhte cleared his throat and sighed. His breath was shaky. "You aren't serious."

"When I said before that we were in a hurry—"

"Gods!" Nekhte bellowed. "You really mean to walk into the Cedar Forest and get killed by a demon?"

Tarlos rolled his eyes. "It's not a demon."

"Yes, it is," said Krastos. "I told you."

"It's just a monster."

"Demon or monster," said Nekhte, frowning, "it's a child of Ablis! Do you know what that means?"

"Nekhte," Tarlos said, "we didn't come here for a sermon. We just want our armor and a sword or two, and we won't bother you anymore."

"His voice is the flood!" cried the blacksmith. "His words are fire; his breath is death!"

"So I've heard." Tarlos frowned at his brother. Krastos wore a snide expression that said *I told you so*.

"This is no joke, princes," Nekhte said. Hidden beneath bushy eyebrows, his brown eyes were wild. "Ablis created Bawa for the sole purpose of terrifying Man."

"And once it's dead, they won't be afraid anymore." Tarlos crossed his arms.

"You'd best fear Bawa if you know what's good for you."

"Can we please have some armor and weapons, or are you going to send us out there with nothing but our wits?"

Nekhte shook his head. "Oh, Tarlos. You were always the ambitious one. I could never convince you to stay. And you're right, I can't send you out there with nothing." He sighed. "Fine. Wait here. I'll be back." He disappeared into a door in the wall of the armory, which connected to his house.

Tarlos smiled at his brother. "He's getting old, I think."

"Older and wiser than us, I guess," Krastos replied.

"Don't believe those stories. People only believe what they want to believe. No one knows the truth of things anymore. We'll be the first to actually see Bawa since—" Tarlos stopped himself.

Nekhte returned a few minutes later carrying several pieces of armor under one huge arm and some weapons under the other. He let them drop to the floor, the metal clattering against the cedar.

"My sons', before they went to fight the Ashurites." He lifted a cuirass up to Tarlos. It was silver, the color of moonlight through a cloud, and scaled with layers of small metal sheets. It would protect everything from his collarbone to his waist.

"It should fit you," Nekhte said. "Just have to make some adjustments to the leather straps. Here, try them on, both of you."

Tarlos dropped the cuirass over his head, and the leather straps fit snugly on his shoulders. Except for some extra space in the chest area, it was almost a perfect fit. Nekhte took no time in cutting slack off the straps and attaching new fastening loops. He tightened the cuirass—Tarlos felt like it had been made specifically for him.

Krastos's armor was the same as Tarlos's but several sizes larger. Nekhte's older son had inherited his massive build, but Nekhte still had to replace the straps with longer ones for Krastos.

The fitting finished, Tarlos and Krastos moved in the armor, testing the bend and swing of their arms. Tarlos touched his toes, twisted his body above the hips.

"You're a miracle worker, Nekhte," he said.

"Thank you, Prince. Now these . . ." The blacksmith picked up two sets of shin guards and handed them over. ". . . should fit perfectly. Let me know if they don't. There should be a finger's worth of space at the bottom, two fingers at the knee."

Krastos shrugged. "Perfect," he said.

"Good," said Nekhte. "Take care of these." He gave them each a spear and a sword, with scabbards to match. "I made this one for my youngest." He pointed to the one Tarlos had picked, and Tarlos practiced some swings at the empty air. "But this was my father's, who gave it to me, and I passed it to my eldest. My father never lost a battle with it, and neither did I. Soske, though . . ." He scratched his beard.

"I'll take care of it," said Krastos. He slid the sword into its scabbard. "And it will come back to you. I promise. Thank you, Nekhte."

"Yes," Tarlos said, putting his own sword away. "We appreciate your help."

"I still think you're damned fools for doing this, if you'll pardon me, princes. But I've been at this a while, and I've watched you go from boys playing in the mud with sticks to men battling monsters in the arena. It's hard for a man to watch a child grow and not care for him just a little." He smiled behind his huge beard, and his right eye twinkled. "Now get on with you, both of you. Before the authorities catch you." He winked at Krastos, and Krastos looked away with a frown.

"We'll come back with Bawa's head," Tarlos said as they left the armory. "And the world will know by whose swords the beast fell!"

But something deep in Tarlos's mind told him that despite everything, Nekhte never really expected to see his sons' armor or swords again.

The main city of Kesh was awake long before the palace grounds. The air was filled with the sounds of the city—donkeys pulling creaky carts over grooved cobblestone roads, salesmen waving their merchandise and shouting at passersby, customers arguing with vendors, children running about playing with their sticks and hoops and painted streamers. And drifting through the streets, the smell of freshly baked bread and honey butter, scorpions and locusts roasted and being drizzled with melted sugar or pepper sauce, the smell of sweaty livestock and dung.

Tarlos took it all in. He hardly ever had a chance to go down into the city, to mingle with the people and taste the street food. But all that would have to wait until he and Krastos returned. The guards—and by now the king—would have noticed that Krastos was no longer in the dungeon and would be searching for him. The princes had but a few minutes left to leave the city walls.

They made their way through the densely packed main street that led to the gate, trying their best not to bump into anyone. But Krastos was the largest man in sight and was having trouble getting through without a struggle.

"Watch yourself!" spat a man after Krastos knocked into him. The man was carrying a basket full of naan, a few loaves of which spilled to the ground. "Now see what you've done! I should have you pay for these. I can't sell them now!"

"I'm so sorry," said Krastos. He bent down to help the man.

People stepped on his hands and bumped his head with baskets and coin purses as they walked by. Wincing, Krastos gathered the bread and stood, rising above the crowd. He gave the loaves to the man, who scowled at him and placed the dirty naan in his basket regardless.

"You ought to watch yourself, man of your size," he grumbled. "Damn stupid foreigners . . ." he mumbled as he disappeared into the crowd.

Krastos lowered his eyes. The man did not know Krastos was his prince. How could he? Krastos did not make it into town often, and the people who lived without the palace would not recognize someone they almost never saw. Even those lucky enough to have gotten front-row seats to their trials would probably not still remember their faces.

Krastos shrugged it off and turned to follow Tarlos. His brother had no difficulty weaving through the crowds—he used his Power to gently move people aside, creating a path for himself. Krastos picked his way slowly through the thick river of shoppers and workers, pardoning himself whenever he bumped into someone, which was often.

Close up, the city walls were enormous. Sixty feet high, the color of amber. The sun peeked over the edge of the wall like half a gold coin. Behind him, Tarlos heard Krastos mutter a prayer to Shar, his grandfather, to watch over them. Or perhaps he was begging the god to change Tarlos's mind about the whole thing.

They approached the stables, which sat nestled in a dirty corner of the city wall, not far from the gates. Tarlos waved at Krastos, hurrying him along, and jogged up to the stable master. The man was leaning against a fence, with one foot resting on a horizontal plank, watching a young boy ride bareback on a grey short-neck.

"Ease up on the reigns, you little fool, or she won't know what you want!" the man yelled. "And quit squeezing her with your knees. She's solid; you can sit on her without falling through, trust me." He saw Tarlos approach and stood up straight. "What can I do for you, young man? Oh! As the sun witnesses, princes Tarlos and Krastos are here to inspect my stock. To what do I owe this honor?" The man kept his thumbs in the waistband of his tunic. He wore an open vest over his muscular torso. A long piece of straw dangled from his mouth.

"What are we doing here?" Krastos asked Tarlos, standing at his side.

"You didn't expect to walk to the Cedar Forest, did you?"

"No, but . . . well, I guess you have a point."

Krastos could sprint faster than a horse when out in the open, but he grew tired like any other man. He could cover at least twenty miles before having to slow to a walk. Tarlos could fly, but using his Power cost energy, same as any other form of exercise. If they did not take horses on the two-day trek across the desert, then by the time they reached Bawa's lair they would be too exhausted to fight.

"Those two will suit us just fine," Tarlos told the stable master. He pointed to the grey short-neck that the boy was riding and a similar brown horse tied to a post nearby.

The stable master nodded, the straw in his mouth bobbing as he spoke. "Two of my finest. They'll serve you well, princes."

"We'll need saddles and tack, too."

"Of course you will. I'll fetch them for you." He cupped a hand over his mouth and shouted, "Boy!"

The boy on the horse, who was perhaps twelve years old and small for his age, half-jumped, half-fell from the horse and sprinted to the stable master. His face was smudged with dirt and his bare feet were caked in mud and horse dung.

"Saddle these two," the man told him. "And be quick about it. Have you finished mucking out the place?"

"No, Father, but I'm almost done. Duck is still walking funny, so I have to redo her shoe before I—"

The stable master clouted the boy on the side of his head, and the boy drew back in pain. "How many times do I have to tell you to stop paying mind to that mare? She's good for nothing but breeding, and I don't need you wasting time on making her comfortable!"

The boy nodded. "Yes, Father."

Tarlos noticed that he never looked straight at the stable master.

"Go saddle these two and be quick about it. And while you're at it, how about minding your manners in front of your princes?"

The boy turned to the twins but did not look at them. He bowed low and quick before disappearing into the main building. He emerged again a moment later with two light leather saddles and wool saddle blankets.

As the boy saddled the horses, Krastos said to the stable master, "Send the bill for the horses and saddles to the palace. Kushim, the money-handler, will take care of it."

"Nay, and say no more," said the man with a wave of his hand. "Kesh and everything she has to offer is yours. Take them. I'll say they're gifts for your coming-of-age."

"Did you see us?" Tarlos asked.

"I did. Told the boy all about it, too."

The boy led both horses by the reins and handed them over to the princes. Krastos took the brown one.

Tarlos jumped in his saddle and the grey stallion whinnied.

"Woah there, boy," he said, and gave the horse a pat on the back.

"Her name is Cloud," said the boy with a shy and squeaky voice.

"Oh, sorry, girl. You have our thanks, stable master."

"Say no more about it and be on your way," the man replied. "No doubt you have important business and I'm keeping you from it."

"Very important," Tarlos said, grinning from one side of his mouth. "The world will sing of it for eternity! Come, Krastos!"

Krastos eased into his saddle, and the brown stallion leered under his weight. He frowned, and Tarlos could see that he felt sorry for the animal. But there was nothing to be done about it.

They led their horses to the city gates that stretched high and wide before them. Two guards pulled open a smaller set of gates that sat within the larger, and the princes galloped through, into the dry desert and the ever-brightening day.

Somewhere deep in his mind, Tarlos knew that he was dreaming, but the part of him that knew he was dreaming was smaller than the part that thought this was all really happening. He was Krastos, and he was fighting the manticore.

He fought the manticore with naught but his godlike strength.

"I don't want to kill you," he told the manticore in Krastos's deep voice. The manticore laughed and threw him aside.

He landed on his chest. His jaw snapped in two places and he bit off his tongue. He screamed in agony as the manticore cackled and the world dissolved around him into tendrils of black substance neither liquid nor smoke.

The manticore remained, and its laughter did not cease. Its spiny lion's body shifted into a mountain of rock with the face of a man.

"I didn't want to kill you," Tarlos said, although his jaw was broken in two places and his tongue lay beside him like the tail end of a dead snake.

The mountain either did not hear him, did not understand him, or did not care. It lifted one giant rocky fist into the air, and dirt and plants rained down from it. Tarlos raised his head and watched as the club of an arm drove toward him, and all went dark.

Tarlos shot upright. He was on the bare ground, the stars above blinking passively. The fire between him and Krastos had fizzled out hours ago, its ashes cold and silent in the pit they'd constructed.

Tarlos's heart thumped. He rested a hand on his chest and took a few deep, steady breaths. He looked to the southwest and saw the edge of the Cedar Forest. They would arrive tomorrow. He wiped cold sweat from his brow and rubbed at his pathetic stubble.

Krastos rolled over on his saddle blanket and groaned. "Wh . . . zh . . . doing," he mumbled.

Tarlos ignored him and lay back down on his own saddle blanket. He stared blankly at the white and yellow stars above—a magnificent, swirling work of art. A part of him wanted to shake Krastos awake and show him the beauty up above—to tell him to take it all in as if water from a cool spring in a desert oasis.

Maybe this wasn't such a good idea, he thought. *We might be killed. But Krastos surely will be if we don't do this.*

Tarlos lay back down and closed his eyes.

He'll miss the stars.

He fell asleep, and his dreams were no better this time.

They had brought no supplies with them, which Tarlos told himself was smart because it was better that they travel light, but he was only making an excuse for being foolish. He had been in so much of a hurry to leave Kesh that he had not thought to bring food or water. They would not starve, though, as there was plenty of desert hare roaming around.

The Cedar Forest was the reason Kesh was the center of civilization in the Fertile Valley. They shipped cedar wood all over the desert to small villages and other city-states in need. The cedar wood trading industry had grown large over the years, and many wells had been dug between Kesh and the forest.

Tarlos found it difficult to comprehend the scale of the Cedar Forest. Where the Fertile Valley ended on the west side, mountains rose and small streams flowed from their slopes. The air was cooler there due to the moisture, and he could feel the dust in his lungs turning to mud. Spending his whole life in a hot and dry desert, it was a strange sensation to get used to. But even stranger were the trees.

The Fertile Valley was not called such because of its vegetation. The two rivers that surrounded the lands around Kesh flooded their banks every year, and the silt left behind was ideal for crops. But the only trees in the desert were those in the palace courtyard, imported there by queen Ningal, Lakaeus's mother and Holder before him. The trees in Kesh were sparse, and they suffered in the heat, not one ever rising above ten feet.

The Cedar Forest could fit three Fertile Valleys within its borders with room to spare. From a distance, the forest was a dark green sea that stretched out to meet the sky. As the brothers came nearer and the air grew cooler, however, they saw the skyscraping trees themselves, each one hundreds of feet high with trunks thicker than ten men standing in a row. The first men to take advantage of this sturdy, pliable resource died wealthier than most kings.

The border closest to Kesh was dotted with stumps and toppled trees stretching inward for several miles before spreading to the sides. They did not dare go deeper into the forest. Anyone who'd grown up in the Fertile Valley knew the reason for this.

The princes halted their horses where the stumps ended and the healthy full-grown monstrous cedars began.

"Well," said Tarlos, "we're here." Krastos said nothing. Tarlos looked at his brother's pale face. "You okay?"

"I was just thinking about Shala," Krastos said. His voice was quiet and reverent. "What if I never see her again?"

Tarlos leaned over to hit Krastos on the arm. "Hey. She'll love you even more when you return with Bawa's head. She'll leave the temple and marry you for sure."

"That's not allowed."

"I'll be king."

Krastos looked at his brother with worried eyes. "Aren't you thinking about Katla?"

This question surprised Tarlos. He frowned for a moment, then offered a reassuring smile. "The same goes for her."

Krastos stared into the forest, noting how the light faded within the trees not more than a hundred yards away. The Cedar Forest was massive, its trees huge. The brothers did not expect to feel so small standing in its shadow.

"I can't," Krastos whispered. "I just can't do it. Tarlos, let's go back while we still can. Please."

Tarlos leaned over and slapped Krastos across the face. "Quit being such a coward!" He'd had enough of his brother's lack of confidence. They had come so far, their revenge in sight. "This isn't the Krastos I know! What happened to the man who fought a lion with his bare hands to protect a shepherd's flock? Who dug a mile-long trench in a single day to irrigate farmers' crops? What happened to the man who killed a manticore with its own stinger?"

"You helped me kill the manticore," Krastos said, staring at Tarlos with hurt in his eyes. "I'd be dead if it weren't for you."

"And I'll be dead if you leave." Tarlos was not turning back. His pride would not allow it. And what would he go back to? A furious father and a battalion of soldiers waiting to place Krastos under the axe. "Do you know what happens when you die? People forget about you. They don't talk about you, they don't care what you did—it's like never having been alive in the first place. Mother's been dead for eight years, and I've heard more mention of her in the last three days than in these past eight years combined. If you go back, you will be executed, and Father will make sure that there is a blot on your legacy so large and dark that no one will remember you."

Tarlos felt heat rise in his neck; could hear his heart beating in his ears. He took a breath to calm himself. "Krastos," he continued, "I'm going to kill Bawa for your freedom and to avenge Mother's death, whether you help me or not. But I need you by my side. What can he possibly do to both of us together? We've already come so far, and only death awaits you should we return without that monster's head."

Krastos was trembling. The sword at his waist vibrated against his armor. "I'm terrified."

Tarlos was also frightened, but he would never let Krastos know that. "It'll be over before you know it. We'll be laughing about it in a few days, beer up to our eyeballs and bellies full of meat; men and women gathered around us asking to hear again and again how we defeated the monster they said no man could kill. Our names will never be forgotten." He punched Krastos on the shoulder. "Stop crying."

Krastos wiped his eyes and took a deep, shaky breath. He stared up into the cloudless sky and closed his eyes. Tarlos imagined he was praying to every one of the gods to protect them, but especially Moleg.

"Fine, brother," he said at length. "I'll go if you'll be at my side."

"Always," Tarlos said and gave his brother a reassuring smile.

They rode on.

The mood and atmosphere changed once they passed the boundary that separated the stumps and hewn trees, and crossed into the full green and living Cedar Forest. The sun all but vanished behind the thick canopy, and strange animal sounds drifted through the trees. The twins never saw an animal, but they heard plenty of chirping birds and yowling cats and singing crickets, all just out of sight.

But they only cared about one creature—and it was not a mere animal.

Five miles into the forest, a clearing opened up in front of them. They stopped to give their horses a break and to stretch their cramped legs. A gap in the trees several yards across spread from north to south. Tarlos squinted at the sun above, feeling its light and warmth on his skin for the first time in hours.

"What do you think?" he asked Krastos. "How do we find him?"

Krastos looked around and scratched his beard. "Follow the trail, obviously. The question is, north or south?"

"What trail?" Tarlos turned and peered around, looking for footprints or broken branches—evidence of a passing monster. "How are we going to find its trail? The forest is massive. He could be anywhere."

Krastos raised an eyebrow and extended an arm outward. "The trail, brother."

Tarlos took another look and finally saw it. The clearing was not a natural one. The several yards of bare ground that stretched north to south was, as he could now see, a trampled path through the cedars. The ground was bumpy and overturned with brown soil and broken branches. Stumps and stunted cedars protruded from the ground every few feet, none tall enough to reach the brothers as they sat on their horses. Tarlos felt the blood rush from his face, realizing now how large Bawa must be. He did not let Krastos see his concern.

He swallowed. "South is the direction of Ablis."

"But he hates his father."

Tarlos nodded. "True, but all things with the innate evil spirit of Ablis are drawn to his ways. Let's follow the trail south for a few miles. If we don't find anything, we'll double back, yeah?"

"Sounds like a plan." Krastos did not look at Tarlos, nor did he smile or nod. He only mounted his horse, kicked it forward, and led the way south down the path of trampled trees and dirt.

The sun began to set and the animal noises stopped. They may have stopped long before the twins noticed—they couldn't be sure. The absence of sound was ominous, but the brothers pressed on.

"What if we don't find him before dark?" Krastos asked, his voice barely above a whisper. Even the sound of their horses' hooves seemed dampened.

"We find a place to spend the night and keep looking tomorrow." This idea scared Tarlos to no end. Sleep in the Cedar Forest while on the trail of Bawa? But they had no choice.

"I think I see a cave ahead," said Krastos, pointing to a small hole in a rock face on a hill a mile or so away. "It's going to be dark within the hour. We might as well bed down there."

Tarlos squinted to see the hole in the low light. It seemed safe enough, and small enough to keep away a monster like Bawa while they slept—or tried to sleep.

They rode south down the trail until they came to the foot of the hill. It was covered in thick rock, and large boulders lay scattered around and in the nearby trees.

"I can barely see in this light," Krastos said. "Are we close?"

"It's just up there a few yards. Leave the horses down here."

They tied the horses to a tree at the foot of the rocky hill, hoping that nothing would scare them away during the night. Or eat them.

The hill was steeper than it looked from a distance, and in the fading light it was difficult to climb without slipping and breaking every bone on the way down. It took several minutes to ascend what was only about a hundred yards. Krastos could have jumped the distance, and Tarlos could have flown, but they were exhausted from riding all day and wanted to save their energy.

Arriving at the cave entrance, they froze. It was much larger than it looked from the trail. Tarlos looked at Krastos and saw that all color had drained from his brother's face. Krastos opened his mouth and closed it again, his eyes so wide they were more white than brown. He tried to say something but couldn't. Tarlos did not have to ask him what was on his mind. He himself heard the breathing coming from deep within the cave. Slowly Tarlos turned his head to see what made that sound.

Red eyes glowed in the darkness. They bounced up and down as the creature walked toward them. Tarlos was stuck, unable to turn or run. He did not have to look at Krastos to know he felt the same. The breathing grew louder, the eyes wider and closer as giant feet slammed into the rock—louder, faster. Tarlos's blood froze in his veins.

Bawa made a strange noise, something between a roar and a purr. It was disgusting, and it sent cold prickles over every inch of Tarlos's skin. The monster approached, towering above the twins. It was at that moment that Tarlos regretted coming to the forest at all. He should have stayed home and fought his father, not Ablis's monster-bastard.

There was just enough sunlight left for them to see Bawa as the creature came to the cave's entrance. Bawa was more or less the shape of a man, with a huge beard and antelope antlers that protruded from his forehead. Bawa walked on all fours; his arms were twice the length of his legs and his knees bent backwards like a dog's. Behind him stretched a whip-like tail, and the claws on his hands and feet scratched the rock as he walked. He was huge, twice the size of Tarlos and Krastos combined.

"What do I see before me?" said Bawa. His voice was deep and smooth. It made Tarlos think of a cow that had learned to speak. "Two young men. One of them with a familiar smell. Both with weapons unsheathed. Tell me, young men, have you come to fight me like so many before you?" Bawa grinned, his smile stretching to his ears, revealing teeth the shape of needles and the color of corn.

Dread surged through Tarlos. Terror flooded his muscles. His legs shook. He forced himself to look to Krastos, and

Krastos did the same. Krastos nodded. Tarlos nodded back. They faced Bawa.

"We've come to avenge Ninsun, our mother," Tarlos shouted. He was afraid he might sound weak, as he felt on the inside, but his voice came out strong and steady. He silently thanked the gods.

Bawa crawled toward them, every step shaking the ground, the entire rocky hill. He lowered his head, which sat atop a long, slender neck. Tarlos could see his reflection in the monster's eyes.

"You are the twins of Kesh," Bawa said with a nod. "I wondered if you might come to me someday. Honor would dictate it, after all. Go home, boys. Do not be fools."

"We will not leave without your head," Tarlos cried, lifting his sword. The moon behind him glinted off the blade, a twinkle in Bawa's eye.

Bawa laughed. His breath made Tarlos's stomach lurch. It was hot and smelled of decay.

"Have you not heard the stories about me? The Mighty Bawa, child of Ablis, the Discarded One." He brought his head closer to the brothers and spoke softly, slowly, as if to children. "You stand before me like a pair of frightened pups. I will tear you limb from limb. I will crush you. I will bite off your heads and leave your bloody and mangled husks on the ground to feed the vultures and crows."

Tarlos swallowed. "If we survive this," he hissed at Krastos, "you don't ever have to follow me again. This was a stupid idea."

"No turning back now," Krastos whispered back. "Don't hesitate. I'm with you until the end."

The world went grey as Bawa leapt at them. Tarlos did not think about his actions, his body reacting to the monster's movements. He felt trapped inside his mind with little or no control, watching the fight as if a spectator from beyond his own body.

Bawa moved like a viper. He swished his tail at them and moved his huge head on his long neck to avoid their swords. He laughed as the brothers swung at him, his breath burning and putrid. He snapped his razored teeth at them whenever they drew near—Tarlos narrowly escaped his jaws more than a few times.

It was all Tarlos and Krastos could do to keep Bawa in the cave. They knew that if he were to escape into the Cedar Forest, he would have the advantage. There, confined to the cave, the fight was as even as it could be.

Bawa came at Krastos with open jaws, and Krastos punched Bawa in the mouth with all his godlike strength. Bawa drew back with a shriek, and for a moment the three of them stopped moving. Tarlos thought that Krastos had stunned the monster. He wanted to move in for a finishing blow, but something within him forced him to wait.

Bawa moved his jaw from side to side and spit out a handful of needle-thin yellow fangs. He smiled, and a trickle of blood ran down his chin and into his wiry beard.

"Such strength, demigod," Bawa purred. "You truly are your father's son." He jumped at Krastos, his deformed dog legs springing forward, and reached for him with his long apish arms, claws at full length.

Using his Power, Tarlos pulled Krastos out of Bawa's path, and Bawa fell on empty ground. He clawed at the place Krastos had been only a moment before and roared with frustration.

"Did your father never teach you that using your Power in battle is unfair?" the monster asked. "There is no honor in it."

Tarlos panted. He walked a semicircle around Bawa and stood at the cave entrance. With the moonlight behind him, he could now see Bawa in all his hideousness—tall and gangly but also brutish and muscular.

"I'm not looking for honor," Tarlos said as he gripped his sword with his mind and forced it at Bawa. It flew like an arrow shot from a bow, aimed at Bawa's slender neck. The monster dodged the sword, moving his neck like a snake avoiding a hawk. The sword planted itself into the rock wall behind Bawa.

Bawa turned his head to the sword and Krastos jumped and landed on Bawa's shoulders. Bawa cried out, flailing and wriggling like a trout in a fisherman's grip. Krastos held on with all his strength, wrapping his arms around the monster's neck and squeezing its waist with his muscular legs. Bawa shook and convulsed, and backed into the wall to try knocking Krastos off.

Krastos squeezed Bawa's neck with the crook of his arm, and with his other arm he drew his sword. Tarlos used his mind to remove his own sword from the cave wall, returning it to his hand. Krastos held his blade to Bawa's neck, and Tarlos approached with his sword outstretched. He was going to pierce the damned monster's heart—if he had one.

Bawa stopped struggling, feeling cold iron at his throat. He saw Tarlos walking toward him with wrath in his eyes.

"Tarlos!" the monster cried. "Son of Ninsun! Have mercy!"

Tarlos paused, not because he thought of granting Bawa any such mercy but because he was not expecting the bastard son of Ablis to beg for his miserable life.

Bawa continued, "Let me live in peace in the Cedar Forest. If you spare my life, I will be your servant. I will cut down the cedars and deliver them to Kesh, and you may honor Moresh and Shar with a temple of such grandeur never seen before in all the world! You will have a glorious cedar palace even more splendid than the one you have now. Men and women will travel thousands of miles and from every country just to gaze upon your kingdom and you, its glorious king of riches and splendor. All this will be yours if you will spare me!"

"Kill him, Tarlos! Kill him now!" Krastos shouted, struggling to hold Bawa with one arm while keeping his sword trained to the monster's throat.

"Krastos!" Bawa shrieked, shifting his red eyes to better see the demigod prince. "Brother! Do not kill me! Let me live in peace and you will have your own kingdom beside Tarlos! Tell your twin to spare my life!"

"Kill him!" Krastos cried. Sweat glistened on his forehead.

Tarlos wondered at that moment why Krastos did not slit the monster's throat. But no sooner had he asked himself this question than he knew the answer. Krastos never wanted to kill Bawa. No matter how evil or corrupt a creature or man, Krastos never intended to kill anything. Suddenly Tarlos felt guilty for helping him kill the manticore instead of subduing it as Krastos had originally intended. Krastos would not kill Bawa. Tarlos would have to make his move.

"I feel your fear, Tarlos," Bawa said, and Tarlos paused. "I see it, smell it, taste it. It is loud in your mind. Death is the end. You know this to be true. And yet you desire to kill me? Your deepest desire is to live forever, as do the Ageless, but you do not fear to deal death. Who are you to issue judgement on me?"

"Tarlos," Krastos grunted. "He's reading your mind. Stalling you. Do it! Now!"

"Your mother died for you," Bawa continued, "and you repay her sacrifice by becoming a murderer."

Tarlos had heard enough. He charged at Bawa, sword stretched out in front of him.

Bawa screamed, "Hypocrite!" and Tarlos halted. The monster wrenched his neck and flicked his long tail, managing to snap Krastos's back. Krastos cried out in pain and fell from Bawa's shoulders. He landed hard on the stone floor. His sword clattered to the ground—Bawa kicked it away, sending it out of the cave. Bawa lifted one huge foot then and brought it down hard on Krastos. There was a snap and a crack, and Krastos screamed in agony. Bawa picked him up with his clawed hands and threw him deeper into the cave, tossing him as if a limp doll. Krastos screamed. Tarlos heard another snap as his brother landed and tumbled in the distance.

From the deep and dark of the cave, Tarlos heard the faint, fading voice of his twin: "Tarlos . . . my back . . . broken. Get out . . . please . . ."

Bawa picked Tarlos up as he had Krastos. He did not throw Tarlos but instead pinned him against the cave wall. With his tail, Bawa flicked the sword from Tarlos's hand and kicked it out of the cave. Bawa laughed, frustrated, exhausted, and relieved all at once. His hot, rancid breath smacked Tarlos's face, caressing his nostrils. Tarlos tasted rotting flesh and emptied his stomach all over Bawa.

The monster grinned sadistically. Tarlos saw the gap where Krastos had knocked out several of the beast's teeth. In their place was a bloody hole as dark as tar.

Bawa opened his mouth and came at Tarlos, arching his neck like a viper. Tarlos used all the strength of his mind to stop Bawa before he could bite his head off. Bawa fought against Tarlos's Power—the monster twitched and shook against the Holder's force of will.

Krastos's voice echoed through the cave again—Tarlos almost did not hear the pained, strained whisper. "Get out . . ."

Bawa's head inched closer to Tarlos as the Holder's Power drained his strength. Lights popped in his eyes as he fought to keep the monster at bay.

"Behold . . ." the voice of Krastos drifted forth, "the strength . . . of . . . a demigod."

With a surge of realization, Tarlos used every last bit of his mental strength to push Bawa away from him, and at the same time he pushed himself away from Bawa, propelling himself out of the cave.

As Tarlos flew, Bawa was forced backwards. He dug his claws into the stone floor and lunged at Tarlos while the Holder remained airborne. Tarlos heard Krastos groan loudly followed by the sound of an explosion that was like nothing he had ever heard. He knew exactly what had happened—Krastos had used the last of his strength and slammed his fists into the cave wall.

Bawa looked behind. Crevasses webbed from the inner cave, spreading from where Krastos lay broken all the way to the entrance. Rocks fell from the ceiling, and the floor beneath them gave way.

As Tarlos fell, landing on the rocky hill outside and rolling away, the cave and indeed the entire hill above him crumbled in on itself, and Bawa screamed his last.

The mountain above the hill groaned as the cracks spread to its peak. With no time to think or process what had just happened, Tarlos flew away from the mountain, not paying any mind to the screaming pain in his head or his depleted energy levels.

The rock face of the mountain crumbled and fell. Tarlos hovered a hundred feet above the rubble as Bawa and Krastos were buried alive.

It started to rain.

Tarlos's eyes went dark, and he fell to the ground.

He woke a mile from the toppled mountain, sheltered beneath a cedar tree. The dust was still settling, and the animals were coming out of their hiding places to seek protection from the debris and rain. He had no idea how long he had been unconscious, only that it was night and raining, the moon a glowing crescent behind the clouds. He was sore and exhausted, and his head pounded with searing pain. His throat was dry and raw, his stomach empty, and the world was silent.

Hours later, Tarlos was able to use his Power to unearth his brother's mangled body and lift him free of the destruction. Krastos's chest was flat, limbs shattered, his clothes torn beneath his flattened armor. Tarlos did not look for any sign of the defeated Bawa.

It was only after Tarlos had landed with Krastos a safe distance from the crumbled mountain, both under shade and hidden from the sun, that he allowed himself to cry. He touched Krastos, ran his hand over his mangled arms and legs, felt the flatness of his torso.

Krastos's eyes were open. Tarlos went to close them, clearing away a stray tooth embedded in his brother's cheek, but paused. He took a moment to gaze into Krastos's dead eyes only to see nothing behind them. No light, no peace, no discomfort either. This body did not know that it was once a living person. Krastos was gone, and that was that.

Tarlos felt something beneath Krastos's shirt and pulled it out. It was the talisman that Lakaeus had given him. By the time Tarlos finished crying, the moon had set and the sun shone through the forest canopy.

The horses were gone, either run away or buried beneath the mountain with countless other animals. Tarlos did not have the mental energy to levitate Krastos all the way back to Kesh, and he could not lift him with his bare hands. Using some fallen branches and Krastos's torn shirt, Tarlos lashed together a sledge upon which he placed his brother's body. He would not leave Krastos there for soldiers to fetch. They had come to fight Bawa together, and they would leave together, too.

Tarlos woke to feathers fluttering around him and the sound of a breeze sifting through dried corn husks. It was dark, but Tarlos saw shadows of grey against a backdrop of black.

One of the shadows approached him. At first, he thought it was some kind of mutant bird, hunched over and walking on two tall legs. But as it neared, he saw that it was in fact a tall man wearing a cloak of black feathers.

"The mountain," Tarlos said in Krastos's voice (was he Krastos?). "I didn't want to kill it."

"That didn't stop you from killing it, though, did it?" the man replied. His voice was dry and hollow like wind blowing through the discarded skin of a snake. His eyes were grey and blank.

The man knelt beside Tarlos and scooped a handful of clay from the ground. He welded his eyes to Tarlos's as he brought the clay to his mouth and took a bite. He chewed, his saliva mixing with the clay. It spilled from his lips, a red-brown liquid that dripped from his chin. Tarlos backed away, disgusted.

He collided then with another person and turned to see a woman dressed in feathers, also munching on clay. Her teeth were black and her eyes saw no light.

Tarlos cried out and ran, but all around him were people wearing feathers and eating clay. They all dwelt in darkness.

"I didn't want to kill him!" he shouted into the abyss, as men and women turned to him, clay falling from their lips and between their fingers as they grasped at the cold ground. "I didn't want to kill him! I didn't want to!"

But then he realized: he was not shouting this. He heard it, but the voice was far away. It was familiar, though, and he ran to it. And there he was (Tarlos, for he was Krastos) kneeling beside a sarcophagus. The other Tarlos cried and pounded the heavy coffin, which was carved and painted to look like a man. Like him.

Like Krastos.

"I didn't want to kill him," Tarlos said over and over and over.

Tarlos/Krastos reached a shaky hand toward himself/his twin and touched the other's shoulder. The other Tarlos turned at his touch, and his eyes were the same dark emptiness as the clay-eaters.

Tarlos/Krastos screamed and ran. The clay-eaters followed him, shambling at a miserable pace, yet they somehow kept up with him.

"Who are you?" he cried out.

Behind him, a clammy hand grabbed his neck and another plunged into his beard, clutching his chin. A hollow wisp of a voice in his ear: "We forget. We forget, and no one remembers."

Tarlos woke calmly from his nightmare, thinking it odd that he was not thrashing or screaming or sweating. His eyes were puffy and stung. He rubbed tears from them until he could focus on the stars and moon above.

"Tarlos," spoke a woman's voice.

He turned to it, and to a blazing fire that had not been there a moment ago. To the other side of the fire sat a woman dressed all in white. Her hair was also white, and it floated around her head as if she were underwater. Her skin, too, was like porcelain. The only bit of contrast was her icy blue eyes.

"Who are you?" Tarlos asked. His voice was cracked, weak from thirst and sobbing.

"I am Hashri," the woman answered, and Tarlos straightened at the name.

Hashri was the goddess of death, she who watched over all souls who crossed into the Nether. Seeing a living, breathing goddess sitting before him did not shake him. Tarlos was fed up with his life and ready for anything to happen. If a goddess had come to take him down the Styx, so be it. He had no desire to live after what had just happened.

"Why are you here?" he asked.

"I thought you might want to know the state of your brother's soul," she said. Her voice echoed in Tarlos's head—the sound made him want to weep for every life that had ever passed.

"He's dead. Please leave me alone." Tarlos turned from her and lay back down beside the sledge and Krastos. "I don't want anything to do with the gods."

An unseen force, however, prevented Tarlos from ignoring the goddess. He tried to turn away but his eyes remained glued to her flawless face.

"Krastos lived a wonderful life," she said. Her voice was even, calm—reassuring, like the sea after a storm. "He brought honor to his name and to his memory, and he overcame the burden of his father's legacy."

This last bit confused Tarlos. He brushed it aside for the moment, though, as he was reminded of something else—something he'd thought of earlier. "Where was Moleg?" he asked Hashri. "He wasn't there to protect my mother, and he wasn't there to protect Krastos. His own son. Where was Moleg when my brother needed him most?"

"My brother Moleg has no mortal children," Hashri said. "Perhaps you should inquire about this when you return home. And you must return quickly, as forces beyond you conspire for the throne. Be at peace knowing that Krastos does not suffer in the Nether. Farewell, Tarlos, son of Lakaeus."

In less time than it took to blink, the fire was gone and Hashri was no more. Tarlos was once more alone in the dark, with the stars and the song of the crickets, and a dead brother.

When he reached Kesh three days later, Tarlos was dehydrated, sunburnt, and still in shock. He wondered if he had blinked even once since leaving the Cedar Forest. The towering walls of Kesh stood before him, a red dot in a yellow desert against a backdrop of stars. He pressed on, dragging Krastos behind him. The sledge was coming apart as the shirt that held it together frayed and tore.

Tarlos stopped at the huge gates and dropped the sledge to the ground. It landed in a puff of dirt, and Tarlos fell to his knees beside it. He looked at Krastos, or what was once Krastos, and felt his bottom lip quiver.

"Made it," he said, and then he fell backwards and slept in the dirt.

He woke to a spear in his face and three armed guards standing above him. He shielded his eyes from the sun rising over the city walls.

"State your business," one of the guards said. The spear inched closer to Tarlos's face.

He sat up, slowly, and coughed. "I'm here to bury my brother."

The three guards looked at Tarlos for several moments before one of them gasped.

"Prince Tarlos!" he shouted, and dropped to one knee. The others followed his example, and their spears fell away.

One of the guards looked to the sledge, and his eyes grew wide. "That's not . . ."

Tarlos nodded. "If you wouldn't mind, I'd like you three to take Krastos to the temple to have him prepared for burial. I'm just going to sit here a minute longer."

The guards bowed, and a stretcher was brought from the guard station on the other side of the gates. They carried away the body of Krastos. Tarlos watched as they carried his brother through the city. Dozens of heads turned, observing the small precession. No one recognized their dead prince.

Tarlos put his head in his hands and breathed. The day was hot, the sand hotter; his skin was burnt and his heart felt frozen. Eyes closed, he apologized to the ground, whispering to himself, to the gods, and to his brother. He did not know if they could hear him, but he did not care either way. He did not care about anything anymore.

Krastos's body was cleaned, embalmed, and wrapped in linens. Nekhte himself crafted a solid-gold sarcophagus in Krastos's image. The priestesses took care when placing Krastos's body into the coffin. Shala, a small and young priestess, held back her tears as she helped. Before the sarcophagus was shut and sealed, Tarlos made sure to lay the talisman Lakaeus had given him on his chest, above his crossed arms.

All of Kesh was required to come to the prince's funeral, and they did. They gathered at the Tomb of Kings, twelve miles south of Kesh. Krastos was carried in by a team of stallions. There they watched and listened in reverent silence as the High Priestess conducted the burial.

She held her palms to her face and raised her chin to the sky. Her voice was loud but respectful. "Hashri, everything that is undesirable of Krastos has been carried away for you." She picked up a vase of water and lightly poured it over the sarcophagus. "Any evil that was spoken in his name, Ilshu has received and cast into the Styx.

"The fluid of life shall not be destroyed in you, and you shall not be destroyed in it. Let him that departs depart with his soul. Hefmut departs with his soul. Moleg departs with his soul. Sekhmet departs with his soul. Sep departs with his soul. Ninety-nine gods and ninety-nine more depart with his soul.

"Krastos, the arm of your soul is before you and behind you.

"Krastos, the leg of your soul is before you and behind you.

"Hashri, I give unto you the offering of Hefmut, that your belly may be filled with the flesh and your body surrounded by the odor."

A small white sheep was brought to the High Priestess, led on a rope by two young priestesses. The High Priestess removed a long knife from her belt, held it to the sky, then slit the sheep's throat. Blood poured over the ground as the sheep bleated and twitched its hind leg.

"This libation is for you, Hashri. This libation is for you, Krastos."

A priestess brought her four sticks of incense, which she lit and waved around the sarcophagus.

"As Hefmut advances, and as Moleg advances, and as Sekhmet advances, and as Sep advances, so shall Ilshu advance with your soul.

"Hail Ilshu, king of the dead. Hail Hashri, queen of the dead.

Hail to the gods of death who live forever, who were born of heaven, conceived of Shar and Moresh. Into your hands we commend the soul of Krastos."

Soldiers placed Krastos in his tomb. Treasures were laid around him, and fresh paintings on the walls depicted his life—from his miraculous birth and childhood, to his many feats of strength and service, to the battle with the manticore, and finally his selfless sacrifice in the fight against Bawa.

The door to Krastos's tomb was sealed shut, never to be entered again.

The sermon was word-for-word the same as every funeral conducted since the beginning of their religion. Tarlos expected no different. But after hearing his brother receive the same funeral as his mother eight years before, with only their names switched, Tarlos felt a small pit of anger in his belly. Why could they not at least take a moment and say something about Krastos's life?

Tarlos stood at the entrance to the tomb and ran his hand over the glyphs carved into the stone above the door that represented Krastos's name. Behind him, the people of Kesh left the Tomb of Kings and made their way back to the city. Tears stung Tarlos's eyes as not one person stayed even a few minutes after Krastos was shut up in darkness forever.

"And just like that," Tarlos said to the door, "you're gone."

The royal concubines lived together in a mansion next to the palace grounds. Like everything else in Kesh, it was built from cedar wood and did not stand apart in terms of appearance. The next morning's dawn cast slats of light onto the grounds and gardens in front of it. Laundry hanging out to dry flapped in the breeze—there was no other movement. The concubines liked to sleep late, and Tarlos did not expect any of them to be awake at this hour. Kamhat would be there, in her private room, confined to her bed. The servants working in the gardens turned their heads and bowed as Tarlos passed them on his way into the mansion.

The heavy cedar doors opened silently. Servants milled

about, cleaning and fluffing pillows and filling jugs with water and wine. More could be heard in the kitchen, preparing a midday meal. A few of them looked his way as he walked through the main room and up the stairs to the topmost floor, but he spoke not a word to them. As much as he respected the servants, he was in no mood to speak to them as he often did, as equals.

Kamhat's room was at the end of the hall. Tarlos approached silently, suddenly aware of the dryness of his eyes and throat. He stopped to compose himself before entering.

She was there, in her bed, just as Tarlos had imagined. Her frail body lay hidden beneath unwrinkled covers—it seemed that she had not moved since the incident. She was thin and sickly, pale with sunken cheeks. She opened her eyes as soon as Tarlos entered the room.

"Prince," she said. Her usual sensual voice was now raspy and weak. "I am sorry."

Tarlos stared at the lump of her body beneath the blanket. He almost felt sorry for her, laying there broken and useless and forgotten.

Finally, he exhaled through his nose, an aggressive sigh, and said, "Why is it that you, a whore and a harlot, get to live after what you've been through—and yet my brother, who never committed a single wrong deed in his life, is now dead and forgotten to the world? Tell me."

Tears welled in her eyes. "I . . . I . . ."

"Tell me what happened that night," Tarlos said. "The truth. I know it wasn't him."

It was plain to see that Kamhat was seriously injured. Tarlos did not think she would ever walk again. But while he felt sorry for her, he waited eagerly to hear what she had to say before extending her any sympathy.

Her eyes wet, she shook her head. "I don't know what you—"

"Just tell me," he spat. "I have had a terrible decan. I watched my brother die, I dragged him across the desert for three days. I stood there and watched as everyone in Kesh left immediately following the sermon at his funeral—not one person stayed to pay their respects. I am livid and in no mood to play games."

"I . . ." Kamhat closed her eyes, sending a tear down her cheek. She turned from him. "I'm sorry, Prince. I don't know what you want me to say."

Tarlos lifted her, and she hovered six feet above his head. She screamed in pain as her legs dangled beneath her, and Tarlos saw the bandages and plaster around her waist and thighs. She cried out and shouted, but through his own rage he could not understand anything she said.

"You're responsible for this!" he yelled over her cries. "This is your fault! He'd still be alive if it weren't for you! I hope you rot in the House of Dust for all eternity!"

She screeched, "Put me down and I'll tell you!"

Tarlos dropped her on the bed. She took several seconds to cry, wipe her eyes, and adjust herself. She could not make eye contact with Tarlos.

Between sobs, she said, "Krastos had nothing to do with it. It was the guards who broke me. With hammers. They told me they would kill me if I said anything, and they told me to say that it was Krastos who did it. Do you understand, Tarlos? They were going to kill me!"

"Why?" Tarlos asked. His blood boiled. "The guards wouldn't do that of their own accord. Who gave them the order?"

"Please, Prince . . ."

"Tell me," he said.

"I don't know!" she cried. "I would tell you! But I just don't know. Who would want to frame Krastos? I can't think of anyone, and I've thought about it a lot." She breathed in, and her breath shook, and she wiped her eyes and bit her lips. "They would have killed me. I am so sorry, Tarlos. So sorry . . ."

Having heard enough, Tarlos left her there, hearing her continued sobs as he left the mansion and made his way to the palace.

The royal house lay silent silent, and almost all inside were still asleep. It was a short and easy walk from a side door in the courtyard up the stairs to the king's chamber. The guards nodded to him, and he opened the door slowly. It creaked low and quiet, opening just wide enough for him to slip through.

He closed it behind him. The room was dark, as it always was, with not even the sun penetrating the thick black curtains. The king's body servant slept in a small private room just a few feet away, which Tarlos locked from the outside then tugged on the door to make sure it would not open.

His father slept in his bed, his small malnourished chest rising and falling gently. The sick and raspy breathing of the king made Tarlos ill. He watched his father sleep for a few minutes, understanding—accepting that this would be the last time he saw his father alive if things happened how he was beginning to imagine.

With a snort, the king yawned and rolled over in his sleep, and the blanket covering him slipped off and revealed his thin legs. Tarlos used his Power to pull the blanket off entirely, and the king shivered. In Kesh, it was hot no matter the time of day or night, but Lakaeus had been suffering chills for several months. This was a sign: his death was near. Perhaps nearer than he knew.

Lakaeus opened his eyes and searched with a wandering arm for his blanket. Tarlos stepped forward. The cedar floor creaked beneath his feet, and Lakaeus stopped in place.

"Someone there?" he asked. His voice was weak and cracking with sleep and sickness. "Abu? Is that you?"

Tarlos whispered, "It's me, Father."

Lakaeus sat up fully, struggling with his skinny, weak arms as he worked to prop himself up against the headboard. "Tarlos! Gods, boy, where have you been? I have so many things to say to you and I don't know where to start . . ."

"I guess you know by now that Krastos is dead." Tarlos took another step forward. His eyes were adjusting to the darkness; he could see his father's eyes clearly. Was the king only tired, or did Tarlos see worry in those grey eyes?

The king cleared his throat. "Yes. Although they didn't tell me how it happened. "

"Bawa killed him. Actually, Krastos sacrificed himself to save my life." Another step forward. The king leaned away from his son. "I need to ask you something, and you need to answer truthfully."

Lakaeus licked his cracked lips and nodded. "Go ahead."

"Was Moleg truly Krastos's father?" He had to whisper the question. He feared that if he used his voice he might cry.

Lakaeus swallowed nervously. He fingered his scraggly beard, then shook his head and looked away. "No," he said softly. "Moleg was not his father."

"Then who was? Because it surely wasn't you."

The king looked at Tarlos, and Tarlos saw clearly the worry in his eyes. Worry . . . and fury. The king lowered his head. "Ablis."

Tarlos stumbled back a step. After a moment's thought, it all made sense. "Mother's life was the price for a son," Tarlos said, finally understanding. "That's why Bawa killed her—because she made a deal with Ablis. You . . . you were responsible for the manticore. You wanted Krastos dead!"

"The manticore should have killed him, even being a demigod," the king spat, using his thin, shaking arms to straighten himself to better meet Tarlos's gaze. "I know you helped him kill it. So, something else had to be done."

"You almost killed Kamhat just to have an excuse to kill Krastos." Tarlos took two steps forward, fire burning in his veins and thunder raging in his heart. "You blame him for Mother's death, don't you?"

"Ninsun would still be alive if that abomination had never been born!" Lakaeus's chest rose and fell tremendously. He put a hand over his heart and coughed.

Silence swelled between them. Then Tarlos said, "I'm going to kill you now."

The king sneered. "Fine. Send me to Paradise. I deserve it after the life I've lived."

"You think you will go to Paradise when only the House of Dust awaits murderous tyrants like you?" Tarlos scoffed. "You will rot in Hell for all time. And when you are dead, I will blot your name from every record. I will make it illegal even to utter your name. Soon, there will come a day when Lakaeus, son of Hestos, might as well have never existed in the first place. Then you will truly be dead."

Lakaeus sniffed and whispered, "Then I shall wait for you in Hell, my son."

Tarlos asked, "Will you try to defend yourself?"

The king raised his head, but his shaking arms gave out and he slumped down into his bed. Lakaeus sighed. "It wouldn't do any good. I'm dying anyway. And I cannot kill you, for the world must have a Holder of Space. Do what you will."

Tarlos pulled the air from his father's lungs. He closed the king's throat, and the king gurgled and choked for a few seconds, then fell over onto his side. His face was blue.

Tarlos did not give his father the honor of being buried. Lakaeus's body was burned, his ashes thrown to the wind.

The High Priestess performed the coronation, and Tarlos was made the new king of Kesh. The crown was cold and a bit too small. It hurt to wear it, so he hardly ever did.

Sleep did not come to Tarlos for many nights, not even with the warm comfort of Katla beside him.

"Just close your eyes and lay down, and sleep will come," the queen would often say to him.

"Why should I sleep when my brother will never wake again?" Tarlos replied one night.

"He's alive in your heart and in your memories, Tarlos."

But Tarlos rolled away from her.

"I have something to tell you," Katla said. "I tried to tell you at the feast after your trial, but it just didn't seem like the right time…"

"I'm not in the mood for talking." Tarlos threw off the blanket and sat up. "I need air. Clear my head." He wrapped a tunic around himself and left through a small back door. Katla said something, but he didn't stop to listen.

A narrow staircase led from the king's chamber down to the palace gardens. The night sky was clear and the stars blinked at him beside the half-hidden face of Moresh. Tarlos breathed in the cool night air as he took the footpath through the flowers, extending a hand to catch a tall one, plucking it and holding it beneath his nose to smell it.

He held the flower gently in his palm and glared at it in the moonlight. It was a foreign flower, given to his grandmother by some ambassador of a faraway land. The five petals were purple and pointed, the center yellow. The flower levitated, floating above Tarlos's hand. One by one, the petals pulled away from the middle, then orbited the stem in a silent dance. Tarlos flicked a finger to the side and the purple pieces fell to the ground.

"That's a shame," came a voice in the dark. "That orchid can't be found within ten thousand miles of this place."

Tarlos turned to see a dark shape sitting on a bench some yards away. "This is a private garden," he said. "You need to leave."

"Ah, but it's such a beautiful night," said the man. His neck bent toward the sky. "Moresh is bright tonight, though she hides half her face. Would you sit with me a moment?"

"Do you know who I am?" Tarlos reached around his waist to a small knife in his tunic. "Your king gave you a command."

"I know who you are, Tarlos son of Lakaeus. Do you know who you are?"

Tarlos stepped toward the man on the bench, though he kept his distance. "Who are you? Speak up!"

The man stood, turned away from the moon, and let his cloak fall to the ground. A dim glow issued from the man's eyes and skin, his toothy smile shone in a red light. As he straightened, Tarlos stepped back. The man towered over him, more than twice his own height. The king shrank as the stranger grinned. Heat radiated from him like a furnace, and Tarlos shielded his gaze lest his eyes melt.

"Do you know who I am?" demanded the stranger in a deep empty voice that conjured up in Tarlos's mind the void between stars.

Tarlos nodded, his hands over his eyes. "Please, I meant no harm." He didn't dare speak aloud the name of the being who now spoke with him—Ablis.

The god laughed, and the heat and light dissipated. Tarlos removed his hands and blinked. "I came to see the new king of Kesh," he said in a voice like dry flame.

"What do you want with me?" Tarlos asked, his voice a mere whisper.

"I want nothing with you," Ablis said. "I want everything from you." The god seethed, and Tarlos felt his anger like a scalding stove.

"What have I done to offend you?"

The heat returned as Ablis groaned in his displeasure. Tarlos knew at any moment Ablis could burn him like a drop of water on the surface of the sun. He silently prayed to Shar and Moresh to protect him.

Then the god answered him: "You were born, Tarlos."

The king shook his head. "I don't understand."

"Look at me." The heat departed again, and Tarlos wiped the sweat from his eyelids to meet Ablis's gaze. "I will try to explain in a way that your finite mortal mind may comprehend. Behold." Ablis extended a hand, and in the palm a small fire sparked to life. The flame expanded into a ball larger than Tarlos's head, though it gave off no heat. Tarlos stared into the fiery orb, watching the red, orange, and yellow flames dance above Ablis's hand. The shapes morphed, and Tarlos watched his own mother in the orb with astonishment.

"Your mother came to the gods for help," Ablis said. The small fire-Ninsun prayed alone. "I answered when no others did." Ninsun shielded her eyes as Ablis came to her in all his burning glory. "I offered her a son, and in return I commanded her to bring me the child after its Power came into maturity. Ninsun agreed, knowing that I would be the child's father."

Ninsun's belly grew, and as time passed her face grew weary and sad. "As the day of the child's birth neared, Ninsun began to regret her decision. She prayed to me many times, but I did not come. A deal once struck cannot be undone." Ninsun carried two infants in her arms.

Ablis growled. "The universe thought to humiliate me by thwarting my plans. Krastos, my own begotten child, was to be an only child. It was he who was meant to hold the Power of Space and inherit the throne of Kesh. Under my guidance,

Krastos was to conquer all of Edorath. The world. Instead..."

Now Tarlos saw himself sitting on the throne, a bronze crown on his head. "My son is dead, and you rule Kesh in his place." Ablis closed his fist and the fiery ball hissed out of existence.

Tarlos blinked and turned away from the infuriated god. He frowned in horror as he saw that the entire garden was dead, the flowers and trees drained of life, dry like a field of snakeskins.

"This Earth was to fall into a new age under my rule," Ablis continued. "Instead, in taking the throne yourself, you have placed Kesh on a road to desolation. Soon there will come a day when none will know that a great kingdom once stood here in the desert. The name of Kesh, as well as the names of Tarlos and Krastos, will fade into nothing."

Tarlos swallowed as he imagined his kingdom blowing away like a pillar of sand. "So," he croaked, "you've come to kill me, then?"

"That is up to you." Ablis shrank to the size of a human, a tunic materializing around him. "I've come here to make you an offer. Serve me where Krastos would have, and I will see that your name never dies, nor that of Kesh."

Tarlos squinted at the god. "You ask me to be a puppet king?"

"I do not ask. I encourage."

"You didn't know Krastos. He wouldn't have done as you propose."

"Then I hope you would be wiser. Tread carefully, King Tarlos." Ablis crossed his arms over his chest.

"I can forge my own legacy," Tarlos said. "I don't need your support, only the support of the true gods. I rebuke you, Ablis. Get out of my sight and never come to me again."

Ablis laughed. Tarlos winced at the grating sound. "You have no power over me, tiny man."

The ground fell from beneath them, and Tarlos drew in a breath to scream, but the air caught in his throat. The desert shrank away beneath them as Ablis brought them into the sky, so high that Tarlos wondered if they may reach the moon. The air grew cold and the wind fierce, and Tarlos's teeth chattered. He had never flown this high. Below, the world curved away in all directions.

Ablis pinched Tarlos's chin between his fingers. "I would have rather let you live," he said. "But I will rule Kesh just the same. Are you ready?"

Finally, Tarlos found his breath and voice. It all tumbled from him in sobs. "Ablis, please! Don't do this!"

Ablis frowned and brought Tarlos's face closer to his. He looked into Tarlos's eyes. With one finger he touched Tarlos's cheek, wet with tears. "You're afraid," he said. "Afraid to die."

Tarlos didn't try denying it. "Please...let me go..."

Ablis smiled. "My son is dead and I've almost lost the very throne of Earth because of you. Perhaps death is a punishment too simple." He placed both hands on the sides of Tarlos's face. They grew warm as Ablis spoke. "I won't kill you, because death is but an instant. But to go on living with a fear of what may come, that is an agony that stays. Very well, King Tarlos of Kesh, I will not kill you. I wish you a very long life."

There was a flash of white light and the smell of burning meat, and Tarlos felt solid ground beneath him. He blinked a few times as his surroundings came into focus.

The vast desert stretched all around him. He scrambled to his feet and spun around. Kesh was nowhere in sight. Nothing was in sight but dunes.

At his feet were three skins of water and a small package. He opened it to find bread and dried cheese. Ablis wanted him to stay alive.

7

The Man with the Wide-brimmed Hat

Tarlos woke to the aroma of food cooking. He pulled on his dirty shirt and filthy trousers, and laced up his sandals. His hair was still damp when he got in bed, and now it stuck out in every direction. He wet it in the bathroom and tamed it as best he could, then rinsed his face to wake himself up.

Downstairs, the tavern was filled with dozens of people. They all spoke loudly and excitedly, laughing and moving from table to table, sharing food and drink. Tarlos stopped at the bottom of the stairs. He wondered how many people like this lived here. At a glance, he guessed there were at least a hundred people.

"Tarlos!" called a familiar voice. "Good morning! How'd you sleep?"

Tarlos held up a hand in greeting to the woman behind the counter. She was dealing out plates of steaming food, the smell of which caused Tarlos's stomach to grumble. On the counter were plates of bread and boiled eggs, and stacks of what looked like thin bread. There were pitchers of fruit juice, coffee, tea, and milk. Tarlos never imagined that there would be such things in the dead country.

"Hungry?" asked the woman. She waved him over, and Tarlos approached the counter. A man with short brown hair and a long nose smiled at Tarlos and moved aside for him.

"Heard you're the new guy," said the man. His eyes were green. Tarlos had never seen eyes that color.

"I'm just passing through," Tarlos said.

"That's what she tells me." The man clapped Tarlos on the back, and Tarlos's eyebrows knit together. "Well, I gotta get back," the man said. "I hope we get to officially meet soon." He nodded at Tarlos, and Tarlos gave him a weak smile in return. The man grinned at the woman. "Later," he said, and disappeared through the crowd.

"Who's that?" Tarlos asked.

"Oh, just a friend from before," she said. "So, what'll it be? Eggs? Bacon? Pancakes? French toast?"

"Um . . ." Tarlos scanned the various plates, recognizing only a few dishes. "What do you like best?"

"Waffles. But we don't have any today, sorry. I'd recommend French toast and raspberry syrup." She made him a plate and poured him a cup of dark coffee. The cup was not glass; it was white and—Tarlos guessed—made of clay, like the cups in Kesh.

"Cream, sugar?" she asked.

Tarlos shook his head, not understanding what she meant, and the woman pushed the plate across the counter to him and handed him an eating utensil. He held it in his fist and gave her a questioning look.

"Man, you really are from the Bronze Age," she said. "It's a fork. You use it to eat, so you don't get your hands messy. Like this." She took another fork and pretended to eat with it. "I'd really like to know about your homeland and your life, when you have the time to talk."

Tarlos choked down the French toast. It was entirely too sweet for breakfast food, but he did not wish to be rude. He finished his plate before moving onto the coffee, now cool enough to drink.

"Is that man here?" he asked.

"The boatman? I think so." The woman stood on her toes and craned her neck to see over the crowd. "Yep, I see him. He's at his usual table. Looks like he chose pancakes today. He always chooses biscuits and gravy when we have it."

Tarlos thanked the woman, and she took his plate and cup away.

The tavern was crowded, with at least four people to each table, all of them speaking and eating. The place was filled with the sound of utensils on plates, beverages being poured, conversation mixed with laughter. The boatman's was the only table that was not full. He sat alone, poking at his food.

Tarlos navigated his way through the tables, avoiding chairs pushed too far back. Hardly anyone looked up at him, and those who did gave him a friendly smile.

The boatman wore a brown hat with a wide brim, and thick-soled boots made of leather. His shirt was plain blue and buttoned down the front, and his trousers were tan and worn at the knees. He bent over his food, the wide brim of his hat covering his face. Tarlos approached slowly, clearing his throat when he reached the table.

The man raised his head. Tarlos noted his pale blue eyes. He had seen blue eyes only once before. Something painful tried to rear its head in his mind; he pushed it away. There was stubble on the man's cheeks and chin. His mustache was thick and long, curled up at the ends. He nodded at Tarlos.

"Have a seat, if you want," he said with a gruff voice. Tarlos took the seat across from him, and the man continued poking at his pancakes and eggs.

"I hear you have a boat," said Tarlos.

The man raised his head once more and pushed his plate away. "I hate eggs. Don't care much for pancakes, neither. I always get biscuits and gravy when I can, but this ain't heaven yet. Yeah, I got a boat. Why?"

"I need to get down the river." Tarlos folded his hands together on the table.

The man sucked his teeth. "Mm-hm. Nothin down there."

"Have you ever been?"

The boatman shook his head. "No, but I been far enough, I guess. Far enough to see that there's no point in goin any further."

"I need to get to the end of the river. I have business in the country on the other side of this one."

"You ain't got no business anywhere but here, son," the man grumbled. He picked up a cup of coffee and drank half of it, sighed and licked his lips, then ran a finger across the handlebars of his mustache. "This is where the good Lord sent you, and you'd do best to accept it and continue your existence in peace. Ain't no use dreamin about what else is out there. You're dead. What else is there to know?"

"I'm not dead."

The man smirked. "That's what we all think at first. There's no shame in it if you're new here. But it's best to accept it as quick as you can. If you put it off too long, it gets real difficult when it sinks in later. And it always sinks in."

"My name is Tarlos," he said with a stern face. "I came to this country through Shar's Mountain, I'm not dead, and I need to get down that river."

The man raised his eyebrows. For a while, he only stared at Tarlos, studying him. Then, after several moments, "Way is dangerous. The river isn't meant to be floated down by the likes of us. It's for the Reaper, only."

"I understand that you float it regardless."

The man nodded. "Yeah, well, I never was one for keeping the rules. They say the water is poison, but that's never been a concern for me. Might be for you, though."

"It might."

The man stuck his little finger into his mouth and picked something from his teeth, then flicked it away. He looked past Tarlos and into the crowd. His eyes stayed fixed to something for a moment. Before Tarlos could turn to see what had caught his attention, the boatman spoke again.

"You say your name's Tarlos. Are you sure about that? It's no name I ever heard before."

Tarlos nodded. "Tarlos, son of Lakaeus, king of Kesh."

This time when the man looked away, Tarlos turned and followed his gaze—to a small woman with olive skin and black hair and angular eyes, like those who lived beyond the World's Spine. She stood reverently at the counter, speaking to the woman there.

"Did you know her when you were alive?" Tarlos asked, turning back to the boatman.

The boatman snapped back and cleared his throat. He finished his coffee and slammed the empty cup down on the table, then wiped his mustache.

"Listen," he said, "I been down the river once, not all the way but further'n anyone else, I think. I told myself I'd never go again. But . . ." His eyes flicked up once more and he sighed.

"What?" Tarlos said.

"I never heard of Kesh. And I never met someone here who remembered their name, neither, but it seems like you're tellin the truth." He cracked his knuckles, and his knee began to bounce beneath the table. "What the hell, I'm dead anyway. Let's go before I change my mind."

The boat was long, slender, and flat. A box on top was large enough for them to stand up in, with a bunk, a chair, and a wash basin. Ropes and posts were strewn about the deck, ready to be put to use should anything need to be shipped up- or downriver.

"Hardly ever go down," the boatman told Tarlos as he untied the mooring from a small wooden post. He gave the boat a shove out into the water, then jumped aboard as the craft floated away. "Hardly anyone in that direction, anyway. I mostly go upriver. Pain in the ass, really. Gotta push against the current with a pole, and it does get mighty tiring after a while. I always thought that after I died, I wouldn't feel tired no more. I guess that's what I get for being philosophical. Should be fun, though, for the most part. At least I ain't alone this time."

The man sat beside the rudder and steered the boat downstream. Tarlos took a seat on deck and leaned against the wall of the box-room. He played with the tooth in his pocket.

"So, Tarlos," said the man. "Never heard that name before, and I been everywhere, or pretty much everywhere. The American frontier, Australia, New Zealand, Edo, even as far as India in my early years. Where are you from?"

Tarlos took the tooth from his pocket and held it in his palm.

"I've never heard of any of those places. I'm from Kesh, in the Fertile Valley."

"Never heard of that, neither. Is it nice there?"

"I suppose."

The tooth floated a few inches above Tarlos's hand and flipped around two or three times before settling back down again. He closed his fist over it and sighed.

"What on Earth?" said the man. He let go of the rudder and stepped forward. He lifted his chin and stared at Tarlos's closed fist. The rudder turned slightly and the boat jerked. He went back to steady it. "Was that thing just floating?"

Tarlos nodded. "I'm a Holder."

"A what? Did you make that move?"

Tarlos lifted his eyebrows. "You don't know what a Holder is?"

The boatman shook his head. "Enlighten me."

Tarlos took a moment to organize his thoughts, then spoke with reverence. "I've been able to do it since I was twelve. I inherited it from my father, and he got it from his mother, and on and on since the first people. The firstborn always inherits the Power."

"Okay," the man said. He tipped his hat back and scratched his forehead. "I guess I've seen stranger things."

"There are four Powers," Tarlos continued. He spoke softly now, not really caring whether the man was listening or not. "Space, Language, Mind, and Time. But the Power of Mind has been lost since—"

"What does the time power do?" the boatman interrupted.

Tarlos glanced at him and shrugged. "Control time. Speed it up, slow it down. But I don't think they can make it run backwards."

"Hang on," snapped the man. "You're telling me there are people from your world who can slow time." It was more of a statement than a question.

"Yes."

"I'll be damned," he mumbled. "I knew a bunch of folks who could do that."

"Do what?" Tarlos mumbled. His eyes closed and leaned

back against the wall.

"Slow time. On my honor, I knew em."

Tarlos opened his eyes. The boatman was grinning, staring across to the south shore, mindlessly steering the boat as it bobbed up and down in the water.

Tarlos said, "You lie."

The man took his eyes from the shore and looked at Tarlos. His smile diminished, the ends of his mustache coming down. "Scuse me?"

"You could'nt have known people who could slow time. There's only one in each generation. Perhaps you could have known two, a parent and a child, or even also a grandparent. How many did you know?"

"Three, four, maybe five or so, and none of them were related," the man said. "They were called samurai and they could slow down or pause time for as long as their strength would let em. I remember there was this one samurai, older'n dirt, who could stop time for days or even longer, I don't know. He used it to meditate for hours and hours without losin a second in the real world, and he'd read every book ever written, I'm sure. The man knew more than was good for anyone. Hey, can I see that?" He pointed at Tarlos's pocket.

"The tooth?"

"Yeah."

Tarlos handed it to him, and the boatman held the tooth close to his squinting eyes. His tongue darted between his lips. "I swear I seen this before," he said with a low voice. "Or something just like it." He gave it back. "Pretty, though."

"Strange," said Tarlos. "The woman at the tavern said the same thing."

The boat floated along the Styx quietly and smoothly. The man talked and Tarlos listened. At least, he pretended to listen. Most of the time, Tarlos was sure that the man spoke only to hear the sound of his own voice.

It must be lonely for him, always floating this river by himself.

He's his only entertainment.

The man had packed dried meat, bread, and water. There were boxes of fizzy drinks, which the tavern woman had given Tarlos before they left. He did not care much for the bubbly flavored water as it was too sweet and the bubbles hurt his throat and nose. The boatman had one every hour or so and belched his approval upon completion. By the fourth day, half the boxes were gone.

The first time the man threw an emptied drink cup—which was made from a very thin metal that the boatman called "sodakan"—overboard into the water, Tarlos watched as it landed in the Styx and began to melt. It sizzled and boiled, and the metal merged with the water around it and dissolved forever.

"Why doesn't the boat dissolve?" Tarlos asked.

"Nothin makes sense here," the boatman replied.

"What would happen if we touched the water?"

The man shrugged as he cracked open another drink. "We'd die, prob'ly."

"But you're already dead."

The boatman swallowed, belched, smacked his lips. "There's dead, and there's dead, and then there's dead."

At the end of the fifth day, as the sun set on the dead country, Tarlos realized that he had not heard the boatman's voice in well over an hour. This was strange to him, and he opened his mouth to ask if everything was all right. But the boatman caught his gaze and raised a finger to his lips.

"You'll wanna be quiet," he whispered, so softly that Tarlos almost did not hear him.

Tarlos mouthed the word "why," and the man pointed downstream. The sky was growing dark, and Tarlos had to strain to see where the man was pointing. The moon was at full face and in view, but the landscape was shrouded in shadow and getting blacker. An invisible bubble covered the Styx and its shores, not allowing in any natural light. On the left bank, Tarlos could make out trees and rocks in the fading light. On the right, he stared into the face of nothingness. Only the faint outline of a building could be seen through the veiled darkness.

The boat neared the building as they made their way down the river. Darkness enwrapped them. Tarlos could now see how large the building was. It was the size of the stone temple in Kesh, or taller. It was made of stone, and the back of it merged with a rocky hillside, giving the impression that the building continued on underground for an unknown distance. Tarlos could almost make out the thick green vines crawling up its sides and clinging to the walls.

The boatman once again held a finger to his lips and kept the rudder steady. Tarlos's breath caught in his chest. He made no sound as they passed.

Then he heard it. He thought at first it was a wounded animal crying out for help. But the more he listened, the more it became apparent—it was no animal.

It was the sound of moaning. A mournful weeping that hung heavy in the air. The intense emotional and psychological pain was palpable. It reminded Tarlos of a mother crying for a killed child, or a son waiting for a father never to return from war. Or the pain a man might feel were he to look back on his life and see only the missed opportunities. It stirred something inside Tarlos, reminding him of all the hurt he'd caused and the people who suffered due to his selfishness.

Tarlos felt his eyes water. The sound stank in his ears and tasted sour in his mind. The boatman held fast to the rudder and wiped a tear from his cheek. Tarlos said nothing until the boat had floated well past the dark bubble and the building was once more invisible behind a bend in the Styx. The weeping and groaning faded, and Tarlos sighed in relief. His breath was shaky, like the breath of one who had been crying for several minutes.

The boatman mumbled, "That's why I never come this way. I guess if there's a Hell, that's it. It's some wonder I didn't end up there, and you better believe I thank God every day that I didn't."

"I think I've heard of that place," said Tarlos. "Although I never really put much effort into imagining what it looked like. And I suppose a part of me never believed it existed at all. The High

Priestess in Kesh called it the House of Dust. I think . . ." He swallowed a lump in his throat. "I think that's where my father is. And it'll probably be where I end up if I don't find the Ageless."

The boatman raised an eyebrow at him. "How d'you figure?"

Tarlos shrugged. "It's a long story."

"Well, we got a ways to go, yet. I'm up for hearing a long story if you're up for telling one."

Tarlos sat for several minutes in silence. The boatman did not press him to speak. Then Tarlos nodded and took his seat against the wall of the boat. After another moment's consideration, he reached for a fizzing beverage and cracked it open using the tab on the top of the strange metal cup.

"I suppose I should first explain that when my father, Lakaeus, was still a prince, he wasn't permitted to marry until his father, King Hestos, was dead."

8

The River

After Tarlos finished his story, the boatman leaned against the rudder and did not speak for some time. The man was a good listener. He never interrupted Tarlos to clarify anything or ask questions; he nodded in understanding during all the right places, and his face showed true emotion by the story's end.

The Styx moved slowly through the dead country. It was wide and stagnant, the trees on either shore dark and foreboding.

"Are there any animals here?" Tarlos asked.

"I think so," the man said. "I hear em, but I never see em. Seen crickets, though. Always one at a time, never a group of em."

"I saw a cricket when I came here."

The man smiled. "Might be it was the same one."

The slow current of the river rocked the boat. Tarlos stood and stretched his legs, and peered into the murky water. A blurry reflection stared back at him, its eyes sad and lost.

"It wasn't your fault, you know," said the man.

Tarlos spit into his reflection. "I made him go. He didn't want to," he said, the sad eyes rippling away.

"He wouldn't've gone with you if he hadn't also wanted it deep down. From what you said, he didn't seem like someone you could force—even if you did beat him at wrestlin a few times."

"He let me win."

"That ain't the point."

Tarlos shrugged off the man's words and lay down on his back, staring up at the cloudy blue sky. The sun was high, but it was not as bright here as it was on Earth—he could almost look straight into it without squinting.

The man cleared his throat and swallowed, hand still on the rudder. "You mentioned in your story those feather-people who ate dirt. . . Does it make you feel any better seein how that ain't what waits for us in the end? We're all perfectly content here. It's just like old times."

Tarlos shook his head. "This is your afterlife, not mine. When I came to your village, there was a sign that read 'Windmill District.' I don't know what that is. And from what you and the woman at the tavern have told me, I don't think our worlds are one and the same."

The man nodded, considering the theory. "I guess that would make sense. After all, I ain't never heard of a place called Kesh. Some of the things you said reminded me of some ancient civilizations from my world, civilizations that existed thousands of years before I was born. But they weren't called Kesh. Egypt, maybe. Or, Meso...Meso-somethin. Never was much of a history buff. Maybe the lady at the tavern would know. She always struck me as an intelligent girl. Shame she died so young. You really should listen to her story someday, if you come back this way." The man cast his eyes out into the trees, seemingly lost in thought.

"How much farther?" Tarlos asked. He closed his eyes.

"This is about as far as I ever been, so I don't know for sure. Can't be much further. I hope not anyway, otherwise I'm comin back empty-handed."

Tarlos did not ask what he meant by that and instead drifted off to sleep.

Two days passed on the wide, flat, stagnant stretch of the Styx. On the third day, rapids appeared in the stream and the trees on either side of it began to thin.

"Never been this far before," said the boatman.

Tarlos picked up a hint of anxiety in his voice. Part of him wanted to laugh at the man. It was Tarlos who would continue to the Ageless Country—if anyone should have anxiety, it was him. No one knew what awaited him there.

Ahead, the pale blue sky met the Styx at the nearing horizon.

"Is it just me or is the river about to end?" asked the boatman, placing both hands on the rudder.

The sound of roaring water filled the air. The man groaned. "Waterfall. Okay, Mister Tarlos, this is where you get off."

Tarlos opened his mouth to protest but kept quiet. He knew sooner or later he and the man would have to part ways, and he did not expect the man to float his boat off a cliff for him.

The man steered the boat to the north bank, and with a crunch of small pebbles and dirt, the boat landed on the shore. He jumped out and tied the boat to a nearby tree.

"Careful not to touch the water," he called back to Tarlos.

Tarlos jumped over the foot or so of water between the boat and dry dirt, landing safely a few feet away from the Styx. He turned to thank the man for the generous ride only to find him double-testing the knot and the rope on the tree.

"You aren't leaving?" Tarlos asked him.

"Oh, I will, soon as I get what I came here for. No offense, Mister Tarlos, but I'd-a never agreed to float down to the end of the Styx if I didn't have somethin else to do while I was here."

"And what would that be?"

"A gift for a friend." He pointed downstream. "Is this the way you're goin? I might need your help."

Tarlos was indeed headed that way. The two of them walked together to the edge of the cliff where the water cascaded down into a small ravine about forty feet below. Beyond the ravine, the water disappeared into a large valley hidden under a dome of dense white fog.

The river ended between two bare trees. The water was white and it bubbled and roared at the base of the waterfall. They could see no trail leading down the ravine. The boatman half-sat on the steep ground, keeping one hand on the dirt beside him as he scooted down toward the water.

Tarlos followed him, using his Power to steady himself and once stopping the man from tumbling into the ravine when he slipped on some loose rock.

"What makes you think it's down here?" Tarlos asked him.

"Seems to be some sort of universal law," the man answered when he reached the bottom. He clapped dirt from his hands and swatted the seat of his pants. "The thing you want most is usually in the place you're most afraid to look."

The two walked downstream for some time, and the ravine shallowed and the walls of dirt on either side became easier to navigate beside the water.

"What exactly are we looking for?" Tarlos asked.

"A flower. Look for a place in the clay, prob'ly next to some big rocks by the water. They like the run-off." The man tipped his wide-brimmed hat back to wipe the sweat from his forehead.

"What color?" Tarlos shouted over the roar of the white water.

"What?" the man yelled back.

"What color is the flower?"

"Blue."

"Like this one?"

The man turned and walked back to Tarlos, stumbling once on a protruding granite rock slick with Styx water. He knelt beside Tarlos and a wide grin split his face.

"That's her," he said.

The flower was a deep blue, the color of the sky after a storm. Tiny specks of white dotted the inner petals, its three layers of petals branching off into two points each so that they appeared doubled. In the center of the blue was a small white bulb, and the whole thing sat atop a short and thin green stem. The flower trembled between two granite boulders as it drank in the moisture from the Styx that seeped through the clay.

"I never thought the river of death could harbor such beautiful life," Tarlos said.

The man took off his hat, and Tarlos had to keep from laughing. Without his hat, the man's head was comically small, and his large nose appeared even larger now. His hair was thin and plastered close to his head, and Tarlos wondered if he had ever had a full head of it or if he had always had that thin spot on top. The man picked a short twig from the ground and gently, carefully, dug a wide circle around the blue flower. He lifted the large clump of clay and the small flower came with it. He placed the whole thing in his black hat, then dumped a little more dirt around the edges to hold the flower in place.

The man sighed and smiled. He wiped his eye with a single finger, then looked at Tarlos. "Thanks for the help. I guess you're goin that way." He looked down to where the water fell into the fog.

Tarlos nodded. "I'm glad I could help. Thank you for bringing me this far."

"Come see us again someday."

"If the gods will allow it."

The man extended his free hand, and Tarlos grasped it. The boatman turned then and made his way upstream where he climbed up the dirt wall of the narrow ravine. Tarlos turned the opposite direction and hiked downstream. Gradually, the ravine grew shallower, and the dome of dense white fog closed in around him as he entered the valley.

He walked through the aspens, which were no longer bare but covered in broad green and yellow leaves. Orange and yellow leaves lay scattered on the ground, and the broken sunrays that pierced through the branches painted various lines and stripes on the floor, igniting the leaves, making them appear more vibrant in the light and even darker in the shadows. Tarlos thought it resembled a beautiful painting.

A small trail appeared beneath his feet after a mile or so. Tarlos was not sure if he had always been walking on the path or if he had stumbled upon it by chance. Perhaps the trail had manifested itself under his feet, leading him through the aspens to where he needed to go. He was not exactly sure where that was, and decided that following the thin track was as good a plan as any.

The path was narrow and steep in some places, and it took Tarlos over hills and between rocks, down short cliff faces and through small canyons. To Tarlos, it felt as if he had been walking for several hours, but the sun had hardly moved in the sky.

To his right, he saw in the distance the cliffs and waterfall, and he wondered about the boatman and how he was faring. The narrow trail led down a series of sloping hills, green with lush grass and wet with dew. The grass gave way to grey and black rocks, then a steep decline—Tarlos feared he would slide down the rocky slope to his death. He wondered, *If I die in the land of death, would I feel any different?*

The hills had now become cliffs, the grass rock, and the path a narrow staircase carved into the living stone. Moving backwards, like descending a ladder, Tarlos placed one foot after the other on the stone steps and lowered himself to the bottom of the cliff, which he estimated to be at least two hundred feet below.

The last few feet of the rocky cliff leveled out into a hill, the stone steps now shallow and wide. Tarlos paused, taking a moment to catch his breath, and glanced to the trees spread out before him. The place was quiet as a winter night—Tarlos could hear only his own breath and, if he listened carefully, his heartbeat in his temples. A breeze blew past him, rustling the leaves of a nearby aspen, but not even that made any sound. He gave his ears a few light slaps to make sure he had not gone deaf.

The trees were not thick, and they did not give prelude to a larger forest like the one that bordered the Styx. He could see light through the trees—they seemed to end just ahead. He brushed low-hanging branches from his face; the leaves were soft, the wood pliable.

The swath of trees stretched several yards across, and Tarlos had no trouble getting through them. Emerging out the other side, his heart skipped a beat.

The land before him was a wide valley of green grass with gold, autumnal trees. Entire gardens of flowers that looked to be made of lapis lazuli, and around them clusters of living coral, dotted the land. From the ground seemed to grow enormous jewels like mountains—emeralds and sapphires, diamonds and pearls, hematite and carnelians. Tarlos marveled at the sight of this alien world. Hope filled his entire being.

He had made it to the Ageless country.

9

Ageless

A river wound through the valley. Tarlos assumed it was a tributary of the Styx. But where the Styx was dark and corrosive, this river was clear enough that he could see all the way to the river bed. Fish darted by, blue and orange and white. Something in his heart knew for certain that this water was safe to drink. He cupped his hands and brought some to his mouth. The water was the sweetest he had ever tasted; it was cool and refreshed him.

Tarlos followed the river as it descended into the valley. He marveled at the crystalline plants and opalescent colors that lay over the place. He was used to a country being all one color of varying shades—the desert was brown, red, and in places yellow with clay. Here were more colors than Tarlos thought possible, all in the same area.

He heard a gentle humming in the air, as if the atmosphere was electrified. The harmony was pleasant and sounded faintly like a woman singing. Tarlos could not help but smile as he walked and listened. He felt it vibrate in his bones.

Tarlos continued for some time until a new sound joined the electric humming. It was a deeper voice, belonging to a man. Tarlos stopped and looked around but saw nothing more than long green grass and a small hill with a single willow tree. The singing continued, and Tarlos pinpointed its location: it was coming from the hill.

He approached with excitement, but also caution. He knew

that he had no right to be in this country, and that the Ageless may not take kindly to his being here. But this is why he had come—this was the purpose of his journey, why he had crossed the desert and run through Shar's tunnel; why he had floated down the Styx with a nameless man. He would not turn back now after having come so far.

Tarlos stretched out on his belly and lay in the long grass, crawling slowly up the hill toward the willow. The humming was deep and sweet, the melody eerie and beautiful. It filled Tarlos with a miriad of emotions: that of a father returning to his family after war, a lost dog finding its way back home, the birth of a child. But the father was missing an arm, the dog was blind, and the mother had died in childbirth. Tarlos lay in the grass and listened to the song, and felt elation and a deep sadness at the same time.

"Do you like to read?" came the voice of the man.

Tarlos remained still.

"You, in the grass, trying to hide. Do you like to read? Come, sit beside me."

Tarlos raised his head above the grass and saw him. The man was seated beneath the willow. His face was wrinkled and leathery from the sun and from age, and his beard was long and white. His eyes were blue, and they sparkled at Tarlos. The man wore a light-orange robe that was draped loosely around him, and on his feet were simple leather sandals. He leaned against the willow, an open book in his lap.

"Come and sit beside me," he said again. His voice was friendly.

Tarlos stood and walked toward the man. He could not feel his feet touch the ground—he became convinced that he was hovering slightly above it. The man stretched out a hand and smiled beneath his huge beard. Tarlos took the hand in his own and sat beside the man.

The man raised his book. "Do you like poetry?"

Tarlos shook his head. "I don't read much."

"Oh." The man clicked his tongue. "That's a shame. I absolutely love it. Couldn't live without it. Listen to this." He flipped a few pages and cleared his throat.

My name is Ozymandias, King of Kings;
Look on my Works, ye Mighty, and despair!
Nothing beside remains. Round the decay
Of that colossal Wreck, boundless and bare
The lone and level sands stretch far away.

"That's by a man named Percy Shelley. Oh, and here's another of my favorites," he said, turning the page again.

Your eyes met mine
And my heart leapt,
as a butterfly from a flower.
How wonderful it is
To be worthy of your gaze

The man sighed and regarded Tarlos with his piercing blue eyes. "Isn't that beautiful?"

"Who wrote that one?" asked Tarlos. He was not really interested, but he felt the question bubble up inside him nonetheless.

"At the time, he called himself Thoth, but he's had many names. He lived many, many years ago, and he will not be born for millennia yet."

"What does that mean?"

The man winked. "It doesn't matter. So . . ." He closed his book and set it aside. "What's your story?"

Tarlos swallowed and shifted his position so that he sat on bent knees. "Are you one of the Ageless?"

"Hmm. I suppose that is one of the names we have. Yes, I am." The man's smile faded a bit.

"I will tell you my story, if you will listen," Tarlos said. "And I have to tell you the whole thing, so you'll understand why I'm here."

The man nodded and waved his hand, signaling for Tarlos to go on. Tarlos took a deep breath and began his story once more.

When Tarlos finished speaking, he felt as if no time had passed. A cricket had landed on his leg at the start of his story, and it was still there when the story was over. Eventually it sprang away. The Ageless man did not look bored or disinterested, but rather worried. He sighed and ran his fingers through his white beard.

"So, you believe that the only thing waiting for you after death is a dark room filled with people who dress in feathers and eat clay." The Ageless shrugged. "I think I can sympathize with your cause." A slight chuckle rumbled in his chest.

"Well, how do I do it?" Tarlos asked, leaning forward on his knees. "How did you become immortal? Show me how. Please."

The Ageless man frowned and shook his head. His beard brushing against his robe made a sound like wind through fallen leaves.

"Why do you want to stretch out your grief for so long?"

Tarlos leaned back, brow furrowed. "What do you mean?"

The man placed a caring hand on Tarlos's shoulder. "Why don't you remember Krastos in happiness, and live the rest of your life in peace with him in your heart? That way he'll never truly die."

Tarlos began to protest, but the Ageless man held up a silencing hand and continued. "Have you ever stopped to think about how blessed you are? You have a body of flesh and blood, and the gods have given you one of their Powers to hold. Already that makes you more fortunate than others. You were prince of a great kingdom, and now you are king. You have riches, and you have subjects who love and respect you. Your parents loved you, as did your brother. While others eat stale bread and drink dirty water, you have butter and wine. While others use old ropes as belts, your tunics are made of silk and cotton, entwined with golden thread.

"Can't you see? You've worked yourself up trying to achieve this goal—a foolish goal, I'd add—and all the while you've forgotten that your life is the true blessing. You're dirty, you're tired, your muscles are about to give out, and for what? You're that much closer to your death."

The old man shifted on the ground. "Life is beautiful and fleeting, and it's beautiful *because* it's fleeting. You wouldn't appreciate it otherwise. Yes, the gods took your brother, but life is meant to be taken. It's meant to end. And yet you build, you create, you fight, you love as if it is to go on forever. Death is a river that floods its banks and takes fallen cherry blossoms down its current." On cue, a breeze picked up and carried some willow leaves over the hill and into the river.

Tarlos listened to the Ageless man, and as he listened a small seed of betrayal grew in his bosom. He was finally in the Ageless country, and he was actually speaking to an immortal man—and what was the man telling him? That his entire journey had been a waste of time. No, not just a waste of time. A waste of life.

Tarlos said, "Then how is it that you and your kind are immortal? Why can't I be like you? Shouldn't that be my choice?"

The man shook his head. "Listen, my young friend. It's a different matter for me and mine. Before the world was created, Shar and Moresh came from the void and created the cosmos. They had children, who became the other gods. They created animals, and they caused them to live and die because it was good for the Earth to have a cycle of regeneration. The animals ate what the Earth gave them, and when the animals died the Earth took their bodies and became more fruitful.

"After a while, the gods decided to make people, and they formed them from stardust. The people looked like the gods, had thoughts and desires like the gods, and they were powerful and immortal like the gods. These people were created especially to be caretakers of the Earth while the gods were the caretakers of the rest of creation—other worlds and peoples. And these first immortal people were the Ageless, and the Ageless cared for the Earth for countless years.

"But Ablis, once the god of balance, thought that the Ageless were redundant. Why have god-like beings to take care of the Earth when there are already mortal animals aiding the planet in its regenerative cycle?

"Ablis took some of the other gods, and they created a new people from mud and wind and fire, and Ablis breathed life into them.

"'Because I have breathed life into them,' Ablis told the

other gods, 'these people shall know the balance of things, and will know good from evil, and their lives will be two-sided: they will spend some years on Earth, tending it, and then they will die as animals do. That is the way of things. Life is a cycle, and Mankind should not be above the ways of nature.'

"But when Shar and Moresh discovered what Ablis and the other gods had done, they rebuked him and cast him out. The other gods fell at their parents' feet and begged forgiveness for creating without permission, and they were forgiven.

"Shar and Moresh looked at this new mortal people and said, 'We cannot destroy this creation, for all life is sacred. Therefore, we will take our original people, the Ageless, and place them in a safe place, away from these mortals—for the mortals know both good and evil and will surely fight one with another, and they will hate and destroy and steal as they love and laugh and sing.'"

The Ageless man finished his story and nodded with a smile. "That's basically what happened. So, as you can see, there's just nothing to be done. You were created as a mortal, and you will die as a mortal."

Tarlos's face flushed red. He stumbled, feeling several things at once. Anger at the gods. Betrayal from the Ageless. Sadness for Krastos. Hatred for Ablis for creating mortal Man in the first place. Tarlos understood everything now. He knew that there was no hope.

In a fit of rage, spying a large boulder at the bank of the river, Tarlos used every iota of energy he had left to rip it from the ground and hurl it across the valley. He watched it soar through the air before landing in a crater amidst a mushroom-shaped cloud of dirt.

The Ageless man stared at him in horror.

"It should be my choice," Tarlos squeaked, tears clouding his eyes. He felt a familiar rip in his head—he'd used the last of his mental energy. He winced, feeling the blood rush from his head, and collapsed.

10

The Gods' Gods

Tarlos woke the next day wondering about how no one knows they are asleep until they wake up. He was in a soft bed, softer than any he had ever slept in before. The sheets were white and softer than cotton or silk, and the blankets were thick and fluffy. His pillow was plump and firm, not at all like his own back in Kesh, which tended to be either lumpy or flat.

Pale morning sunlight streamed through a window beside the bed. It was made of a transparent material that Tarlos did not know. At first, he guessed it was made from the same glass as the cup that the woman at the tavern had given him. But he touched it and it vibrated ever so softly, light colors dancing around the spot where his finger met the window. The room was an off-shade of white, accenting the bed, and the sunlight coming through the window made the walls look yellow. Beside the bed was some sort of chest, and on it were pictures of the Ageless man alongside a woman. Tarlos stared in awe at the details. Whichever painter had depicted them was a god of art. He could not believe how realistic they looked—like a moment in time had been captured and stuck to paper.

Tarlos sat up in the bed and the blanket fell to his waist. He was wearing a blue shirt made of a strange but soft material. Someone must have changed him as he slept. This thought unnerved him. He stepped out of bed and walked to the bedroom door, upon which a large sprawling tree had been carved.

He twisted the brass knob and the door opened without a sound. Immediately he was struck by the smell of food wafting through the place. Tarlos's stomach growled and his mouth watered.

He followed the smell of food down a hallway and to a room where a woman stood over a stove, or what he guessed was a sort of stove—there was no fire or smoke to be seen. On the stove was a pan, and something in it sizzled and popped.

The woman turned as Tarlos entered the room. She beamed at him.

"Oh, good morning! You woke up just in time for breakfast, albeit four days late. Did you sleep well?"

"I didn't even realize I was asleep," Tarlos said. "I didn't even dream. I feel more rested than I have in a long time."

"Good!" She smiled even wider. Her hair was long and grey, pulled back in a single tail behind her head that reached to her waist. She was thin, and her aged skin was stretched over her limbs. Her eyes were a stark, icy blue, wrinkles surrounding them and continuing down to her mouth. "Pancakes are already on the table," she said. "Bacon is almost done. My husband is already eating; go and join him at the table."

Tarlos remembered the French toast from the tavern in the dead country. The thought of such a sweet breakfast made him cringe. He hoped that these pancakes would be different and more suitable as breakfast food.

The Ageless man he had met under the willow sat at a small wooden table. He was reading a book—a different book, Tarlos thought, than the one from before. In the middle of the table was a plate stacked high with flat round cakes.

The man looked up as Tarlos sat down. He smiled, though it was not as genuine as his wife's. Tarlos wondered what was bothering the man.

"Sleep well?"

"I did, thank you. What are you reading today?"

"It's called *The Epic of Gilgamesh*. It's a story from a world not unlike your own in many ways. Your story reminded me of it, and

I thought I would revisit it, along with some other thoughts."

Before Tarlos could inquire further, the grey-haired woman approached the table with a steaming pile of bacon on a plate. She set it next to the pancakes and helped herself to a few strips.

"Go ahead, dig in," she told Tarlos, and he did. "Do you like syrup on your pancakes?"

"I don't know." Tarlos poked at his pancake with the metal prong. *Fork*, he reminded himself.

The man said, "I've always preferred peanut butter on mine. Have you ever had peanut butter? No, I guess you couldn't have. Here, try some."

He gave Tarlos a jar with the word *Jif* written on the label in bold red letters. Tarlos scooped some of what was inside onto his pancake—first a bit and then a heap after he tasted it. They ate, and after four pancakes and nine strips of bacon Tarlos's stomach finally stopped growling.

"You passed out after throwing that rock," said the man. He used a finger to lap up the last bit of peanut butter from his plate, then licked it from his finger. "I figured you could use a soft bed and a meal. After what you've been through, my goodness."

Tarlos set his fork down on his plate and pushed it away. He closed his eyes and sighed. "What am I going to do now?" He was speaking to himself, but the question came out of his mouth anyway. "Go back to Kesh? To being a king?"

The man said, "Yes, why not?"

"What's the point? If I'm going to die anyway, why even live?" Tarlos felt a lump in his throat, and his breath staggered. "Everywhere I turn, I see death."

The woman and the man looked at each other, and for several seconds they said nothing. Tarlos swore that they were communicating with each other through their eyes. At length, they looked to Tarlos again.

"I mentioned that I had to consider other things," the man said. He laced his hands together on the table. "There was one thing about our conversation the other day that I couldn't stop thinking about. You claimed that it should be your choice whether or not to be immortal, if that possibility existed. As the Ageless, we're endowed with every attribute of the gods, but confined to this world only. I hold all four Powers, as does every other Ageless. I can hear the thoughts of your mind and heart, and I can feel your pain. I think it's only right to give you that choice. Or rather, a chance to make that choice."

Tarlos's eyes opened wide and he stood from his chair, knocking it backwards. "A chance for immortality? But you said it was impossible!"

"For most mortals, yes. But you're a Holder, and that means you carry a small bit of god blood in your veins. You also mentioned to me that your mother was thought to be descended from the Ageless. It's not impossible, as some of us do choose to have children, but it's rare. If it isn't true, you still have a chance. If it is, you have a greater chance. But it's only a small one. And it's . . . rash."

"What is it?" Tarlos put his hands on the table and leaned forward. "Whatever chance there is, I'll take it. I don't care if I have to swim to the bottom of the ocean."

"Oh, it's nothing like that." The man smiled, and the woman smiled with him. "Nothing that easy. Sit down, Tarlos."

He sat, and the atmosphere of the room turned reverent, the air thick and solemn. Their smiles faded, and they grasped each other's hand.

"Tarlos," said the man, "who created Earth?"

He paused for a moment, only to consider that this might be a trick question. "The gods."

The man nodded. "And mankind?"

"The gods."

"Animals? Plants? The stars and moon and sun and everything in the cosmos?"

"The gods."

Another nod. "And who created the gods?"

Tarlos's eyes narrowed. He sat back in his chair. The question made no sense to him—it was like asking what color hunger was. He shook his head. "I don't understand."

The man continued, still holding his wife's hand. "Your world is one of many, Tarlos. You met people from another world on your way here, yes?"

Tarlos nodded. "They spoke of things I didn't understand. Places I've never heard of."

"An infinite number of universes lie beyond the veil of this one. The gods Moresh and Shar, and their children—all the gods you worship—created and care for this universe. But as the Ageless care for this Earth while the gods care for this universe, there are other entities that care for *all* universes."

Tarlos frowned, and there was a funny buzzing sensation in his throat and belly. "Do you mean . . . are you saying that the gods . . . have gods?"

The man tilted his head. "I guess that's one way to put it. The elder gods created the younger gods, just as the younger gods created mankind."

"Do they ever speak to mortal men? Do they give blessings the same as gods?"

Both the man and the woman shook their heads. The man asked, "Have you ever sat to watch ants crawl in the dirt?" Tarlos nodded. "They're so tiny, compared to you. And so stupid. They have no idea what goes on in the minds of humans, if they could even comprehend your presence. Imagine two ants walking opposite directions around a rock. You're looking down at them and can see them walking around the rock, but from the ants' perspectives they don't see each other—you know they will bump into each other before they do. They know nothing of the man watching them, who to them would appear as far away as the sun to us. They know nothing of astronomy, of the weather, of the existence of billions of colonies just like theirs around the world. Yet, from their perspective, they are intelligent, loyal to their family and to their queen; they hunger, they protect, they live and they die, and that's enough for them. It's a simple existence compared to that of a human, but it's all they know.

"As an ant is to a human, that is how a human is to an elder god. You are but one ant in a colony of trillions spread throughout the universe, which is only one of an infinite number of universes. You understand the mind of an elder god as well as an ant understands yours."

The man finished, and the room fell into silence. Tarlos took a few seconds to drink in what the man had told him. "So, why would one speak to me?" he croaked.

The smile finally returned to the man's face. "Because you're a Holder, and a possible descendant of the Ageless. You carry in you a small piece of the gods—you are more closely related to the elder gods than other men. There may be a chance, albeit a small one, that you could be granted an audience with an elder god. After all, it was they who created the concept of immortality in the first place, long before the gods were created."

Tarlos had a thousand questions, but he ignored them all in favor of the only one that mattered. "Where can I find the elder gods?"

The man made a gurgling noise in his throat, part groan and part chuckle. "They don't live in a *where*, exactly. They're all around us, everywhere at once, beyond the realm of this physical universe, in the same way that a person lives outside a pond full of fish. But there are certain places within our worlds that act as doorways to their realms. I know of one. It's a book, and the book is inside a mountain to the southeast of here. Read from the book, and you will be taken to the realm of the elder gods—if they choose to acknowledge your existence at all."

"But they care for humans?"

"As I said before, no more than a man may care for a specific ant that lives in a hole four thousand miles from his house." The man laughed. "But they have a deep connection to all things, because everything in creation—all worlds and universes—came from them. And as I said, you are a Holder. I think that gives you a better chance than most. But the chance is still small."

Later, after the food was eaten and the dishes washed and put away, the Ageless man brought Tarlos outside. Tarlos saw that the house was small and modest—not at all what he would have imagined for an immortal being. It was one story with only a few small windows, and the roof was low and covered with black tiles. The door was slender and red, and it bore the same carving of a tree that was on the door to Tarlos's room.

The yard around the house was full of luscious green grass with small patches of flowers of every color. Fruit trees were scattered around with bees buzzing from flower to tree, coming and going between a series of man-made beehives several yards from the house. Small wooden birdhouses hung from the branches, frequented by swallows and sparrows bringing food back to their young.

"Is this all yours?" Tarlos asked.

"It is. And it takes more work than you'd think."

The man led Tarlos around the back of the house. There, a wide flat field spread out in front of a large barn or stable. Various animals wandered about. Tarlos recognized swans and geese, even an ibis or two, and there were horses and cows as well, lounging in the noonday sun.

"Where are the other Ageless?"

"They have their own homes elsewhere. This way." He opened a door on the side of the large barn-like building and followed Tarlos inside.

Inside was musty and smelled like dung and straw and mud—smells that reminded Tarlos of Kesh. Tools hung on the walls and equipment was spread across the dirty straw-covered floor. Saddles and harnesses sat on wooden stanchions.

To the right of the door was a row of stalls, similar to the stable in Kesh, though these stalls were enormous—large enough for a person to live in one comfortably with his entire family.

"Now don't be shocked," said the Ageless man. "She's big, but she's gentle and friendly. Give her a minute to get the smell of you before you go petting her. And don't touch her around the eyes, if you please."

He opened one of the enormous stall doors, which swung backwards. Tarlos stepped inside and craned his neck around the corner of the stall. There, in the corner, the largest black horse he had ever seen was lying on the dusty floor, her legs folded beneath herself. She was more than three times as big as any horse in Kesh.

"What is . . ." Tarlos whispered. He was not afraid of the giant horse, but he would rather it did not awake until he knew exactly what it was.

"This is Calliope," said the man, and at the sound of her name the horse raised her enormous head and shook the sleep from it. "A pure descendant of the first horses that Poseidon created, from a world parallel to yours." He reached into his pocket, produced a large carrot, and held it out. Calliope stood, back stretching like a cat after a nap, and sauntered over to them. She ate the carrot in one chomp. "She knows the way to the mountain."

"You want me to ride that thing?" Tarlos asked, still whispering. The horse towered above him, all muscle. Her legs were thick and heavy, the joints around her shoulders wound tight with rope-like tendons that created the look of small hills beneath her skin. She was a powerful creature, and he did not want to offend her.

"I told you, she's gentle. Hold out your hand. Here." The man gave Tarlos another carrot, which Tarlos held out to Calliope. She lowered her massive head and sniffed the carrot with her huge black nostrils. The air blew Tarlos's hair back. He swallowed his nerves.

She reached for the carrot with her lips, careful not to bite Tarlos's hand, and swallowed it. She raised her head and shook it again, lowered it down to Tarlos once more and gave him a sniff and a huff, and then nuzzled her nose against his forehead. Tarlos could not help but smile.

The Ageless man smiled as well. "There now! What did I tell you?"

Tarlos rubbed Calliope's cheeks and patted her thick neck. Her mane was grey and had been trimmed close.

"Let me just get her saddled and ready to go, and you can be off as soon as you're ready." The Ageless man walked across the stall to a door on the other side. He pulled out a cart carrying a large seat with straps hanging from it.

"You don't have to do this, you know," Tarlos said.

"Do what?"

"Let me use your horse." Calliope nuzzled against Tarlos's shirt, searching for another carrot. "I mean, I appreciate your help. I do. But I don't understand why you're helping me."

With the help of a crane-like device leaning against the stall wall, the Ageless man lifted the saddle into the air and Calliope positioned herself below it.

The man asked, "Do you think the world is mostly good, or bad?"

"I never thought about it."

"Yeah, I'm not sure myself. I've never been to any other world in the Continuum, so I can't really compare humans on our Earth to the humans on others. But I think for the most part they're good. Are you good?"

Tarlos thought about his life in Kesh. He was a good person, wasn't he? He had done good things, right? Thinking hard, Tarlos was surprised and disappointed that he could not remember a time when he went out of his way to do a good deed, to help someone in need, to give a compliment, or to raise the spirits of a sad friend.

And I killed my father. And caused the death of Krastos.

He frowned, feeling heat rising in his throat, stinging his eyes. "I think . . . I'm . . . I don't know."

"A good answer," said the man. "A bad man thinks himself righteous; a good man is not so sure." He strapped the huge saddle around the horse. The saddle was built like a padded chair, with a raised and rigid backrest. There were loops in which to place one's legs and straps around the chest and lap to hold the rider in place. There were no reins.

The ageless man held up a closed hand and Tarlos extended his own to take whatever was being given. The man dropped Tarlos's tooth into his hand. Tarlos smiled. "Thank you!"

"I didn't know what it was, but it was in your pocket, so I saved it for you. Seemed important."

The man checked the straps on the saddle one more time, then gave Calliope another carrot and a pat on the neck, and ruffled her short mane. He left Tarlos alone with her and went back to the house, returning a moment later with a heavy coat made from a thick wool-like material. The woman came as well, carrying with her a small sack of food—bread, cheese, apples, and water. Tarlos thanked her, and she brought him in for a hug.

"Good luck to you," she said. "I hope you find what you need, and not just what you're looking for."

Tarlos gave her a kind smile in return and put the heavy coat on. The man helped him climb the several feet onto Calliope's back and strapped him in. When finished, Tarlos could not move his legs or bend forward. He felt secure and comfortable.

"Remember, you can back out any time. Any last words?"

Tarlos snapped his gaze to the man, but the man was laughing.

"Kidding. Good luck out there."

Tarlos nodded. "Thank you. For everything."

The man and the woman held hands, and with his free hand the man slapped Calliope on the rump. "Get on with you," he said, and Calliope galloped at full speed from the barn.

11

Otherwhere

Calliope was an arrow shot from a bow.

Tarlos had never flown this fast on his own. The ground beneath him was a colorless blur, and he clutched at the saddle and closed his eyes against the momentum. His knuckles were white, and his stomach was in his bowels. All the blood in his head rushed to his feet, and he thought he might be sick. The wind screamed past them, and Tarlos's ears popped as his stomach lurched.

He had no idea how far away this mountain was or how long it would take to get there, regardless of the bone-snapping speed at which Calliope ran, but he knew he wanted to experience the ride as little as possible. His eyes closed against the blurring shapes and piercing winds. When Calliope whinnied, Tarlos peeked.

The space around them seemed to fold in on itself. Entire forests, rivers, mountains all appeared as flat paintings, and the wall on which they hung telescoped inward. Tarlos's mind was unable to comprehend what was happening, but he knew that Calliope was now running faster than even Imep, the messenger of the gods.

How long the great horse galloped Tarlos didn't know. After some time he stopped feeling her run beneath him and instead felt still and watched the world race past. His awareness faded, and time became meaningless.

Calliope eventually called Tarlos with a loud whinny. The world had stopped moving and Calliope stood patiently on solid ground. Tarlos looked around, panicking for a moment when he realized he could not move his legs. Then, remembering that he was strapped in, he calmed down enough to undo the straps and slide off the horse's back. It was a long drop, and he landed on his rear end.

He stretched, feeling his spine pop in several places. It felt wonderful. He did not know how long he had been riding Calliope, but he was surprised that he was not sore at all, as was always the case after riding a horse for more than a few hours.

"Are we here?" he asked the horse; she did not respond. "Where are we?" He looked around.

It was nighttime. The stars were bright, but the constellations were unfamiliar. He was still in the Ageless Country, or a country neighboring it in this Otherworld. The moon was full and larger than he was used to, and he could see the faint outlines of Moresh's smiling white face.

Years before, an emissary from an eastern land came to visit Kesh and pay homage to the king. He brought gifts from his homeland, which he called Nis. Among these gifts were trees that the king tried to have planted in the gardens, but they did not survive. The trees were strange to Tarlos and all who lived in Kesh, as they had no leaves but thousands of tiny green spines. The emissary called the tree an evergreen because they stayed green even in the winter. The forest that Tarlos now found himself in was nothing but evergreen trees. They gave off a pleasant, musky smell, sweetening the forest air.

Tarlos turned around and had to crane his neck to see a looming mountain, the base of which Calliope had landed at. The mountain cut a black triangle from the starry night sky, piercing the clouds with its towering height.

"So, this is the place?" Tarlos asked the horse. She did not acknowledge him and simply walked behind him and gave a gentle nudge with her nose, pushing him to a small dark spot at the base of the mountain a few feet away.

Tarlos moved a few fallen evergreen branches aside. He felt his adrenaline escalate upon spying a small cave entrance.

Calliope nudged him again.

"Down there?"

Calliope whinnied, stomped at the ground with her foreleg, and then turned and galloped away. After only a few seconds, Tarlos could no longer see her through the forest. He held up a hand in thanks.

Tarlos stepped into the cave entrance, which was almost straight down into the ground. He climbed down the rocks at the opening, and after a few feet the cave leveled into a stone tunnel with an ancient dirt floor. The ceiling was low, and he had to crouch as he walked.

The tunnel reminded him of Shar's Mountain. He shook his head, thinking about how it had only been a decan or so since he was last there. A decan since he had been in the land of the living.

Tarlos was not sure if he'd spent hours or days walking through the narrow tunnel. In the darkness, time was almost impossible to keep track of. The ground beneath his feet crunched with small broken bits of rock, then after several hours changed to soft sand. He was not sure how long it had been since he last slept.

The air became thin and electric. It prickled his skin and made his lungs sting and his throat sore. He had to stop four times to catch his breath and coat his throat with fresh saliva before continuing.

The narrow tunnel ended at a small crevice. Tarlos sucked in his chest and belly as much as he could to squeeze through, the rock tugging at his clothing as he moved. He emerged on the other side in a large round room, the ceiling perhaps three yards above. Dotting the walls were tiny shells of all shapes—some conical, others spiraled, and others still pointed and shaped like many-armed stars. All these shells were embedded in the walls as if placed there in mortar by some ancient mason. They glowed faintly with an eerie green light.

The ground was hard, smooth stone that sloped downward slightly. Tarlos followed it down. In the distance, he heard the faint drip of water, the sound echoing throughout the cavern.

Set into the far wall of the cavern, at the bottom of the sloped stone floor, was a small door about half Tarlos's height. He bent low to squeeze through and came out the other side into another huge cavern with more shells in the walls here, their green glow not enough to see the impossibly high ceiling or even the far wall. He kept his right hand on the wall beside him and began to walk the perimeter.

He stopped at a large pillar and ran his hand over it. It was not rough and bumpy like the cave walls, but smooth. The soft glow of the shells provided enough light for Tarlos to see that this pillar was not natural, but had been carved by people—or at least intelligent beings. This entire cavern must have once been a building. *Maybe even the entirety of the mountain*, Tarlos thought, shivering at the idea.

Continuing along the cavern wall, he encountered a dozen more pillars like this. It was only on the last three or four that he noticed intricate symbols had been carved into them. He did not understand them, though, and was confused by this; he had been able to understand all languages since he first entered the dead country. But this writing was alien to him, and he could not make sense of it.

Finally, Tarlos came to a doorway of proper dimension carved from stone. He entered, and immediately the hallway ahead of him shrank to such a size that he had to crawl on his hands and knees. The hallway sloped downward and wound in a spiral, and his feet were always at a higher level than his head. The glowing green shells lit his path, but they did not help his intense claustrophobia. On several occasions his body wanted to stop and take a break, but he forced himself to keep going lest he panic in the tight space.

At last a faint orange glow appeared ahead, and Tarlos hurried after it. The tunnel widened, and he was able to stand at full height, grateful to be free of the tiny tunnel. He stretched and continued toward the orange light.

The stone tunnel opened into another spacious cavern. Sharp bulging stalactites pointed from the cavern ceiling, stalagmites rising from the floor to meet them. A smooth level path led through the pointed rocks. Tarlos followed it as far as it would take him.

The path took him around several bends that obscured his view of whatever lay ahead, and all the while the orange light grew brighter. And then the path ended, and Tarlos was in awe.

The cavern was empty, save for a stone arch about the height of a person. It was a natural arch, not built by intelligent people but carved slowly through eons of erosion.

But what filled Tarlos with such amazement was that the arch glowed orange, like a fire, the light flickering different shades of yellow, orange, and red, like flames lapping up wood. A faint humming came from the arch. Tarlos swallowed and cautiously walked around it, inspecting it from every angle. It was just a stone arch, free from any structure and standing on a flat piece of smooth ground.

Tarlos could not see through the arch. There was only black. Walking around to the other side, it was the same—the arch was hollow, but he could not see through it. His curiosity outweighing his caution, he extended a hand and poked a single finger through the arch. He yanked it back.

His finger tingled, like a limb after blood flow has been restricted. It did not hurt, but he did not like the idea of his entire body feeling like that.

"I'm here," he told himself. "Bring on the tingles."

He walked through the arch. . .

. . .and emerged on the other side feeling intense sensations like pins from his hair to his toes. Looking around him, he was a bit confused. He was still in the same room as before. This made logical sense, but he'd expected the strange archway to at least transport him somewhere—to where the elder gods were, perhaps.

He looked back at the arch and paused. On the other side of it now stood a stone podium with a book on top. A tiny pinprick of light a hundred feet above him came through a small hole in the ceiling, enveloping the book in yellow light.

Tarlos approached, feeling the tingles rush out of his system.

He relaxed. Behind him, the arch continued to hum.

The book was of a fashion that Tarlos had never seen before. The pages were not papyrus but smooth and white, its cover thick and covered with something that resembled leather. Drawn on the cover in gold was a symbol for which Tarlos had no words—he could not make sense of what he was seeing. It was completely eldritch, shapes that no human would have ever thought to create or imagine. He turned his head in every which way, looking at it from all angles, trying to decide what it was. When he squinted, he thought it almost looked like the tree carving at the Ageless man's house.

Tarlos reached out with a tentative hand and placed a finger on the brown cover. Nothing happened. Slowly, he lifted the cover and opened the book.

A shock thundered through his body—a shock that he felt in his bones, in his mind, and in his soul. His teeth rattled and his brain turned to jelly in his skull. His fingernails rotted and fell from his fingertips, and his bones turned to dust. His skin liquefied, and the cavern around him became an inside-out globe made purely

out of space

and time

and thought.

Tarlos saw himself

from

every

angle,

staring back at himself.

The cavern turned

itself

even

more

inward

until

the walls tore   with a sickening

s l u r p

and
the
universe
around
him
transformed
into
a
mobius
strip.

Tarlos's consciousness was taken through the third dimension,

where
he
beheld   and **all**   the   planets   in
Earth   his
                                     own   solar

                                                   system,

and then all the stars and planets in the galaxy, and he saw nebulae of every color—not just in the visible spectrum, but the entire array of possible light, colors writhing and spinning around him in a riot that seemed to peel his eyes to their very roots—and he continued through the third dimension until he could see the entire universe as an undulating infinitely-faceted snake that writhed and curled around him, coiled and shrank. More coiled snakes joined the first one as Tarlos was dragged up ever onward into the fourth and fifth dimensions, packed in a grid so tightly that there was no longer any space between them. Farther and farther out Tarlos flew, until the grid of coils was nothing more than a flat plane, and the plane folded in over itself to create another shimmering mirrored globe. He descended onto the globe, touching both the inside and outside surfaces, and traveled along in a straight line. To either side, and below and above him, other entities that he could find no means to explain traveled in parallel to him, and then their paths merged as he ascended once more. Globe became snake, snake became coil, and coils became a flat plane that curled in on itself to create another series of globes, and he could see that his universe was not the only universe and he was not the only him and infinity

was a number he could
count to if only he knew
how to treat infinity as
something. He wanted to
scream at the sight of all
of creation—

not just the
universe in which he lived
but every conceivable
reality

that had happened,

is happening,

and could or will
happen,

and then everything
reduced to a marble and
the marble shrank to an
indeterminate point
without length or width or
depth and everything
around it was orange and
smelled like burnt
almonds.

And then—

The elder god.

Hello Tarlos

He did not hear the voice. The voice existed—it was inside him and everywhere.

"Who is that?" he asked. He did not have a voice, and he had no mouth with which to speak. He was an essence, floating in the orange. "Where am I?"

No

"What's happening to me?"

Be still Tarlos

You are safe

That is all you need to know

"Who are you?"

Yes

Tarlos tried to close his eyes, but he had no eyes to close; he tried to swallow, but he had no throat. "Did you bring me here? What is this place?"

You read from my book

There is no here

It is everywhere

And nowhere

Location is meaningless in the eleventh dimension

"Why is—"

You have many questions

I cannot answer them in ways you would understand

We must do what needs to be done

What you came to ask of me

"Why can't I see you? Where are you?"

I have no physical form that you could comprehend

Would it be easier for you if I did

"Yes. I don't know. Maybe. I'm so confused."

The orange melted away, but the smell of burnt almonds remained. Around him, on the canvas of space-time, colors dripped like rain and painted the nonmaterial walls around him—they swirled, giving depth to pictures, and it seemed to Tarlos that he was standing on a sandy plain among mounds of sand rising up and taking shape, so that before long he was back in Kesh, in the palace, in his bedroom. He had a body once more, and he was sitting on his bed. He could feel his silk sheets, the cool breeze through the open window; he could see the yellow light of the sun outside and the red and yellow dirt of the desert beyond.

He touched his arm. He was solid, real.

There was a knock on his bedroom door.

"Don't be afraid," called a familiar voice. "I'm coming in. Are you ready?"

At the sound of the voice, Tarlos stood from his bed and crossed the room. The door swung open before he could reach it and a man walked through.

The hair, the muscles, the brown eyes and the smile. The way he swung his arms as he walked into the bedroom, the way he placed his weight on his legs and leaned against the bedpost.

"Is this better?" Krastos asked, smirking.

Tarlos sobbed. He wiped tears from his eyes and cheeks and spit from his lips. "You . . . you aren't . . ."

"I'm not Krastos," the elder god said. "I thought this would make it easier for you, talking to a familiar face. Come on, you need this." He extended his arms, and Tarlos ran into his embrace.

Tarlos held his brother and hugged him tightly, not able to reach fully around his massive chest. It was so real—his voice, his smell, his demeanor, even the energy that he'd carried with him in life. Tarlos wanted to talk to him, to tell him what he had been through these last few decans—about the dead country, the Styx, the Ageless. He wanted to sit with Krastos and vent, to be happy that he was back. To apologize.

But this was not Krastos. Tarlos understood that. He hugged the elder god tightly just the same, and he snuffed his cries away.

"Okay, all right, you're fine." Krastos drew away and ruffled Tarlos's hair. "Would you rather I change into someone else?"

"No!" Tarlos said. "It's fine. Stay like this. I . . . I miss seeing him. It's been so long..."

Krastos nodded and sat on the bed, then beckoned for Tarlos to sit beside him. Tarlos did, never taking his eyes from the likeness of his twin.

"The man," Tarlos said. "The Ageless man. He didn't think there was a good chance that you would speak to me."

"I usually don't speak to your kind," said Krastos. "It's nothing personal, I just have a lot to worry about. That's why we created your gods, to handle those details. But you're a special case."

"Because I'm a Holder? Because my mother was descended from the Ageless?"

Krastos smiled from one side of his mouth. He shook his head. "No. It's because of the part you're playing in the Continuum. You're a very important character. You are the start of a very long narrative."

Tarlos focused on Krastos's eyes. They were different from his brother's. These eyes were unfathomably deep. He feared that if he stared into them too long, he might go mad. Multiple eternities' worth of knowledge were contained within.

"I don't understand."

"I know you don't. You don't have to. Now, please ask me what you need to ask."

Tarlos gripped the silk sheets in a fist. "Will you make me immortal?"

Krastos tilted his head in consideration. "Immortality and the power to be a god go hand-in-hand, Tarlos. The Ageless are immortal because they hold all four of your gods' Powers, and they hold those Powers because they are immortal. In order for you to become immortal, you must hold all four Powers. Do you think you can?"

Is it that easy? Tarlos thought.

"No, it's not easy at all, but that's the price."

"Yes, I can. I think I can. Can you give them to me?"

Krastos shrugged. "Yes, of course I can give you the Powers. The question you need to answer honestly is if this is what you really want. If you truly think that by gaining this trait and these Powers, your life will be better."

"Yes."

"Are you sure?"

"Can't you just look into the future and tell me if I turn out okay?"

Krastos shook his head. "There is no future, Tarlos, just as there is no past. There is barely a present. I can see every outcome of every universe, every possible choice and every path that each subatomic particle and vibrating string of energy might take, and I know the probabilities of those paths. By your definition and perception of time, yes, I know the future. But I know all futures, and they are all happening right now, and they have already happened, and all of them will happen, and none of them will."

"That doesn't make any sense."

"Things don't have to make sense to you in order for them to be true. You have free will, Tarlos. All of your parallel selves also have free will. I'm asking you to choose whether or not to take these Powers. With the Powers comes the understanding of how to use them. I advise you not to, as using a Power you were not born with can drive a person mad."

Tarlos stood. "I've come too far to say no. Give them to me. This has been my goal since you—since Krastos died."

"Your goal is to live forever, or to defeat Ablis?"

"Both. Ablis told me that I would someday fade into nothing, along with any memory of Kesh. If I live forever, I will have proved him wrong. And I can use the Powers to drive him away."

"You didn't know you'd be getting the Powers before coming to me," Krastos said. "What was your plan for dealing with a god?"

Tarlos shrugged. "I guess I'm lucky this is how it works, then."

"Oh, I wouldn't call you lucky. Remember, Tarlos, when you hold all four Powers, you will be no different than a god. Shar and Moresh will be your equals, but I can't speak for them regarding your place among them. They cast Ablis from their presence for using his Powers in ways they disagreed with. Would you risk alienating yourself from all humans and gods for a chance to regain your kingdom?"

"I've come so far," Tarlos said. "I'm not going to say no to this chance."

"All right, then." Krastos stood, and the bed creaked as his weight came off of it. "Give me something."

Tarlos looked around. "From here?"

"Something back on your world, with your body if possible. Anything will do."

"I don't think I have anything but my clothes. I had a sack full of food but I guess I left it with the horse . . ."

"Your clothes will do."

"Wait!" Tarlos remembered, holding up a hand. "I have a tooth in my pocket. You can have that."

"I don't want to keep it; I just need something to help you hold the Powers. This is a bit of a trial run—you'll be holding the Powers without immortality, which is usually not allowed. You need some kind of . . . shall we say, talisman to hold the excess energy you'll be wielding. You can also use the tooth to call me."

"How do I get it to you?"

"It's already done. The cow's tooth is now your personal physical incarnation of me. It will act as a connecting point between us and will help you hold all four Powers. When your task is done, hold the tooth and think of me."

Tarlos nodded and looked around nervously. "What happens now?"

"Now, you go home." Krastos placed a hand on Tarlos's shoulder, and Tarlos felt his emotions well up once more.

"Just like that?"

Krastos nodded. "Just like that."

The room popped out of existence, and Tarlos woke as if from a dream. He lay on his back in the desert, the high walls of Kesh just a short walk away. The tooth was at his neck, having been made into a necklace. It vibrated with life.

A cricket hopped onto his leg and chirped.

"H—hello," Tarlos tried.

"Good luck," said the cricket, and it hopped away.

12

No Place Like Home

The moon was dark and the stars were veiled. Tarlos stood from the cool sand, feeling like his muscles and blood vessels had been taken apart and put back together again. The great walls of Kesh were not far off, a blacker shape than the night sky behind them.

The world was silent. The gates were closed, which was normal for night, but it was not normal for there to be no lit torches lining the walls. A small breeze pushed at Tarlos's back, urging him onward to his kingdom. He obeyed and approached the gate.

He cupped his hands around his mouth and shouted, "Hey up there!"

Two helmeted heads popped out from a small window above the gate. "Who's there?" called one of them.

"Your king! I've returned!"

There was silence from the guards. Then, "Who did you say?"

"Tarlos!"

"Who are you? Where did you come from?"

"What are you talking about? Hurry up—it's cold out here and I'm tired and hungry."

The other guard said, "If you need shelter and a meal, we would be happy to provide. But you must tell us who you are. That is our law."

"Dammit, open the gate!" Tarlos yelled. "You know I can open it myself, but like I said, I'm exhausted and I'd rather you just help me out. Is no one glad to see me?"

"Is that a threat to Kesh?" the first guard asked. "You dare speak of breaching our walls?"

"They're my walls! This is my kingdom!"

Another guard, standing on the wall to the left of the guard tower, stepped from the shadows. He pulled back a bow, and a sharp arrow glinted on the string, ready to fly.

"That's enough of that," said the archer. His voice was familiar, but Tarlos could not place it at that moment. "Turn back the way you came, stranger, and do not come back. Leave, and no harm will come to you."

Tarlos picked up a small stone and hurled it at the archer. The man dodged it and let loose the arrow. It flew whistling at Tarlos, who stopped it in midair a few inches from his face.

The two tower guards gasped—horrified. A strange whispering echo sounded throughout his head:

gods gods did you gods did you see what he did you see what he did he stopped it he stopped it in midair demon in midair he stopped it in midair it's a demon a demon demon

Tarlos rubbed his tingling temples. The guards disappeared into the window, and Tarlos waited for them to come down the stairs.

There was a series of clicks and a thud behind the gate, and Tarlos sighed in relief. He was finally home, after decans of traveling through the desert and the Nether.

The gate swung open and four guards ran through—two brandishing spears, two with swords. The spearmen took position, aiming directly at Tarlos while the swords were raised in defense. The captain of the guard stepped forward with his own sword extended. His bow was slung over his shoulder.

"Who are you?" the captain asked.

Finally, Tarlos could see his face. "Lugal?" Tarlos said. "You have a beard! How?"

Lugal stepped closer. He brought the tip of his sword to Tarlos's chin. "How do you know my name, demon?"

could could it could it be oh please gods please gods gods

"It's me!" Tarlos said, his voice breaking. "Lugal, look at me. I'm Tarlos. How can you not see that? Has everyone gone mad?"

Lugal put his sword away. "You do bear a certain resemblance to the king. Your tricks are clever, demon, but not clever enough. Guards!"

At that, the remaining three guards each pulled a chain from their belts. The chains had fetters on their ends.

"What is this?" Tarlos asked Lugal. He was no longer merely annoyed. He was becoming furious.

if if it's if it's you please you please forgive forgive me if it's you forgive

"The High Priestess will know what to do with you," Lugal said as the guards cuffed Tarlos and locked the chains tight.

Tarlos's hands were bound together and his ankles chained a few inches apart. One of the guards kicked him behind the knees and he crumpled to the ground. Tarlos winced in pain as his knee landed on a pebble.

"You're all going to feel so stupid . . ." Tarlos mumbled.

"Quiet." Lugal turned to the other guards brandishing a sword. "Go and fetch the High Priestess. Tell her that some sort of demon or jinn is outside the gate. Tell her to hurry, we don't know how long we can hold it."

"Can we not bring it to her?" the guard asked. "Seems like a waste of time—"

"Jinn can enter an enclosed set of walls only if you bring them in or invite them," Lugal interrupted, his tone stern. "I don't want it in my city. Do as I say."

The guard saluted and took off through the gates of Kesh.

"You two," Lugal said to the other two guards. "Run upstairs and get more chains. I don't think these are enough."

The two nodded and jogged up the steps to the guard tower.

Lugal wrapped a strong hand around Tarlos's upper arm and pulled him toward the gate. "Come on. Don't say anything."

"What are you—"

"I said don't talk!"

He led Tarlos through the gate, keeping an eye out for the two guards he'd sent upstairs. He stepped lightly, and Tarlos followed his example. Once through the gate, Lugal picked up his pace, and Tarlos struggled to keep up with his fettered feet.

"Can you unlock these?"

wish wish I wish I could could yet not yet

"Not until I know for sure. I won't tell you again to be quiet."

Kesh was dark and silent like the desert that surrounded it. Tarlos understood that it was the middle of the night, but the streets were usually alive with teenagers and stray animals, or citizens who liked to stay up all night. But no light came from any windows; there were no dogs or cats running through the dirt roads, and not a single person could be seen.

"W—" Tarlos caught himself before he spoke. He wanted Lugal on his side, so he obeyed his wish and remained silent. *Where is everyone?* he wondered. Hopefully this would all make sense soon.

As they made their way down the main street, the stench of rotting meat filled the air. Tarlos gagged. He looked every which way, expecting to see the streets lined with dead and putrefying animals. Seeing nothing on the ground, he looked up.

Dozens of thick ropes and chains crisscrossed the city, going between buildings and tall wooden poles. Hanging from the ropes were metal cages, and inside the cages . . .

Oh gods, no. What in Shar's name . . .

Dozens, perhaps a hundred bodies rotted away in the cages above the city, their sour smell wafting through all of Kesh. Tarlos stared in awe and disgust, grateful that it was nighttime and he could not see their dead and detailed faces.

Lugal pulled him onward. They wove between small buildings and thatch-roof houses, into small alleys and places that even Tarlos was not familiar with. At last they came to a squat cottage with a straw roof and mud walls. Lugal, hand still on Tarlos's arm, walked to the wooden door and knocked twice.

A deep voice shouted, "Trying to sleep, thank you!"

"It's me," said Lugal.

A silent moment passed, and then the sound of something heavy being dragged along wood, and the door clicked open. There stood Nekhte, the royal blacksmith. Tarlos craned up to see the giant man, wondering how his beard had gotten so grey since he had seen him last, why his eyes looked so tired, and what was he doing in the lower city and not at his palace apartment?

Nekhte pointed a meaty finger at Tarlos. "Who is that?"

please gods please please gods maybe could maybe could it be maybe

"Let us in," Lugal said. "They'll be looking for us."

Nekhte stepped aside and the two of them entered, and Nekhte closed the wooden door behind them. He moved a large bronze chest in front of the door, scraping the old wood floor beneath as it moved. Inside, the house was black and smelled of mildew.

"One moment," Nekhte mumbled, and Tarlos heard him shuffle around the room. There was a spark, and Nekhte lit an oil lamp. The room was bathed in a soft orange light.

Nekhte squinted at Tarlos, holding the lamp above his head to give better light. He took turns looking at Tarlos and Lugal, and after five or six takes asked, "Is it him?"

"I think so," said Lugal. "He stopped an arrow with his mind."

"You shot at him?"

"That's my job."

"Jinn can stop arrows."

"I know, but—"

Tarlos lifted his chained hands, calling for silence. "Would someone please tell me what's happening? And take these off me!"

"Not yet," said Lugal. "Tell us something only the real Tarlos would know."

"What?" Tarlos looked back and forth between the two men. "This is all getting a little too—"

Nekhte boomed, "Will you stop wasting time and do what we ask?"

Tarlos's mouth snapped shut. He nodded. "What kind of thing would you like me to say?"

"First of all, what's my name?"

"Nekhte. You're my family's blacksmith. You live on the grounds. Or at least you used to. What are you doing out here?"

Nekhte continued, "I gave Tarlos something, not long before he disappeared. What was it?"

"A few things. A sword, some armor, some words of caution . . ."

"Were you alone?"

Tarlos shook his head. "No. My brother was with me."

Nekhte nodded. He raised an eyebrow at Lugal. The guard took a turn.

"What was my position when Krastos was still alive?"

Tarlos licked his lips. "You were his door-guard."

"Did I have a partner?"

"Yes. Marhemnu." The chains were beginning to rub his wrists and ankles raw. "Anything else?"

Lugal nodded. "Two more. Who is the only woman Tarlos ever loved?"

Tarlos frowned. "Katla."

"Fine. Last one. Who was Krastos's father?"

Tarlos took in a deep breath. "That has two answers. Everyone thinks it was Moleg. But I know the truth."

"Say it."

Tarlos stared first into Lugal's brown eyes, and then Nekhte's. "It was Ablis. But there's no way you would know that, so what does it prove?"

Lugal took a silver key from his belt and undid the cuffs around Tarlos's arms and legs. With a few clicks, the chains crashed to the floor. Tarlos rubbed his wrists.

"Now," Tarlos said, "can one of you please explain—"

Lugal wrapped his arms around Tarlos and held him tight for several seconds. When finally he came away, he looked at Tarlos and said, "You have been missed, my king."

Before Tarlos could respond, Nekhte grabbed him and spun him around, and he too squeezed Tarlos in a bone-bending hug.

thank thank the thank the gods the gods thank the gods

He let Tarlos go, and Tarlos panted for air. "What in the name of Shar is going on?"

Tears formed in Lugal's eyes, but they did not fall. "Where have you been, Tarlos?" he asked. His voice was a whisper.

"I've been . . ." He searched for an answer they would understand. "I've been away. There were questions that needed answers, and I was looking for them."

"And did you find what you were looking for?" Nekhte asked.

"I don't know yet. Anyway, I've only been gone for a few decans. What's all this fuss about?"

Lugal placed a hand on Tarlos's shoulder. "You haven't been . . . Tarlos, it's been three years."

Tarlos almost laughed. He looked from one man to the other, searching for a hint of humor in their faces. He found none. "You aren't serious."

wish wish we wish we weren't weren't

"Everyone thought we were crazy, didn't they?" Nekhte said. "Still do. But we knew. We knew all along. You were still out there, and that thing on the throne is a hoax."

"The thing on the throne—what do you mean?" Tarlos's voice was rising, and he felt his heartbeat quicken. "And why are there . . . the cages . . ."

"Wait here," Lugal said. "Nekhte, keep an eye out."

"Hurry back," Nekhte said. He moved the bronze chest from the door, and Lugal disappeared into Kesh.

Nekhte smiled at Tarlos beneath his huge beard. "I'm sure glad to see you, King. Sit down, I'll get some tea. By the way, what happened to your hair?"

Tarlos ran a hand through his shoulder-length hair. It was dry and tangled. He brought forth a lock from above his ear and blinked at it. He was not sure if it was a trick of the light or not.

"My hair is white," he said evenly.

Nekhte nodded. "Looks good on you."

Within an hour, the small house was filled with people. Most were servants, including Patnu and Basmem, who used to wash his and Krastos's hair and trim their beards. They looked at Tarlos with silent wonder, and Tarlos regarded them sorrowfully. Basmem had always been missing his thumbs, but now the small bones at the ends of each finger were missing and the wounds had already scarred over.

Palace guards arrived as well, ones that had kept watch over Tarlos's bedroom door or escorted him through the lower city. They all looked tired and saddened, even as they seemed relieved to see Tarlos there with them.

The priestess Shala also came, and she was taller and more mature than Tarlos remembered. She was dressed in a yellow robe, paint on her eyes and beads in her braided hair. She took one glance at Tarlos and then looked away.

The last to enter was a huge man that Tarlos had never seen before, standing at least seven feet tall with shoulders like a ship's anchor and skin as black as obsidian. Around him a purple blanket was wrapped, and seated in the blanket like an infant child was a crippled Kamhat. Tarlos felt his breath catch in his belly when he saw her. He expected her to cry at the sight of him. Instead, she smiled warmly.

"Well," she said. Her voice was softer than it had been before her injuries, but it still carried with it a certain sass and flirtatiousness. "He decided to come back after all. Did you miss us, Tarlos?"

Tarlos now stood in the center of a large group of people, all of whom stared at him with confusion, and some with happiness. A few wore expressions of betrayal.

Tarlos asked Lugal, "Where is Katla? And Mez?"

Those collected glanced sadly at each other.

Lugal adjusted his belt. "Mez is dead."

The blood drained from Tarlos's head as if water from a cliffside. He stumbled. "No. No. How?"

"This is why we meet in secret. The new king—who poses as you—doesn't tolerate shaking faith that he is in fact you." Lugal looked at the floor, then at the palace guards. "Mez was the first of us to notice that something about the false king wasn't right. He spoke out against him, refusing to serve anyone but the real Tarlos. The king made an example of him." Lugal swallowed and stared through Tarlos. "His bones are still in the cage that hangs over the city square. He was loyal to you until the end."

Tarlos tried to swallow, but there was no moisture in his

mouth or throat. "And Katla?"

This time all eyes were cast to the floor, and the air was filled with a knowing tension. Nekhte broke the silence: "She is still queen. She lives with the king. She and her son."

Tarlos stammered. "She and this false king . . .?"

Nekhte shook his head. "She was pregnant before you left. The boy is yours."

Tarlos did not feel his knees give out, but he crumpled to the floor just the same. His head fell into his hands and he thought he might cry. He could not, though. He looked at each person individually, seeing the hurt in their eyes. He could hear their thoughts with his new Power of Mind—they were sad and many, so much that he could not make out individual words. His head was filled with a buzzing white noise of echoing voices, and no matter how much he tried, how much he wanted to, he could not look away from these people. His people.

"Why are you all here?" he asked.

Kamhat smiled. "We're the only ones in this whole city with brains, it turns out. The only ones who know that the king who claims to be you really isn't. We all held hope that you would return someday."

Tarlos frowned at her. "Kamhat, I'm so sorry about—"

"Don't you start that," she interrupted. Her voice cracked. "Only the gods understand what you've been through, and I forgave you long before tonight."

Tarlos shook his head. "And the empty streets? Is that the king's law?"

Lugal nodded. "Curfew is sunset. Anyone caught outside after dark is placed in solitary for three days without food. The second offense is banishment or death. The offender gets to choose."

"And how many have been banished?"

"None. Being banished means being set free in the desert, naked, with no supplies or water. Death is easier."

"Tarlos," Nekhte said, stepping forward. He placed a large hand on Tarlos's shoulder. "You're back. You're the king. Take back what's yours, for all our sakes."

Emotion welled up inside him like a geyser bursting through frozen ground. "It's all my fault, isn't it? If I had been here, Mez would still be . . . oh gods . . ." And the tears came, and Tarlos sobbed. Everyone waited with patience and understanding until he caught his breath again.

Tarlos wiped his eyes and cleared his throat, then stood once more. His eyes stung, and his hands shook with anger—anger at the false king, anger at the gods for allowing any of this to happen. Anger at himself for blaming anyone but him. This was his doing, and he would make it right.

"Take me to him," he told Lugal. "Let me see this false king."

Lugal nodded. "We'll have to be sneaky. Can you pretend to be a jinn for a while longer?" He picked up the cuffs and chains. "And you'll have to put these back on."

13

The King of Kesh

It was difficult for Tarlos to know how long he'd been in his cell. He was beginning to get used to being in dark spaces for unimaginable lengths of time. But at least in Shar's Tunnel and the cave beneath the mountain, he was always moving. This cell was small and there was nowhere to go. He counted the drips of water from the stone ceiling as they splashed to the damp stone floor. So far, he had counted over four thousand.

Lugal had chained him up as before and led him through the city toward the palace and dungeons. On their way there, they came across a group of a dozen guards, all in a frantic search for the jinn and their missing captain.

"He got through the gate," Lugal told them, "but I caught him. Help me take him to the dungeons, and then we'll see what the king has to say."

That was hours ago. Now, Tarlos sat on the cold hard floor and leaned back against the freezing stones of the wall. The guards had not given him a cell with a bench or a stool, or even a bucket in which to relieve himself. It was miserable; he was hungry, and he rubbed his arms and listened to his stomach growl. Even his father had never denied prisoners food.

A small scurrying sound approached. Tarlos straightened up and listened intently. The tiny steps came up to him and stopped.

"Hey," said a small, hissy voice. "Hey, hey you, you, you, hey you."

"Who is that?" Tarlos asked, trying to spot whatever was

sitting in front of him, but it was too dark.

"Got food?" the weird voice asked again. "Food, huh? Where is food? You got any? Bugs? See any around? I'd like a bug. You got food? Doesn't have to be a bug." Whatever it was spoke very fast, and Tarlos had a hard time keeping up with it.

"Tell me who you are first," Tarlos said.

The thing ran around him once, dipping under his bent knees and circling his feet, then jumped into his lap. Tarlos cried out in surprise—it was a large black rat.

"Oh yeah, I can understand you." A smile came to his face, and he let out a small chuckle. "A lot of good that will do me down here, though. Do you know what's going on up there?"

"You got food? I'm hungry. Hey, why don't you answer me? Food?"

"Who is king up there?"

"I don't smell food. No bugs. No food. Thirsty. I'll have water. Fill my belly. Can't find food." The rat pounced from Tarlos's lap and ran away with the tiny pitter-patter of paws that sounded through the stone halls.

What's the use of being able to speak to animals if animals are stupid?

Tarlos leaned against the wall and sighed. He tried closing his eyes for a nap, but his roaring stomach would not let him sleep.

Deep in the dungeon halls, a heavy door opened and thudded against the wall. Light flooded the place for a moment, and then it was dark just as before. Footsteps sounded through the halls. Tarlos stood and grasped at the metal bars around his cell. He waited patiently as three figures came forward. Tarlos could not see them in the darkness, although the one in front carried a torch. The light from the flames silhouetted them.

As they neared, Tarlos saw that two of them wore armor. They were guards.

"Have you come to bring me dinner?" Tarlos asked. "I hope it's boar. I haven't had that in decans. Years, apparently."

"You will remain silent in the presence of the king unless asked a direct question," spoke the guard holding the torch. The dancing orange light glimmered on his helmet and bounced off the walls.

Tarlos nodded to the guard and backed away from the bars. The guard took a large key from his belt and unlocked the gate. It swung open, squealing on rusty hinges. The third figure, not wearing any armor, stepped forward.

"Thank you," the shadowed figure said to the guards. At the sound of his voice, Tarlos felt the entirety of his skin erupt into goose flesh. "You may leave us now, I'll be all right. Just wait outside."

The guards bowed, handed the torch to the man, and left him there with Tarlos.

The man smiled, face lit by flame.

Tarlos stammered. "What . . . how . . . who . . ." He did not understand anything that was happening. The man standing before him, smiling sinisterly with perfect white teeth, was Tarlos. It was him, down to the last detail—his thick brown hair, his straight nose, his high cheekbones, the scant beard that he could never manage to grow as fully as he was expected to. Right down to the way he stood and shifted his weight on his feet. Tarlos stared at himself as if looking into a mirror. His knees buckled and he crumpled to the hard floor. He could not take his eyes from his double, although it made him sick to look.

"I know," the double said. "This must be very strange for you. I'll give you a moment to compose yourself, and then you need to come with me."

The blood returned to Tarlos's head and he followed his double out of the dungeons and through the main palace building.

"Please, keep your head down," the double said in Tarlos's voice. "And don't speak to anyone. This is confusing enough as is."

It must have been the early morning still as no one was awake and walking around the palace except for the servants, and they avoided eye contact altogether. Only once did a servant—who Tarlos did not recognize—glance up and offer a brief glimpse of confusion before looking away again.

They came to the king's chamber, and the double glared at Tarlos. "Any sound from you and she dies."

Tarlos was about to respond when the chamber door creaked open a few inches and a soft voice sounded from the other side.

"Tarlos?"

Katla. He would recognize her voice anywhere.

"Is everything all right? What's happening?" She locked eyes with the real Tarlos, and a startled voice echoed through his mind.

Tarlos Tarlos is that Tarlos what is what Tarlos is that what is this who is Tarlos that who is that

He almost answered out of reflex but kept his mouth shut instead, fearing what would happen if he didn't. The double answered for him.

"Everything is fine. Go back to bed."

A small voice came from the room behind the door. Katla turned as the door opened another foot and a small naked toddler ran into her arms. The boy wrapped his little arms around her neck and her white-yellow hair. Tarlos's mouth gaped and his throat dried up.

"Go back to bed," the double said again, stronger this time. Katla nodded and closed the door.

Tarlos hissed at his double, "Is that—"

"No speaking. Not yet. I promise I'll explain."

The false king led Tarlos through the palace and into the gardens that his grandmother had planted many years before. The sun was beginning to rise, and the sky was pink in the east. The air was still cool, but it was already beginning to warm.

They walked through the gardens, and the servants avoided them and bowed their heads to the ground. Tarlos said nothing, and the man who looked like him did similar. The double took Tarlos to a small door in the wall behind the gardens. It was a door almost no one knew about—it led outside the city walls and into the desert beyond.

The double held the wooden door open for Tarlos. "After you," he said.

Tarlos stepped out of Kesh and into the desert, and the double closed the door behind them.

"The first thing you should know," said the man, "is that your hair is white." He pointed at Tarlos's head.

Tarlos ran a hand through his hair. "I know."

"Second," the man continued, "you've been gone for some time. Did you know that?"

"Yes," Tarlos said. The sun was higher now, the pink fading into a light blue. It would be a clear day, a hot day. "But I thought it was only a few decans."

The man laughed. The sound made Tarlos's skin squirm.

"I'm afraid not, Tarlos. It's been three years. More than that, actually, but not by much. I won't bother you with the exact time down to the second. Your son is two years old. His name is Messu, if you were wondering."

Tarlos did not know where to begin with this person. He decided to start with the obvious. "Ablis," he said.

Ablis bowed sarcastically. "In the flesh."

Tarlos backed away, staring at the cast-out god who had taken his image, his kingdom, his wife and son. "What happens now?"

"Hopefully a lot," Ablis answered, still circling the true king. Tarlos turned, keeping eye contact with the god. "Honestly, you coming back never factored into my plans. But now I've thought about it a little, and I can see how it might be better this way." The Discarded One leaned forward and took a deep, long smell of Tarlos. He felt his soul within him tugging at his bones. "I don't know how," Ablis said, "but you hold all four Powers, don't you? Yes. Interesting. Well, so do I."

Tarlos remained quiet. It took all his energy to fight the heat of the sun and keep from passing out.

"Forget Kesh," said Ablis. "Think about the Fertile Valley. Think about Edorath. Think about Earth. Or more . . ."

Tarlos felt a familiar sensation of being sucked through his own body, and he heard the slurp in his head as the world folded in around him. He emerged on the other side to the cosmos in all its glory—planets, stars, nebulae, and supernovae. Worlds without number circling each other in circles within circles. The universe extended forever in every physical dimension as stars were born and burned in dazzling colors, then exploded in horrifying shows of fire, or else collapsed in on themselves and became a void. Light shone from every corner of the universe, accentuating the dark places and warming the life that seemed from every part of creation. Tarlos and Ablis ascended to the highest point of the cosmos and looked down on everything that occupied their corner of reality.

And then they stopped moving. Tarlos waited for more, waited for the higher planes and dimensions that he had seen before meeting the elder god.

"This could be ours," Ablis said. "Just imagine it. A god and a Holder of all four Powers. Think of what we could accomplish together. Think of what we could become."

The vision melted away and Tarlos found himself back in the blistering heat of the desert. It was still early morning. So why was it so hot already, and why did the sun appear so high in the sky? Tarlos swayed on his feet. He spread his stance to keep his balance.

"You've had time to consider my offer since last we met," Ablis said. "I would consider it a sign that we met again. I never give second chances. What do you say?" He smiled, and for a moment Tarlos caught a glimpse of the true Ablis in his double's brown eyes. It filled him with pity.

Tarlos gave one slow shake of his head. "I didn't come back in order to join you."

The smile on Ablis's face turned to a grimace. "Think about what you're saying, Tarlos. I'm offering you the world. I'm offering you all the worlds. We could have them. Co-rule this universe. Join me." He extended a hand.

Tarlos stared at him. Sweat dripped into his eyes and his skin burned in the sunlight. "Why don't you go away? Nobody likes you."

This brought back Ablis's smile. He lowered his outstretched hand. "Fine, Tarlos. Have it your way. But then, I used to be the god of balance. Now that I think about it, there really is no need for any other Holders when you yourself hold all four Powers. You think it's necessary that Messu lives?"

This gave Tarlos pause. He sneered. "You will not—"

"Or what?" Ablis taunted. "You might have all the Powers,

but you're still mortal. I'm a god. I am eternal."

Tarlos probed inside his mind, feeling for that spot that moves objects, that speaks with rats and crickets and hears the thoughts of others. He found something else there, something new, and flexed it. Suddenly, the air around him dampened and slowed like syrup. The sun's fiery fingers stopped shimmering in the sky, and the clouds far above stopped in place.

The Power of Time.

Ablis was caught mid-blink, mouth agape. Tarlos groaned, the thickness of the air and his own fatigue weighing on him, and he launched a missile made of wind at Ablis. Normally, the blow would have knocked an opponent across Kesh's walls. But the air was thick and time was slow, and the force of his strike barely moved Ablis. Tarlos released his hold on time, and the invisible fist of air struck the god head-on. When the dust cleared, however, Ablis remained in place, one eyebrow raised.

"Oh ye of little faith," said Ablis, motioning toward Tarlos with a single finger.

Immediately, Tarlos felt a force seizing his every atom and he was launched a hundred yards from Ablis. He soared through the air, trying to gain control over his own Power to fly or to at least slow his landing. He felt Ablis in his mind, prodding around like a fisherman trying to get at the meat in a mussel. He was blocking Tarlos from using his Powers, and Tarlos fell to the hard and hot desert, landing in the middle of a patch of cacti.

The prodding ethereal finger of Ablis left his mind, and Tarlos levitated out of the cactus plants. He was covered in numerous thin thorns, each one a burning sensation. He groaned inwardly, biting his tongue until he tasted blood, and worked to remove the thorns with his mind. But he could not focus on all of them at once. He would have to remove them individually.

"I bet that feels icky." Ablis materialized beneath Tarlos. He reached down into the brambles and plucked from it a dried stick about a foot in length. The stick straightened in his grip, thickened, and sharpened itself to a metal point at the end.

"Like I said," Ablis shouted up to Tarlos, "no need for all these Holders." He launched the spear.

Tarlos felt a sudden pressure in his chest. He fell to the ground, though it seemed to him that he fell slowly. Ablis laughed as Tarlos looked to his chest and the spear protruding from it. His body cried out for oxygen but his lungs would not expand. Blood pooled around him.

The tooth.

The elder god could help him. He just had to call him.

Tarlos felt for the tooth around his neck, only he did not find it. As he lay in the dirt, he turned his head to the right as far as it would go. There it was—the tooth was caught on a cactus.

"You're still afraid," came Ablis's voice, though Tarlos could no longer see him. "After all that, you're still afraid..."

The sound of Ablis's laughter fresh in his ears, Tarlos stared up into the sky and was comfortable. The day was hot, but he did not feel it anymore. He was quite cool. All the blood that had been in his body only moments ago was now soaking into the thirsty ground, but Tarlos felt fine.

So this is it, he thought. Sort of like falling asleep, except . . .

Tarlos closed his eyes and died.

14

Devil's Food

Sort of like falling asleep, except . . . except I . . .

. . . I'm . . .

. . . what was I saying . . .

. . . what is . . .

He floated. Drifted. The space around him was clad in silver, and there was no apparent source of the silver light.

His sense of balance was not working. No—it did not exist. He floated and drifted, but he did not know in which direction. He felt a sort of current around him, and the silver light rippled in shafts. It was like the sun shining through a clear pool of water.

He traveled onward, knowing he was moving but not knowing where. Perhaps there was no where. Perhaps he was drifting through the dimensions, like that time he spoke to the elder god. How long ago was that? Days? Centuries? Seconds?

There was no linear movement. The shafts of silver light did not move or break as he drifted onward. There was a lack of time—he drifted for centuries and also less than a moment. A moment and a thousand years, both and neither. Every second happened at once, and his human mind attempted to sort them into sequential events.

Something brushed his arm. He was intrigued. It had been an eternity since he'd felt the touch of anything. The something wrapped around his arm and dragged him upward, or what he assumed was upward, the silver shafts of light widening, brightening as he neared the nonmaterial edge of this in-between place.

A strong arm pulled him from the Styx, and Tarlos sputtered as he came out from the water. He felt a solid surface supporting his body, and he rolled over and panted.

"You're fine," said a soothing voice. It was old, kind, and calm. "Try to sit up. You'll regain your balance faster."

Tarlos tried. He leaned against the wall of what he now saw was a small boat. His vision was blurry—the sun was bright, and it took several moments for his eyes to adjust. When finally he could see clearly, he looked up at the tall thin figure next to him.

The man was pale, his hair white and his eyes blue. He towered over Tarlos, more than seven feet tall, and his limbs were thin and stick-like. He was draped in a billowy cloak from neck to ankle, the color of it shifting between shades of black and purple. The tall man held a long pole in his hands, and he used it to push the boat forward. Tarlos thought the man resembled an ibis.

The boat itself was made from reeds and thin branches lashed together in the shape of a canoe. It felt sturdy, if not a little wobbly, and Tarlos settled on its edge, facing the man.

"Who are you?" Tarlos asked. "Where am I?"

"I am Ilshu," the tall man answered. His voice was wind through a cavern, not a whisper but not fully voiced. It was oddly comforting. "You are dead. I am taking you to your place."

"Oh." Tarlos looked around inside the boat. The river was calm, and it moved what he assumed was eastward at a steady rate. On the banks of the river were reeds and weeds and flowers, and beyond those trees of every kind he recognized and many he didn't. All of this seemed familiar.

"Have I been here before?"

The god of the dead nodded slowly. "You have, though you were not supposed to. Your memory will return shortly."

"That's good. I don't even remember my name."

"I am afraid that will stay lost."

"Oh." Tarlos felt that this should worry him, but strangely he was unbothered. He waited patiently as Ilshu pushed the reed boat along the Styx, and the trees and landscape crawled by on the shores.

"So where is my place?"

"Down the river. Almost at the end. You passed it on your previous adventure here."

Tarlos nodded, short shadows of memory ghosting through his mind—shapes and feelings but nothing substantial. He decided to wait patiently until his memories became solid again.

He leaned against the side of the boat and watched the landscape drift by. The boat ride lasted for several hours, and they passed many villages on their way downstream. Wooden signs lined the river at each community, and Tarlos could understand the strange foreign words as they passed by.

Streetlamp District
Watertower District
Searchlight District
Lighthouse District

At this last village, he saw a man seated on the bank of the Styx, skipping rocks across its surface. He was average height, with short brown hair that thinned on the top. He wore a simple shirt that buttoned down the front. As Tarlos and Ilshu floated by, the man stopped skipping rocks and lifted a hand in greeting. Tarlos waved back, and the man smiled.

"Who was that?" Tarlos asked.

"He does not matter," Ilshu replied.

Tarlos frowned. "That's not very nice."

Ilshu turned his head to Tarlos. "He does not matter to you. He is not from your world."

"And you're taking me to mine?"

"I am taking you to where you belong. At the end of the river."

A shock of memories cascaded through Tarlos's mind like ice dripping down his spine. He remembered Kesh, he remembered his brother—though he could not remember his name. He remembered the journey across the desert and the dead country and floating down the Styx with the boatman. He remembered the blue flower and the House of Dust—

"Oh no," Tarlos said. "No, please not there." He stood and placed his hands on the reed railing of the boat.

"It is not for me to decide," Ilshu hummed. "My duty is to ferry souls to their place; it is not to judge them."

"And who will judge me?" Tarlos demanded. "When?"

"That Which Judges. And in time." Ilshu did not slow or speed his pace. The long pole dipped in and out of the water as the boat floated down the Styx.

"I'm not going to that place." Tarlos approached the god. He stopped when he felt a static force surrounding the being. It made him feel sick to get too near. "Take me anywhere but there. Anywhere."

"That is not the way of things."

Tarlos looked across the river, over the banks and into the trees beyond. Tiny houses dotted the way, smoke coming from their chimneys, lights in the windows.

"Why can't I go there?" Tarlos asked.

"That district is not for your world." Ilshu continued to push forward. He did not turn as he spoke.

Tarlos leaned over the railing to get a better look, shielding his eyes from the sun. A familiar landmark lay ahead. He gasped.

"The bridge!" he shouted at Ilshu. "It leads to the Windmill District! Drop me off there!"

"No."

"They know me! I have friends there! Ilshu, please, don't do this to me . . ."

Ilshu did not respond.

Tarlos stared into the Styx. It's poison, he reminded himself. *But I'm already dead. And I was just in there.*

The bridge approached. The boat would slip right beneath it, and Ilshu would have to duck to clear it.

"I can hear your thoughts," said Ilshu. "If you do it, I will not be there to pull you out again."

The boat reached the wooden bridge, and Tarlos jumped onto the edge of the boat. The boat rocked in the water, and Ilshu turned.

Tarlos leaped as the boat came under the bridge, and his fingers grazed the edge. He grasped, trying to hold onto nothing, and fell backwards into the Styx. The boat passed on without him.

The water was cold, colder than he remembered, and foggy white shapes drifted past him like seaweed. He kicked hard, trying to reach the surface. One of the white shapes brushed against his leg. It sent electric prickles up through his body, and he seized in surprise. He swam upward, and the white cloudy things drifted by.

The surface was near—he could see where the river met the shore just a few yards away. He turned in that direction, and his lungs began to pain for air.

One more white shape wafted toward him, and something made Tarlos stop and watch. The cloud came near, and it swirled and turned as the formless wisp took shape. The face of Lakaeus appeared in the thick white mist, and his body formed below it. Tarlos opened his eyes wide as his father's soul reached out for him. Lakaeus's eyes were sad, apologetic, and filled with regret. He reached to Tarlos with ghostly fingers, and Tarlos could almost hear his father speaking.

My son . . . come with me . . . let me make it right . . .

Remember me . . .

With his mind, Tarlos forced a current at the ghost of his father, propelling himself toward shore at the same time. He collided with the ground and grasped blindly above the water for purchase. He managed to lift himself out and fell on his back in the dirt, sputtering and coughing.

He looked to the river, half expecting to see Ilshu in his boat waiting to take him away. But he was not there. Tarlos was alone.

He removed his clothes and squeezed as much water from them as he could before putting them back on. The clothes were freezing and damp.

Up ahead was the Windmill District. He needed a drink.

He put his hand on the round brass door handle but did not twist it. There were voices inside—many voices. He heard laughing, the sound of glass clinking, and loud conversation. He smelled meat, pastries, coffee, and beer. A party was happening inside the tavern. Tarlos hesitated before easing the door open.

The noise hit him like a gust of wind, as did the smell. The tavern was packed with at least a hundred people, and none were sitting; there was no room for tables or chairs. Some people held plates of food in their hands, which they ignored as they talked and laughed with each other. Those who did not have a plate of food held a glass of foaming beer from which they drank gladly.

Tarlos inched over to the wall beside the fireplace and leaned into the corner. He had no idea what was going on here, and he did not want to interrupt.

A voice in the crowd yelled, "Ladies and gentlemen, I'd be ever so grateful to have yer attention!" A short man jumped up onto the counter, and Tarlos caught a glimpse of the brown-haired woman behind it. The man had a strange accent, one that Tarlos had never heard, and he wore a funny flat hat.

Atop the counter, the man took off his hat and waved it in the air. "Now listen, you lot! I need your help with this one!"

"Oh please, not another one! We're already queasy from drinking," shouted a woman.

The crowd laughed, as did the man. He put his hat back on, one hand on the bill in front and one hand on the back. He secured it tightly on his head and adjusted his pants, which were sagging off his hips despite his suspenders.

"Now I know ye all know this one. 'Twas one of his favorites, and I think it's only right that we end the party tonight with it. Ye all know which one I'm talking about."

"Wild Rover!" yelled a man.

"Aye! And you'd better belt it this time so he can hear you from wherever he is!"

The man began to stomp a beat on the counter, and everyone else joined in by stomping on the wooden floor. Those who had no food or drink clapped along. After a few bars, the man on the counter took in a deep breath and began to sing, and when he sang the others sang with him. Soon, the tavern was filled with joyous song.

I've been a wild rover for many a year
And I've spent all me money on whiskey and beer
But now I'm returning with gold in great store
And ne'er will I play the wild rover no more

And it's no, nay, never
No, nay, never, no more
Will I play the wild rover, no, never, no more

I went into an alehouse I used to frequent
And I told the landlady my money was spent
I asked her for credit, she answered me "Nay,
Such a custom as yours I could have any day."

And it's no, nay, never
No, nay, never, no more
Will I play the wild rover, no, never, no more

I took from my pocket ten sovereigns bright
And the landlady's eyes opened wide with delight
She said "I have whiskey and wines of the best
And the words that I spoke you were only in jest."

And it's no, nay, never
No, nay, never, no more
Will I play the wild rover, no, never, no more

I'll go home to my parents, confess what I've done
And I'll ask them to pardon their prodigal son
And when they caress me as ofttimes before
Sure I never will play the wild rover no more

And it's no, nay, never
No, nay, never, no more
Will I play the wild rover, no, never, no more

The tavern erupted in shouts and whoops and applause, and the man on the counter applauded his audience in turn then flipped off his flat hat and bowed theatrically. He jumped off the counter and received several slaps on the back. Tarlos remained in his spot by the fireplace. He did not smile.

After, the party grew quiet and the atmosphere became tired. People began to file out, slowly at first and then in groups. They said goodbye to each other on their way out and yelled their goodnights to the woman behind the counter. A few stayed behind to bring out the tables and chairs and set them out as they were before. Then, one by one, they put on their hats and flipped up their jacket collars, and hugged a woman who stood at the counter.

She was small and short, and very thin. Her hair was black and straight, her skin a light olive. She wore a simple black tunic trimmed in white. A small voice somewhere in Tarlos's mind—like that of a memory—whispered, *Kimono. It's called a kimono.*

Tucked behind the woman's ear and threaded through her black hair was a blue sun orchid, the same deep shade as her eyes. Tarlos's frown deepened at the sight of the flower—he recalled how he had helped the boatman find it. He turned his head in every direction. Had he seen the boatman since he arrived? It was a large crowd, surely he was there. Tarlos must have just missed him. He stood on his toes to see over the remaining heads.

With no sign of the boatman, Tarlos relaxed on his feet and slumped against the wall. The party was over, and everyone was leaving. What should he do now? This was not his after-world—Ilshu had not meant for him to be here. Would there be a place for him to stay? Would he fit in with these people from an alternate Earth? He looked to the tavern woman and wondered if he should ask her for help. Perhaps he could stay in the bedroom upstairs.

"Hey!" she called, and Tarlos snapped to and focused his eyes on her. She smiled and waved at him, then came over to the other side of the counter. Tarlos met her halfway, and she gave him a friendly hug. "What the heck are you doing here?"

Tarlos shrugged. "I died."

Her eyebrows shot upward. She tried to hide a laugh behind her hand, disguising it as a cough.

"It's not funny," Tarlos said, his frown now a scowl. "It's all over. I failed. This wasn't how it was supposed to end."

The woman nodded sympathetically and took a calming breath. "Of course. I'm sorry. I guess that's why I don't remember your name."

"Ah, I was hoping you would. Oh well."

The woman motioned for Tarlos to take a seat at a table. She walked away then, returning a moment later with the woman with the flower in her hair, and the woman smiled a greeting at Tarlos.

"This is my friend," said the tavern woman. "I'd introduce you properly, but I don't know either of your names. She knew the boatman when they were both alive, and I was good friends with one of her descendants. Well, I guess I'm still friends with him..."

Tarlos stood to greet the small woman, and she gave him a polite bow in return.

The small woman said, "He told me that you helped him find this." She touched her orchid reverently. "Thank you." Her voice was soft, and it made Tarlos want to lean in to hear her better.

"You are very welcome," Tarlos said. "So, you knew the boatman in life?"

"I did. We were close friends. He was a wonderful person. One of the most selfless I've ever met."

Tarlos took one more glance around the room. "Where is he tonight? Does he not like parties?"

A solemn look crossed her face. The barkeep woman rubbed the back of her neck.

"Did I say something wrong?" Tarlos asked.

"He's gone," the barkeep answered.

"Gone? What do you mean?"

"He's dead. It happens. People die, they come here, and

then after a while they disappear again."

Tarlos frowned. "Where do they go?"

"No idea. Just like no one knew we'd end up here."

Tarlos sat back down and scratched his head. The flower woman bowed. "If you'll excuse me, I'm very tired. It was lovely to have met you. Goodnight." She gave them both another bow, and Tarlos watched her tiny slippered feet shuffle beneath her kimono as she exited the tavern.

A silence passed between Tarlos and the tavern woman. She sighed. "We got a lot of leftovers. Want some chocolate cake? It's amazing. Devil's food."

"Sure," Tarlos said. He did not care about eating, but he had nothing else to do, and he needed something to distract him from his disappointment.

The woman patted Tarlos on the shoulder, then disappeared into the room behind the counter.

Tarlos studied the grain in the wooden table. He picked at it with his fingernail.

How can the dead die?

"Excuse me," said a voice behind him. Tarlos turned and met eyes with a pale bald man. "Do you mind?" He gestured to a chair opposite Tarlos.

"Not at all."

The man thanked him and took a seat. He held two steaming mugs, and he handed one to Tarlos. "You looked like you needed something hot to drink. Go ahead. It's just tea."

Tarlos sipped the hot tea and felt warmth spread through his body. "Thanks," he said.

"You're going to love this cake," the bald man said. "It's my favorite."

The man had a peculiar look that Tarlos could not figure out. It was not that the man looked strange or deformed. He appeared normal enough, except for his eyes—they were a rainbow of green, blue, grey, and brown, with every shade of each in concentric circles that bled into each other. They were ancient. His skin was smooth and without wrinkles, except for around his eyes and mouth, which was stretched into a permanent smile. His nose was neither big nor small, and Tarlos could find no fault in the bridge of it. His skin was pale but no more so than the skin of the woman he'd left in the living world. His fingers were nimble and still, and they grasped the mug of tea like it was his best friend. His clothing was simple, grey and perfectly tailored. His shirt had no buttons, and his pants had no belt or fasteners. Tarlos could not make up his mind about the man. Did he look different than any other human, or did he look like what a man would be if all humans in existence were combined into one person?

"Ah, here it comes," said the man as the barkeep brought out a plate and set it in front of Tarlos, along with a fork and a paper napkin.

"I suppose you want a slice, too," she said to the man.

He smiled. "You know it's just a waste of breath when you ask."

The woman stuck her tongue out at him and went behind the counter once more.

"Eat. And be amazed," the man said to Tarlos.

Tarlos scooped a bit of the chocolate cake with his fork and brought it to his nose. It smelled sweet, filled with too much sugar. But he took a bite anyway. The dark, rich chocolate touched his tongue, and he paused and stared at the man in disbelief.

"What . . ." he tried to say around his mouthful.

The man laughed, and his vibrant eyes sparkled. "Told you. Isn't that the best chocolate cake you've ever had?"

Tarlos swallowed. "I've never had chocolate cake before."

The woman brought a second slice for the man, and Tarlos finished devouring his before she could walk away. He touched her wrist. "Cah ha s'more?" he said with his mouth full.

The woman laughed. "Well dang. Yeah, there's a little bit left. I'll just bring it out and you two can finish it off. Save me a few trips."

While waiting, Tarlos cleaned his tongue with his teeth, savoring the aftertaste of the cake and the chocolate frosting. The tavern was all but empty now.

Tarlos looked around. "This wasn't a party after all," he said. "It was a funeral."

The man tilted his head in consideration. "Can't it be both?"

The rest of the cake was placed on the table in front of them, and Tarlos and the man each took a slice.

"But he was already dead," Tarlos said. "Why die again?"

The bald man shrugged. "Just the way of things, I guess. There's always an ebb and a flow. Always needs to be opposition, yin and yang, that sort of thing. Nothing stays one way forever. When it's time to move on, you move on. The journey is never over."

"But . . ." Tarlos waved a hand. "He was already dead. You can't die again."

"Oh, but you can. It's happened many times before, and it will continue to do so until the final quark fizzles out. It will happen to me, and to you, and to her." He pointed to the counter. "All of us. Some take longer than others."

Tarlos shook his head and put down his cake-covered fork. "What's the point then? If even death isn't the end, why even do anything? What's there to live for?"

"Everything!" the man said, suddenly booming. Tarlos startled. "We have everything to live for. Do you have a family?"

Tarlos licked his teeth. "I did."

"Did you love them?"

Tarlos nodded.

"And you still love them."

Tarlos shrugged. "Yes."

"The ones we love never really leave us. I'm sure you've heard that before, but that's not the point." The man sighed and took another bite of cake, which he chewed thoughtfully. "I don't think life has an objective meaning. You have to find your own. It's like winning a game. The winning isn't really the fun part. Playing the game is."

"But aren't you sad when the game ends?"

The man shook his head. "Sometimes, I suppose. But the point of something fun is that it doesn't last forever. Just like life. Life is beautiful and fleeting, and it's beautiful *because* it's fleeting."

Tarlos felt like he had heard that before, but the memory of it was hidden beneath a fog in his brain. He shook his head. "I'm still . . ." His gaze drifted to the table in the corner. He could almost see the boatman there, face hidden beneath his wide-brimmed hat. "I don't understand how someone can die twice."

"I have a theory about that," said the man. He pointed his fork at Tarlos. "But it's just a theory, so don't take it as gospel. We all die twice. The second time is when someone says your name for the last time."

That sent a cold shudder up Tarlos's shoulders. Tears burned at the corners of his eyes. He took another bite of cake.

The bald man let out a small chuckle.

"What is it?"

The man swallowed some cake. "I was just thinking about this story the boatman told me once. He was always telling me funny stories about his family in Oklahoma, but this one always stuck with me."

"Can I hear it?"

"Sure, just let me put it together in my head real quick." The bald man closed his eyes for a moment and then began speaking.

"The boatman had hammer toes—grew up with them, suffered near his whole life. Finally, when he was thirty or forty, he went to the doctor.

"'Doc', he said, 'I need you to fix my toes. I can't hardly stand em no more.' So, the doctor takes him into the operating room, cuts each of his toes down the middle, breaks the bones, resets them, and sews them back up.

"He was laid up for a while, not able to walk or work. Could barely even hobble enough for his necessaries every morning and evening. Then finally, a few months later, his toes were healed and he went out in the cotton field to do some work. And wouldn't you know it, he stepped in a gopher hole and broke his foot!"

Tarlos smiled. The man chuckled and continued.

"Anyway, fast forward some years. He's about sixty now. His

wife died some twenty years earlier, and he'd been living alone ever since. This old woman starts calling on him near every day. She brings him beans and cornbread, 'and boy-o do I love me some beans and cornbread,' he told me. 'But whoo-ee! Was she ugly! And old! And she was always wantin to kiss on me.'

"But she was only a year or two older than you, I told him.

"'Well sure,' he said, 'but who wants to kiss an old lady?'

Tarlos and the man laughed, and the man took a swallow of tea.

"Well, this went on for some time. He gave her enough attention to keep the beans and cornbread coming, but not so much that he'd have to kiss her.

"Well why didn't you ever kiss her in a friendly way, I asked.

"He told me, 'If I'd'a done that much, before you know it, we'd be sleepin together, and I can't be sleepin with a woman like that.'

"Why not, I asked.

"'Because, I'd prob'ly wake up one morning and see that old hag in my bed, and take off runnin and prob'ly break my damn foot again!'"

Tarlos laughed into his cake, the bald man into his tea. The story made Tarlos feel a bit better about his situation and he took another slice.

"This is really good cake," he mumbled.

"It sure is," said the man, shoveling another huge bite. "It's a shame that it'll be gone once we eat it all."

15

Not for the World

The sun was setting on the dead country, and soon Shar would enter the tunnel in the mountain to rise again in the east of the living world. The air was still and warm, and the brightest stars had already begun to poke through the purple sky. The Styx was steady, gurgling over rocks, insects buzzing its surface.

Tarlos took a deep breath. The air seemed so fresh despite its belonging to the dead. He smiled as his lungs filled, and he let it out slowly. This might be the last he would see of this place, and he wanted to savor the feeling. Some distance away, at Shar's mountain, the sun was nearing the gate.

The bald man stood beside Tarlos. He wore a grey hooded shirt with a large pocket on the belly in which he kept his hands. The hood was up, and, facing west, the red light of the setting sun illuminated his kind features.

"Are you sure about this?" he asked Tarlos, watching as the king enjoyed his last breaths of the dead country.

Tarlos nodded. "I'm dead, but my friends in Kesh aren't. Their whole lives are ahead of them—especially my son. I won't be able to rest until Ablis is gone. It's my fault he's there to begin with." He sighed nervously. "The boatman once told me that the thing you want to find is often in the place you're most afraid to go. I have one last thing I need to do, and after that . . ."

The man nodded and patted Tarlos on the back. "Best of luck to you. I don't think we'll be seeing each other again, but in the grand scheme of eternity I guess anything is possible."

Tarlos shook the man's hand, and the man's grip was firm and warm.

"Goodbye," Tarlos said. "And thank you."

With a blast of air, Tarlos launched himself into the sky toward the mountain. The bald man watched from the ground, using a hand to shield his eyes against the sunlight. A small green cricket pounced on his shoulder and chirped.

The man said to the cricket, "I'm glad I got to help someone one last time," and the cricket chirped once before jumping away. The man waved to Tarlos, knowing Tarlos could not see him, and then turned and headed back to the village.

The sun had entered the tunnel only a few minutes before. Tarlos slowed down to give it a head start. The sky darkened and the stars came into full bloom. Tarlos counted to one thousand before deciding that he had waited long enough. He flew into the hole in the mountainside.

This time it was not so dark. He kept pace with the sun, leaving a thousand feet or so between it and himself. The sun lit the tunnel with a red and yellow glow, and Tarlos saw for the first time just how mind-numbingly enormous the cave was. Even with the light, Tarlos could hardly see the stone ceiling high above, and it was just as spacious to the left and right.

But he had no time to appreciate the magnitude of the sun or its tunnel. He focused, speeding on through the mountain with the sun just ahead. He did not count how many seconds had passed before the sun squeezed through the other side.

A cool morning breeze brushed Tarlos's face as the sun rose into the sky above the desert and the Scorpion Gate opened before him. Only moments after the sun passed through, the gate began to materialize back into the mountain, and Tarlos pushed harder to make it through in time.

The morning air of the living world slapped him to attention, and the shock caused him to stumble and drift to the ground. He took a moment to catch his breath.

"Hey!" called a voice.

Tarlos turned and saw next to him a young boy with black eyes and hair who'd not been there a moment ago.

"Hello again," said Tarlos. "Remember me?"

"You can't just leave," said the boy. He grimaced, annoyed and angry.

"I promise I'm coming back. I just have to do something first."

"You had your whole life to do something," cooed a different voice. Tarlos looked up to see the girl hanging upside down from a tree branch. "No second chances."

"Sorry." Tarlos raised himself a few feet into the air. The children screamed painful screams, and Tarlos drew back farther into the sky.

Below him, the jinn twins twisted into sick caricatures of their young and innocent selves. Their mouths grew wide, their faces splitting across the middle. Their small white teeth rusted to a dark red and grew and stretched into sharp fangs. Their brows protruded over their black eyes and their hair receded to reveal wrinkled scalps covered in sores and dark spots. Their arms grew long and their fingers became claws, and they reached toward Tarlos as he put more and more distance between them.

The jinn spoke in unison, their voices the wails of Hell. Their words were screeches and growls, and Tarlos did not understand any of it.

It was their job to keep anyone from going into or coming out of the dead country, and Tarlos understood that. The jinn twins were frightening and disgusting, but he held no ill will against them.

"I promise I'm coming back," he shouted from his vantage point. "Today, tomorrow, someday. I will come back."

The demons cried as Tarlos flew west, and they shrank back to their common forms. The girl lowered her head in defeat and sat beside her climbing tree. She brought her knees to her chin while the boy kicked a rock and sent it skidding along the yellow grass.

"What will . . . *he* do to us?" asked the girl.

The boy looked up at the sky with his black eyes. "I have a feeling we soon won't have to worry anymore."

With the dead country behind him, the dead king of Kesh laughed. "My name is Tarlos!" he shouted into the wind.

The desert was a blur beneath him. Wind in his hair, on his face, stinging his eyes. How long had it been since he had flown like this? In the open air, the ground as far below him as the sun was above?

After a while the sound of the wind faded into the background, and to him the world was silent. Peaceful. He would return to the dead country. But first, one last thing.

Kesh was a small circle, a red coin surrounded by yellow sand. Tarlos positioned himself above it, taking in the sight of his kingdom. He studied the brickwork of the walls, the ancient roads, and the stone temple that reached so high. He saw the fields of grain and corn just beyond the wall, and the lush garden beside his cedarwood palace. This would probably be the last time he would see his home in full. He took his time.

Gently, slowly, he lowered himself to the city, and the walls and buildings came up to meet him. He stopped, level with the top-most floor of the cedar palace, where the royal chambers were. The shutters were closed, and the curtains did not move in the calm noon air.

Ablis, Tarlos thought.

The curtains drew back, pulled by an invisible hand. The shutters opened, slamming against the walls. A child cried. Tarlos swallowed.

The being who called himself king floated out of the window, sneering at the real Tarlos. His hair floated as if underwater, and in his eyes Tarlos saw a burning—annoyance, anger, and hate.

"I cannot believe," said Ablis, "that you would be this stupid." His voice was no longer the voice of Tarlos. It was the sound of rocks grinding together in an avalanche, of lightning cracking over a storming ocean. A tornado ravaging an empty plain.

"I need to finish this," Tarlos said. His voice did not shake or tremble. He was past the point of fear or worry.

"You're dead already," Ablis howled. "I won't harm you—I will destroy you. Your spirit will not return to the dead country, nor will it suffer in the House of Dust. I will wipe every memory of you from your family and the world, blot your name from every record. I will make it a sin even to utter your name. Soon will come a day when Tarlos, son of Lakaeus, will cease to exist. Then, truly, you will be dead."

Tarlos did not respond. He turned to the wall behind the great garden in the courtyard and flew. Ablis followed behind, shouting curses in languages Tarlos did not understand.

Tarlos led Ablis over the wall and to the small area where he had died. He landed there in a small crater of sand, which erupted in a plume upon his landing. His body was nowhere to be found. At least Ablis had had the decency to keep it from being scavenged by birds and desert wolves. Tarlos ran to the nearby patch of cacti.

"There is no use in running," Ablis said at his back. Tarlos turned to meet the hellish voice just as Ablis grabbed Tarlos by the throat and squeezed. Tarlos tried to cough or wheeze, but no air was allowed to escape. "Tell me," said the god, "before I destroy all memory of you: What did you hope to gain by coming back?" He loosened his grip just enough to allow Tarlos to answer.

Tarlos took a swallow of air and coughed. "Needed . . . to . . . fix . . . what I . . . did," he panted.

Ablis smiled, his teeth sharp. "Your task is futile. Were I to fall and your throne to return to you, Kesh would disappear beneath the sand and the wind would erase your name from stone. You cannot stop me without killing yourself."

Tarlos wrapped his fingers around the necklace, and the tooth dangled in front of Ablis's face. "Don't you know?" he asked Ablis, then he thought as loud as he could.

Elder god!

Something pulled from behind Ablis's stomach, and his eyes

widened in horror. The god tried to pry his grip from Tarlos, but an unseen force kept them glued together. With a too-familiar *slurp* sound, the two were pulled upward and inward through dimensions. The physical universe turned inside out and back again, curling in on itself like a snake and unfolding into the next dimension, over and over, and all the while Ablis screamed in astonishment and panic. Tarlos brought both his hands to the one around his throat and pulled it away.

"You didn't know," Tarlos said. "You didn't know all of this was here, just outside your sight, space folded inside itself." He laughed. "The god Ablis, drifting with me through the Continuum, and he's afraid to die."

"You're just as dead!" Ablis cried out, his eyes wild and burning.

"That's fine. I enjoyed the chocolate cake." Tarlos pushed at the Discarded One, and Ablis drifted away into an unknown dimension. He cried out at himself and to the other gods, to his parents Shar and Moresh, but they were far beyond them now, and no god heard his pleas. As the multiverse became a series of small mirrored marbles around them, Ablis floated away between them, and when the multiverse became one again Ablis was gone—a being lost in the void of voids, the space between spaces, the collective of universes, the tide and current of the Continuum.

Orange.
  The smell of burnt almonds.

Hello again

"It's done," Tarlos said. "I did what I meant to do. Ablis can no longer harm my world, my family, my kingdom."

Is that what you wanted

"Maybe not at first, but now I know what's important to me."

Good
Now what

"I'm dead, aren't I? Aren't you going to send me back to the dead country?"

If that is what you wish
But you have also earned your immortality
Will you not take that

"I . . ." Tarlos searched for the right words to explain his change in perspective. But surely this god of gods understood. Knowing the thoughts of Tarlos's heart and mind would be effortless. "Kesh needs a king. Katla needs a husband. Messu needs a father. Send me back to Kesh. Let me live the life I should have lived all along, and when my time comes, I will embrace death." Tarlos smiled to himself despite having no mouth. "Life is beautiful and fleeting, and it is beautiful because it is fleeting."

It is your choice whether or not to wear the tooth
Remember the responsibility that comes with it
Keep it safe

"Tarlos!"

He felt a few light slaps on his cheek, and he opened his eyes. He lay on the sand, where he had died, staring up into the blue cloudless sky.

"Oh, thank the gods, he's okay!"

A series of gasps sounded all around him, and Tarlos lifted his chin to his chest. A group of people surrounded him, including half a dozen guards, several servants, and Katla, holding Messu. Lugal stood over him, his face inches from Tarlos's.

"That was some hit you took," Lugal said. "Try to sit up."

He helped Tarlos to sit and he gave him a bag of water to drink.

"What happened?" Tarlos asked, then took a drink. It was delicious.

"We saw your fight with Ablis," Lugal said. "We thought he was going to gut you with that spear, and that there was nothing we could do about it." He wiped his sweaty forehead and laughed. "But I guess he changed his mind and left. We ran out to get you as soon as he was gone. You've been out for a few minutes."

Tarlos felt his belly where the spear had gone through—where he'd died his first death—and felt nothing. He was clean and rested.

"Can you stand?"

Tarlos nodded. Lugal helped him to his feet, and Tarlos took another drink of water.

The group parted, and Katla stood now in front of him with her young son in her white arms. Tarlos stared at her. He approached her and looked to Messu, busy sucking on his fingers.

"I hope," Tarlos told Katla, "that in time you'll be able to forgive me for leaving you."

A single tear slid down Katla's cheek. She smiled at Tarlos then handed Messu to him. He held his son awkwardly at first—Messu wiggled uncomfortably and wiped his wet hand on Tarlos's face before finding a comfortable position, then placed his head on Tarlos's chest. Tarlos felt a lump in his throat as he held his son for the first time. He looked up to see everyone staring at the two of them.

"Welcome home," said Katla.

Emmett Burgess is a student of history, linguistics, geology, and literature. He spends his time writing, reading, studying dead languages, and sharing a quantum-entangled id with two other beings. He lives in Utah with his spouse and child, ca. 13 BA.

Emerson Grey was born and raised in Jemston, New Amrika. He attended the University of Jemston where he studied literature, history, and linguistics, earning advanced degrees in Ancient Terran History and Culture. He is now a tenured professor of Terran Literature at the University of Jemston, as well as a senior member of the Windmill Writing Fraternity. He lives in a small cottage on the Robert Grey Memorial Estate with his wife Matilda, ca. 9340 AA.

John Talbot's favorite animal is a giraffe.

You can connect with me on
Threads **@authoremmettburgess**
Instagram **@authoremmettburgess**
Facebook **@emmettburgessauthor**
TikTok **@authoremmettburgess**
www.goodreads.com/emmettburgess
and at **www.windmill.ink**
Reviews are always appreciated.

Read on for a preview of

The Form and The Shatter:

Being the **Second Movement**
of the
Song of the Crickets

Taken from the Epic
Sos Mao Brikhweg
by **Kanwas**

Adapted and translated by
Emerson Grey

—here transcribed by
Emmett Burgess

Prelude

On the coast near the taiga, there lives a song.

No one knows how it came to be there, or how long ago it was written. No one has heard it in its entirety. It is difficult to find, and if you find it you would be lucky to hear even a single verse.

Those who have heard it say it is elegant and sad, layered and haunting. It is chasmic, complex as a concerto and familiar as a fairy tale. Some hear deep tones from a duduk while others are convinced the chief instrument is a sorathryu. Most agree that several instruments play the song, and some even hear the lyrics.

As with any mystery, those who know of the song cannot make any sense of it. Those who hear only music cannot agree on which instruments it is played, and those who hear lyrics cannot understand them. No one knows why the song is there, what purpose it serves, or even whether one should hear the song at all.

But the song is there. You can find it if you listen for it.

Often you can find it at night when the moon is full and the night-ribbons dance across the sky. Look out over the water and listen to the surf wash against the shore while the owls hoot and foxes yip in the dark wood behind you. All these are parts of the song, so listen.

Then, žužžánije. This is what the locals call the chirring of insects. If the night is warm, which is rare on the taiga coast, žužžánije will be steady.

When you have listened to žužžánije for enough time that your mind places it in the backdrop of sensation and you lose your focus on all that is around you, the song will begin. Or rather, you will hear it then—the song has no beginning.

The melody will rise and circle you. Perhaps you will hear the *thump-thump-thump* of the drums, and the bass will hit you in the heart like an iron-tipped spear. You may hear a lute played with light notes that border on the sound of tiny silver bells. And you may hear the lyrics. Don't worry if you do not. Those who do are often disappointed when they find they cannot understand them.

But you will feel these things:

Harsh sunlight against hot sand, and winds that bite in the snow.

Excited for young love, saddened at loss, the joy of fast friends, and the dreadful crawl of slow death.

The curiosity of holding a new instrument. The betrayal of dying before playing anything worth hearing.

The sting of tears that slide down your cheeks as you struggle to choose between duty and love—the shame of choosing duty and having to hide your face in public.

The taste of salt spray from an ocean that many claim has no end. The pride of discovering what lies beyond.

An uneasiness in the belly that comes with the sound of a sour-milk voice.

Razor claws that rake and tear flesh from bone.

The color orange.

The smell of burnt almonds.

You will forget what brought you there, the choices that shaped and formed your sorrows and joys, that determine where you will journey next. And later you will forget the music. You will forget the lyrics if they came to you. The experience will fall through your memories like snow melting in sunlight. You will remember only that the song exists, and that you were lucky to have heard a single measure.

I am not lucky.

I have heard the entire song.

This is a small piece.

www.ingramcontent.com/pod-product-compliance
Lightning Source LLC
Chambersburg PA
CBHW031217260626
47169CB00007B/2085